MW00989912

Unhappy Endings

Tales from the world of
ADRIAN'S UNDEAD DIARY

Volume One

Edited by Chris Philbrook

Unhappy Endings: Tales from the world of Adrian's Undead
Diary, Volume 1
Edited by Chris Philbrook
Copyright © 2015 Christopher Philbrook

All rights reserved. No part of this book may be
reproduced or transmitted in any form or by any means,
electronic or mechanical, including photocopying,
recording, or any information storage and retrieval
system, without prior written permission of the author.
Your support of author's rights is appreciated.

Published in the United States of America

First Publishing Date 2015

All characters in this compilation are fictitious. Any
resemblance to actual persons, living or dead, is purely
coincidental.

Cover illustration by Ian Llanas

Cover design and interior layout by Alan MacRaffen

Also by Chris Philbrook:

<u>Elmoryn - The Kinless Trilogy</u>
Book One: Wrath of the Orphans
Book Two: The Motive for Massacre

Coming Soon:
Book Three: The Echoes of Sin

<u>Reemergence</u>
Tesser: A Dragon Among Us

Coming Soon:
Ambryn: & the Cheaters of Death

<u>Adrian's Undead Diary</u>
Book One: Dark Recollections
Book Two: Alone No More
Book Three: Midnight
Book Four: The Failed Coward
Book Five: Wrath
Book Six: In the Arms of Family
Book Seven: The Trinity
Book Eight: Cassie

A.U.D. Anthology: Unhappy Endings

*Don't miss Chris Philbrook's **free** e-Book:*
At Least He's Not On Fire:
A Tour of the Things That Escape My Head

TABLE OF CONTENTS:

Foreword:

What a journey.

I've been writing in the world of Adrian Ring since late 2010, and others have been right there alongside me, creating stories set in the world that somehow slipped out of my mind, and onto the website so long ago.

It all started with the AUD forums and a contest for folks to write some fan-fiction to win a shirt or something. Just as with the success of Adrian's Undead Diary, I had no frigging idea how big the concept of AUD fan-fiction would get. The first contest got dozens of entries, and each contest I ran got bigger and bigger. Now, as I write this, there are over a hundred fan-fiction stories still on the site.

Some are… clearly written by people who wanted to share a story but didn't know how to, and some are written by people who didn't know they knew how to tell a story. I'm thankful for everyone's visions of my world, and I love reading the stories.

I wanted to share the best of these with the larger audience that has come into the world of Adrian Ring, as well as bridge the gap between the events of AUD book eight: Cassie, and the new trilogy I'm working on.

Unhappy Endings serves as a way for me to achieve both.

There are fifteen stories in Unhappy Endings that fans and friends wrote for the site, or for the anthology directly, and I love them all for various reasons. The people, as well as the stories they wrote. From me to them; thank you very much. You're good people. I don't care what your parents say about you.

Officially, I grace their words in this tome as AUD official. What they've written here, has happened. It is no longer fan fiction, it is AUD canon. Stick that in your pipes and smoke it.

Mixed into their stories like ice with whisky are a series of side fictions that I've written. Most notably are the two original Eddie Smith stories that are/were premium on the site, as well as two more, never-seen Eddie Smith stories. Eddie and his group of survivors from Longview Texas play a major role in the new AUD trilogy I'm working on, and the stories in Unhappy Endings bring them into the fold further. If this is your first visit to the world of Adrian Ring, I highly suggest you run back out and pick up Dark Recollections, and start at the beginning. You can read this first, but some of the stories could spoil some details for you, and as we know, the Devil's in the details.

If you enjoy Unhappy Endings, please, please leave it a review on Amazon and/or Goodreads so I know you liked it. I'd like to do more in the series, but I need to know you enjoyed it before I do this again. Turns out publishing an anthology is a lot of work, and kind of expensive. Please let me know your honest thoughts.

So yeah. What a journey. Thank you, readers, for all the time you've spent gallivanting around inside my imagination, and with Adrian, and now, please enjoy a little time inside the imagination of some great people who shared their thoughts with me, and now you.

Chris Philbrook, May 2015

FEAR

JOE TREMBLAY

I'm Michael Turner, I'm a cubicle zombie at the local phone company. I sell shit for a living and just recently started reading 'The Secret.' I am on a quest to lead a more positive life now. This morning I was thinking to myself, *today is going to be a really great day!* Wednesdays are usually very shitty days for me, but I figured what the hell, give positive thinking a shot. So it's Wednesday, June 23rd and I walk out of my apartment building in San Diego for my morning cup of coffee at the Starbucks across the street. The first positive sign I get for my hopefully awesome day is that the place is empty! Weird, but hey, no line! Positive thinking is working already!

Hippy-kid Jerry, as I like to refer to him on account of his ratty hairstyle and tie-dye shirt, is at the register barely even aware that I am standing there waiting to place my order. Instead, his eyes are glued to his cell phone watching some video.

"Everything alright?" I ask. He looks through me as if I'm not actually standing there.

"Naaah maaan... It's like Dawn of the Dead out there, you been watching the news?"

He holds up his phone to show me what looks like an amateur video of two disgusting looking people ripping some older man open with their teeth. The video was raw and made me instantly sick to my stomach. The same kind of feeling I used to get when I watched Faces of Death videos when I was a kid.

"That's fucking sick man," was all I could think to say. Although at this point, I'm just thinking it's some kind of prank and how nice it would be to get my fucking coffee.

Right about then, two cars crash head-on into each other just outside the shop and I realized that if I listened closely, I could hear police and fire sirens and... were those gunshots? I knew instantly that panicking would lead to my untimely demise so I ushered Jerry to fetch my coffee, which he did with an "are you fucking serious?" attitude. Yeah I was fucking serious. This might be the last Grande Mocha with whip cream I ever get to drink. He got it to me and told me don't worry about the money. He grabbed a bunch of pastries and bottled juices and took off and told me to be careful to not get eaten by one of the "dawn of the deads."

I then decided to call people and pulled out my new awesome flip phone. I hit all the speed dials on my phone one after the other and got nothing but busy circuits dial after dial. I left the store thinking that maybe I was just dreaming. As I hit the sidewalk and looked around, I noticed how surreal it all was. People were everywhere suddenly. Like some kind of impromptu city block party. People ran, walked and screamed maniacally from every alley, corner and storefront. I swigged some mocha and pinched my cheek just to be sure this wasn't all some fucked up nightmare.

Out of nowhere a black haired Korean woman carrying a kid appears in front of me and I see the kid is bleeding badly from his neck. She grabs my arm with an impossibly strong vice like grip.

"PLEASE help my Billy!!!" *Damn woman almost made me spill my coffee.*

"What the hell happened to him?" I say as I wrestle my own throbbing arm away from her. I look at Billy and Billy looks like shit. His neck has an oozing tear in it and his clothes are drenched in blood. I gently place my coffee to my side, grab the kid and toss him on the ground to look at the wound, he was bleeding badly and man do I hate blood. I kept staring at the blood oozing out of his neck and I felt an awful sensation of terror march up my spine.

"He got bitten by a very sick man!" she whines frantically.

"Bitten" There's the word. I don't like this, matter of fact, positive thinking is completely worthless if this is what happens. I should have probably woke up thinking only the worst can happen and then maybe I'd have won the lottery or something.

I'm looking at the kid, but all I feel is the sun hitting me hard and I hear screaming from distant areas of the city and the clatter of chaos everywhere. The kid was bad. I was bad. I hate blood and gore. It makes me sick to the point that my body goes into shock and I knew that I couldn't help him; it was too much for me. I started to get the nausea and gut wrench feeling which told me that if I stuck around this dying kid and crazy woman any longer, I was dead. I don't want to be dead.

I look the lady straight in the face and say, "I can't help you and if you stick around your dying son, he's going to turn into a zombie and kill you." I then grab my coffee and I run from her as fast as my shaky legs would let me. I could hear her screaming at me as I fled and I tried very willingly to get a grip on the new reality being force-fed into my scrambled mind.

I come around the corner on G-street and Kettner Boulevard where I experience my first ever, heart stopping shock in life; a horde of zombies. Freshly minted dead people, able to get up and kill. Fucking zombies... I was terrified. I can't explain it, but you ever see a kitten get circled by a bunch of hungry stray dogs? I'm feeling like I am that kitten at the moment.

Hilariously enough, I was one of those people who would often say, "Yeah baby, bring on that zombie apocalypse! No more laws, bills or taxes! Just kill or be killed and take whatever the fuck you want!" What's not to love about that?

Well, being about fifty feet from 20 or 30 undead changes the way you think about things dramatically. The first hard lesson is that I'm alone and that my family and most of my friends are probably going to die and become one of these things. Second hard lesson is that for as cool as I thought I was going to be if I ever was going to deal with a zombie apocalypse, I was wrong. I was stuck in the middle of San Diego with no gun, no water, no vehicle, backpack or even a fucking Swiss Army knife. I had a cup of coffee and my phone and the stupid fucking phone wasn't ever going to work again. Did I mention that zombies were just a stone's throw away from my still living body?

All in all, people say they can't wait for this shit and then when the shit does actually happen they shit themselves. There is nothing cool about blood, guts, ripped skin and death being around every corner unless it's on the flat screen being run off a PlayStation. There's nothing cool about it when it's real because it's the most disgusting feeling ever. Just remember what it was like to lose someone close to you and how much it hurt that you'd never see them again and then imagine losing EVERYONE. It's gut-wrenching misery. There's also nothing cool about the fact that I'll probably never get to have Starbucks Mocha again. That really sucks.

Okay back to the problem at hand, the undead don't see me because they are currently occupied with chewing the skin off some obese guy's hairy back and legs. I'm reminded of this nature series on the discovery channel featuring those mangy, starving wolves in the winter feasting on the one skinny deer whose blood is all over the pure white snow. I got sick and threw up the little bit of coffee I'd drank. *This sucks*, is the only thing going through my head. That and *What the FUCK am I going to do?*

Where do I go, should I get a fucking boat? Nah, fuck boats.

Should I find a Wal-Mart? That's probably not a good idea. I imagine there are a thousand other people who think that's going to be a great place to have to their own, killing any other survivor who tries to get in. Greedy materialistic bastards. Jesus I had to do something before I was surrounded with nowhere to run.

Just then, a man appears behind me screaming, "RUN FOR YOUR LIFE!" I turn and he's being chased by another mob of undead. As I'm turning to confront him, he pivots left and runs right where I just came from and where there is the bigger

12

group of dead people. I try to scream to him not to go that way, *it's worse*. He can't hear me, his mind is gone and into the hungry wolves he goes. Christ, nothing is going well. I decide to down my coffee and really get my head in the game. *Positive thoughts, Michael, positive thoughts.*

First fucking problem, how do I get out of the city? Scratch that, how the fuck do I get away from the zombies this old man brought in my direction? Those ugly, shambling, bastards all had that glazed look in their eyes. They were horrid to watch with their bloodied faces and necks. I felt like they exuded this kind of aura that made me think and move much slower than usual. The curse of terror I suppose and it actually made me realize why in every horror movie, the girl trips. It's legit now those movies make great fucking sense!

First rule is cardio. Thank you Zombieland! I was dressed in my New Balance shoes and khaki cargo pants, so running would be easy. Although it was hot as balls outside today, so obviously water was going to be a priority if I was going to be doing a lot of running. And so I ran, as fast as I could. Lucky for me the dead people were kind of slow, but the problem is they were just about everywhere I was heading. I remember running and hearing screams from all over. There were nonstop sounds of vehicles crashing, horns honking, sirens blaring and the trolley train. The damn train was filled with people, but it would just move five or so feet, stop, move five more feet, stop… Imagine being on that train with the urgency that I feel. Maddening. Didn't seem like a good method of transportation. At random I'd see two or three zombies eating some poor fuck or some woman or God forbid, a kid. It was all so sickening to the stomach that it took all I had not to just flop on the ground and give up completely. I'm so glad my adrenaline was on, or else I'd have done just that.

My first inclination was to get out of the City by darting through it on foot, but then I thought, why go empty handed and on foot? Being that I live in the city, I didn't own a car, so I needed to find one. Then I could simply drive it back to my apartment and get some spare shit. *So fuck it, let's get a car* I thought or at least a cab. There are usually taxi cabs by the Hyatt Hotel only a block away. The Hyatt is right next to the Convention Center where they have the ComiCon every year and it's usually bustling with activity. I just knew there was going to be zombies, but I had to take the risk. Getting a vehicle to ride my ass out of town was my only shot to retaining some of my sanity. Not to mention, I was in a major city and based off the illogical actions of our government's history with bombs it wasn't farfetched to think that they would be dealing with this major disaster with a nuclear BANG! I mean was San Diego the only place this was happening? Or was this worldwide?

Within minutes I am right near the Hyatt, the tallest building in the city. As usual there are scores of white and yellow cabs situated just outside of the main entrance. I can see that there are actual living people scrambling about attempting to get the fuck out of Dodge. This is a good thing; it meant I still had time. I run up to the long series of cabs and all the cab drivers are screaming and shouting at each other. I think they were quickly realizing that competing for fares was utterly useless. Zombies have a funny way of making money obsolete. One by one as I got near, the cabs started taking off in a hurry with no passengers. *Shit.* I approached a driver and told him to let me in the cab. He looked at me, spit on ground in front of me and sped off. I watched him speed down the road to the first light, which was red, run it and get T-boned by an SUV which is a scene straight out of the new Dawn of the Dead remake. I almost laughed until I understood that this time it wasn't a movie. Man shit was bad, but oh well that guy was a douche.

At this point I know beyond a doubt that it's survival of the fittest. If I don't take one of these fucking cabs by force, I'm going to die today.

There were still about a dozen cabs there. I grab the driver of a white cab. He looks to be a middle-aged Hispanic man and he has this nervous look in his eye. Like he just shit in his pants and is worried everyone can smell it off him. Or maybe just that he couldn't fathom the events happening. When I tried to talk to him all he could do was mumble Spanish under his breath and kiss the cross on his necklace. As far as I was concerned, he was a goner. Most cab drivers keep their cabs running even when they're standing outside of them. Such was the case. I pushed him aside and got in his cab. He looked at me in disbelief.

I said, "Shut up." That's all that I could think to say to the guy, nothing personal. He lifted his shirt and pulled a gun on me and started screaming in Spanish.

Fuck, I pick the cabby that's packing a gun. I put my hands up over the steering wheel. I had no idea what he was saying, but I think he wanted me to get out. I was about to, I really was, but I looked past him to the section of the city I'd just come from and noticed there were hundreds of undead shambling our way. I pointed and yelled at him to look. He looked quickly and angrily. He then looked back at me and his face was pale. He fell down on his ass and started sobbing violently. For a moment I had pity, but as I looked out the window I noticed the dead were getting oh so closer. A lot of them mind you. I looked at the ID tag in the cab and it read, Jorge Gonzales.

"Jorge, get in the fucking cab!"

He looks at me and tilts his head a little. I know that look. You know that one, where the mind is sufficiently overwhelmed and all sanity exits back stage. The kind of look you would get from a father who just lost his daughter or from someone who just lost their legs on a land mine. The dead were creeping closer and Jorge was blanking out of existence. In 45 seconds the cab would be surrounded. I reached my hand out the window, grabbed Jorge's gun and took it. He didn't even notice.

I could smell something awful headed my way. I could hear their heavy and deathly, ominous footsteps. I was transfixed for a moment as I looked upon them. Where was the zombie sound? Why was there no sound? They should be making a moan sound or something. Was I going insane? It didn't matter; I would have died just sitting there. Worrying about the noise a zombie makes isn't appropriate when they're THIS FUCKING CLOSE. Gear; Drive. Gas pedal; down... I was off. I didn't want to go fast because that could lead to being T-boned. I looked into the side view mirror at Jorge. Poor Jorge. The mob attacked him in the same way you'd expect to see a bunch of ravenous loonies attack a psychiatrist at an insane asylum. Strange to see otherwise slow moving dead people operate at light speed when they're devouring their prey. I puked out the window. Fucking Zombies...

I had to drive carefully. I skipped going to the apartment after all. I felt that if I did go there for my stuff, I'd just get myself into trouble, possibly dead. If I could make it to the outskirts of town then I could hit the back roads and avoid the highways. They'd probably be jammed in a time like this. Last thing I needed was to be stuck in traffic during a zombie apocalypse, as if people weren't crazy enough just in a jam.

The rear view mirror of the cab had a plastic cross hanging from it. I don't know why, but I got the feeling, we were being punished. Like Judgment Day was upon us. I was hopeful for my friends and family up in the New England area, hopefully they'll be okay. There was no way I was trucking there though. By the time I ended up getting there it'd be too close to winter and if the zombies don't get you, the cold will.

Jorge kept a clean cab. Right on the floor of the front seat he had a cooler with water and a couple of sandwiches. I guzzled some of the water right away. He had a box of 9mm ammo and a flashlight in the glove box. Now that I thought about it, I had just scored really big. The odds of finding water, a car and a gun all at once were pretty damn awesome. The positive thinking thing might not be totally out of the question.

Driving out of town wasn't as bad as I thought it would be. The side streets were relatively clear and I made my way outside the city proper in less than 15 minutes. It's a mess though. The way out of the City was like watching a movie about a world that suddenly loses all government. Chaos everywhere. There was so much bang and holler from the exhilarated looters that it hid the horror of the zombies. It would of course only be a matter of time before the initial sense of liberation fades and the zombie horror starts to overwhelm.

I could see helicopters and small planes all over in the sky. The city has a few large military bases so who knows what they're doing about all this. There were a good number of army vehicles, but too much confusion for them to be effective.

I don't know where I'm going or what I'm going to do, but I survived getting out of the city. So we're off to a good start.

Only a few things I wish I'd done differently.

Grabbed as much free shit from Starbucks as I could.

And put a bullet in Jorge's head before the zombies got to him.

PART TWO:

Less than a week ago, I stole a cab and headed outside the city of San Diego. I made it, but wound up running out of gas in the middle of nowhere. I think I made it about 200 miles. It's good I took the back roads at first, but eventually I hit a dead end and had to get on the highway. Highway 8. The amount of crashed cars is pretty intense. People just don't think before they act. I've seen a few zombies, a few people running from zombies, a few people killing zombies, a few zombies killing people. *Sigh.* I've seen some crazy shit just in those 4 hours of driving than I ever cared to. *People are stupid.* The hysteria has set in and no one is acting sensible. I probably should have tried to help this one unfortunate guy who was stuck in his crashed up car, but his legs looked mashed up pretty good. Which means he would have been useless and probably died. I don't need anyone in my company dying and biting into me as I sleep. *I'm safer on my own,* I told myself as I left him to face a horrifyingly lonely death. *What's wrong with me for that anyway?* I can't figure out how I can be so horrible as to let people die in such awful ways. I have a gun, I could have shot Jorge and the mashed leg man. Both would have been better for it. I didn't though. I feel bad about that. I gotta keep thinking positive

17

thoughts though. Maybe mashed leg man was rescued by a doctor and maybe Jorge... well never mind about Jorge, but leg man... he had a shot.

Before I abandoned the taxicab I made sure to grab the gun, bullets and bottled water which is all I had left when the taxi ran out of gas the other day. The last sign I saw was Yuma, which is in Arizona. "310 to Yuma," with Russell Crowe. Boy I miss life the way it was already. Movies were my favorite. When I finally get settled somewhere I'm making damn sure I hit a Best Buy first and grabbing all the movies I can.

I was on foot for almost 2 days in the sweltering heat and I was feeling pretty hopeless especially when I ran out of water. Starving and thirsty I shambled on. The highway was empty and the world was still. I stopped to catch my breath and as I wiped the sweat from my forehead I realized that my body reeked like shit. So this is what it's like to be homeless. I knew I was ruined if I didn't find some food and water and if possible, some clothes that fit me. I was really starting to regret not hitting my apartment now. I also didn't want to be stuck on the highway for the rest of my life. There was an exit 14 miles ahead to a rest station. They have those little snack machines and bathrooms. Great fucking plan I thought. So I walked and five long hours later I was walking up the ramp in this exceptionally hot night to get to the rest stop building.

I heard a gunshot. *Man what the fuck I just want some Twinkies and water.*

I took the gun out of my cargo pocket and got the flashlight in my other hand. I slowly tiptoe up the road until I can see what is going on. At first all I see are a few cars, a pickup truck and one of those giant Mack trucks. Then, another gunshot sounds off. It was particularly loud because the night was so quiet. The lights from the building showered down into the small lot where a few bodies lay on the pavement. I didn't see the motherfucker with the gun though and that had me anxious as hell. I crept up a little closer and paused for any kind of movement. Then, coming from the inside of the open building I saw him. He was about my height, almost 6 feet and he was training a rifle around every corner until he got to the lot. I also noticed he had a pony tail. And that's about all I could make out about him because of the damn light. He was stabbing the bodies with the barrel of his rifle and kicking them I guess to make sure they were good and dead. Well, another survivor I thought and I may as well try to make friends. Pony tail or not. I get up from my crouch and signal my flashlight down at him and say, "Hey there".

BANG! Something whizzes right by my skull.

I fall on my ass and drop the flashlight. I still had my gun, so I lied there on my back, in the dark gripping the pistol with both my hands, finger on the trigger pointed up. I waited. It seemed like I could have watched all the Lord of the Rings Movies in the time I was laying there but he finally came upon me. He is outfitted with just a pair of jeans, dark boots and a flannel shirt. He wears a slightly scruffy beard and his hair, is tied into a ponytail. He didn't look pleasant. Standing three feet in front of me with his rifle pointed at me I felt beaten. I had the gun pointed at him, but I didn't know if I had it in me to pull the trigger. At least not until after I talked with him,

"Don't shoot me man," I said.

He looks at me and slowly bends down, rifle still pointed at me, he picks up my flashlight and points that at me too. Now I feel like I am a deer caught in the headlights of the evil hunters.

"Where you coming from?" he asks.

I told him I was coming from San Diego and that my car ran out of gas awhile back. He moves the flashlight up and down my body looking for something and then he asks if I'd been bit or scratched by any zombies. I tell him no, been on my own since the shit went down.

"What's your name?" he asks in almost a friendly tone.

I tell him I'd feel better if I could get up and talk.

"What's your fucking name MOTHERFUCKER?!"

I take a deep breath and steady myself. This was going to be difficult; this man was obviously a little on edge. "My name is Michael, Michael Turner".

That seemed to calm him. He straps his rifle to his back,

19

pockets my flashlight and extends a hand. I eye him for a few moments, put the gun in my pocket and grip his hand to be lifted up. I can't see shit. All I can see is the memory trace of the bright flashlight in my eyes.

"Nice to meet you Michael my name is arrrrghhhh!"

He screams bloody murder and I am promptly dropped on my ass back onto the hard pavement, again. His screaming is ear-piercing. I hear his body drop to the ground and his rifle clatter nearby. He went on and on with the screaming. This was bloody murder. Then I heard another thump. I can't see shit and swiftly I am back to being terrified.

He was growling and struggling on the ground.

"Help me!!! Get it off me!! Please man!! Help!!"

"What the fuck, what the fuck?"I am saying, still blinded. "I can't fucking SEE you! What's going on?"

"You mother fucker! You fucking motherfucker!" his voice is getting weak, "I'm a fuckin kill you, I'm a fuckin…" and then he was silent.

My stomach turns on me and I get light-headed. I feel like I am dwindling into the gloom of an eternal misery drenched hell. I hear him now gurgling and bubbling and also the distinct sound of chewing and jaw smacking.

My vision comes back to me and I can see now what has happened. A deceased lady had come up behind him -silent like the plague- and chewed into him when he was lifting me up. These fucking zombies are so quiet you can't hear them. I look down and she is still chewing on his neck. Blood is flowing around her face, spitting into her hair and pooling on the road. I am frozen sick.

Then she slowly looks up and stares right into me.

She quietly and meticulously forces her corpse up and starts to walk towards me, ever so slowly. She has long, brown, bloody hair and looks to be no more than 20 years old. Her chest area is stained black like she'd been shot there. I wanted to cry out for help. I wanted to scream for her to go away. I was more scared then I'd ever been. I had thought it was scary to see a horde of these things in San Diego during broad day light.

I thought with all the chaos of that day that I'd faced the worst, but no. This was the worst. The pale, blood soaked face of this monster staring at me with hunger and hatred in the still, dark night made my bowels let loose all the piss and shit I'd been accumulating for days. With my shaking hands I pointed the gun at her head and I pulled the trigger.

Nothing happened.

The gun is not firing. Her hand is grabbing my arm. The gun is not working. Her face is moving into my shoulder. The fucking gun won't go BANG and end this zombie from killing me. Her teeth find the center of my bicep. It doesn't make sense, it won't even make the click noise when I pull the trigger. There is pain jolting up through and down my entire arm as her teeth bite into my tender flesh. I know there are bullets, why hasn't the fucking thing been firing?

"Oh My Fucking Lord, I've been bitten!"

Scared even more then I was moments ago, I rip her mouth off my throbbing arm and turn and run back down the ramp. As I'm running, I feel the two pounds of shit creeping down my leg and I'm worried I'm going to get some into my socks. Stupid thing to worry about because I end up losing my footing and plowing into the pavement hard. I knew if I lied there that fucking monster would be on my ass in no time. What difference does it make now though, *I've been bitten! I'm going to die.* All I could picture was her mouth. Her dreadful mouth chewing at my arm and then my neck. Then my neck bleeding into her mouth. I got up in a frenzy and continued running down the ramp. Whatever happens, I cannot allow her to bite into my neck. She got arm and that's fine, but there is no way she's getting my neck. By now my night vision was kicking in full force and I could see that I put a good distance between me and the zombie.

I look up into the night sky and the clouds part to reveal the brilliant, full moon. The light is shining down brightly and I look upon my wicked gun of treason. I point it up into the sky and squeeze the trigger and get nothing. Why?? I examine the gun thoroughly for signs of anything broken and it looks fine.

21

It has bullets, it just won't fire. Meanwhile the zombie is getting closer. I look at my arm as it drips blood and radiates its screaming pain to the treacherous brain who failed it. My brain. Then I ask my brain why it has failed my arm and it tells me that my eyes have failed us all. I ask my eyes, what didn't we see and look closer at the gun.

And as she's 30 feet from me, like a fucking moron, I finally see my mistake. How incredibly stupid… Right near the trigger above the handle is a little switch called the safety. I hit the switch and it reveals a little red dot. I squeeze the trigger.

BANG! *The fuck…*

I need to protect my neck. *That zombie is going to try and get my neck.* She is only about 15 feet from me now. Not far behind her another form is sluggishly following. I knew who it was when I saw the silhouette of the pony tail.

"Shoot it in the head man, shoot it in the head."

Dawn of the Dead, 1978. The swat guy is telling his swat buddy to shoot the zombie in the head in the section 8 apartment complex they just raided. All I had playing in my head as I pointed the gun at her lifeless face; Shoot it in the head man, shoot it in the head.

I shoot her in the head. She falls. I walk up to Ponytail and shoot him in the head. I feel good now, despite my arm, I feel great. My neck is going to be fine. My arm is mad at me, but fuck it, my neck is going to be great and it's happy with me.

I walk up the ramp and fire off the remaining shots. It doesn't matter now anyway, I've been bitten. I really need to find something to eat though. One last yummy snack before I turn. As I approach the building, I toss the gun into the trash. I hear the sounds of florescent lights and see cockroaches scurrying through the blood splattered floor. As I enter the building I see the vending machine is completely filled over in the far corner. I walk to it and break the glass. I have my choice of all the different types of candy bars, mints, chips and peanuts. I also see there is a soda machine I can bust open. I am thinking positive thoughts now, not long from now I'll be able to play a zombie in whatever new reality it is we have going. I hope I can eat as many people as possible before I'm shot in the head. Yeah, no one ever thinks, that maybe being the zombie is the more fun part of the game. I open a Reese's-Pieces peanut butter cup and start giggling. *Yes, it won't be long now. Not long at all.*

Oh and what do you know, had I not been such a fucking coward and actually mustered the courage to kill Jorge and the mashed leg man, then I would have known about the safety. If I'd know about the safety, I wouldn't have been bitten, because I would have shot that girl in the head long before her teeth got into my arm. Yes, this is the price of karma. This is the price of not doing what's right, of being afraid, too afraid.

Those are such negative thoughts though. I must see the positive side to this.

I'm so tired. Positive thinking... yawn. I can't wait to eat people. Fucking Humans...

In the Arms of the Dead

Christopher MacDonald

The humidity hung heavily in the warm June night. Alan pulled at his sweat stained t-shirt, trying to detach it from himself as he gazed up at the star filled sky, waiting. He had been watching her for several months, learning her after work patterns and habits. Emily was a petite, raven haired beauty with soft features who worked as a bartender at a popular watering hole in town. In Alan's opinion, the place was only popular when Emily was serving drinks. She had this friendly and caring demeanor that--accompanied by her good--looks drew in large crowds. Men and women alike.

He remembered the first time she caught his attention. He'd been exiting the town's little convenience store and a little girl, maybe eight or nine years old lost control of her bicycle and tumbled over its handlebars. As the little girl sat on the ground, holding her skinned, bleeding knee and crying her little heart out, he saw Emily who appeared from out of nowhere rush over to her. Kneeling beside that little girl, he watched as she pulled some tissues from her purse, offering one to the little girl to dry her eyes and with another she gently cleaned the girl's knee. A few minutes later, the girl got up, her face all red and puffy from crying and hugged Emily. Emily hugged her back and smiled as she watched the girl get back on her bike and peddle off.

It was at that time he knew he had found his next target. He began observing her and eventually learned about her bartending job.

He knew that on Tuesdays she would finish work at 9:00, have a margarita with extra salt, down two glasses of water and by 10:00 she would be traveling down this back road on her way home. The road had murderous potholes for car shock absorbers and was out of the way but she favored it because it shaved fifteen minutes off getting home. He felt thankful; it would make things so much easier. He looked down at his watch and noticed that Emily was five minutes late. Alan frowned in the darkness. He hated waiting.

He saw the headlights of an approaching car. His heart raced as he stepped away from his white Jetta and waved his arms, trying to get the driver's attention. The car slowed and pulled over to the side of the road just in front of his car. He smiled as Emily slowly emerged from her silver Camry.

"Car trouble?" Emily asked Alan as she approached.

"Yeah," Alan said as he looked down at his feet and ran his hand through his short dark blonde hair. "Everything was fine and then all of a sudden it started making a knocking noise and then it died on me. It was a real bitch to pull over to the side too."

"Yikes! That's not good. I had something like that happen to me last year. I spent more money than I wanted to get my car fixed," Emily said as she shot a glance over her shoulder at her car.

Alan swore under his breath and kicked the tire of his car in mock frustration. "Not exactly the news I wanted to hear."

Emily's eyes got big as a look or recognition came over her face, "Hey, you're that dude who comes into the bar on occasion. Adam, right?"

Alan chuckled. He was always misremembered or not even remembered at all. He took pride in that. Blending in and being unrecognized was useful for his hobby. He was just average. He wasn't short, but he also wasn't tall. He was neither thin nor fat. He even had people argue as to whether his hair was blonde or brown. "Alan actually, but that was pretty close," he said, pausing as if thinking something over. "Hey, if it's not an inconvenience, could you possibly give me a lift into town or let me use your cell phone so I can call Triple A? I left mine at home," he asked using his best pleading look.

"Yea totally. Car's a bit of a mess, but if you don't mind that, I can give you a lift," she said smiling brightly to Alan before turning and heading back to her car.

When Emily turned her back to Alan, he reached into his back pocket and pulled out a Taser. Before Emily knew what happened, 50,000 volts of electricity coursed through her body. She dropped to the ground convulsing as Alan pulled a roll of duct tape from his car and quickly bound her hands and feet with it before slapping a piece over her mouth to keep her silent. Alan scooped her up easily in his arms and carried her to the back of his car. He popped the trunk and gently set her inside. Her eyes were glossy and unaware as he reached down and gently brushed the hair out of her face.

"Thank you so much dear, sweet Emily. We are going to have so much fun together," he said lovingly to her as he closed the trunk shut.

*****

Years ago while doing some work on his home Alan had found the hidden room in his basement. He had heard the stories about how the Underground Railroad had run through the town and that some homes had secret rooms that had been used to hide the terrified slaves as they made their way North towards freedom. Never in a million years had he dreamed that he would be lucky enough to find one of them. The unremarkable old room sat 15 by 15 feet and was accessed by a hidden door in the floor of the basement. The former residents who built that secret sub-basement had done excellent work at concealing it. For 150 years it had remained hidden until he accidentally stumbled across it. Alan had cleaned it out and

27

managed to squeeze in a small bureau, some portable work lights and a bed. Beautiful Emily was bound and gagged to the bed.

Sweet, beautiful Emily. She reminded him so much of his younger sister Beth. The curve of her hips, the swell of her small, but firm breasts. She even had the same thin shaped lips. He could almost believe that Emily and Beth were twins. Beth was twenty eight, just two years younger than him. He had always loved his sister, just like any big brother should. But when she hit her teens and came into her beauty, that love changed. He would sneak outside her window at night and just watch her as she got ready for bed. She was the first girl he ever saw naked. That same night he had stayed up late; fantasizing about her naked body and all the things he would love to do to her.

It took a year before he had the courage to act on his feelings. Their parents had left for a week to go on vacation and it was just Alan and Beth home alone. One night they got into their dad's booze and got good and drunk. Without warning, he took his sister in his arms, pulling her close to him, pressing her firm young body against his. He kissed her full on the lips, one of his hands sliding up to cup her breast. She pulled quickly away from him with a look of confusion and disgust all over her face. She called him a sick pervert, a freak and a lot of other words that broke Alan's heart into a million pieces. She never told anyone what had happened that night, but from then on, their relationship had crumbled before his eyes. She made sure she was never alone with him. If their parents went somewhere she stayed at a friend's house. The worst part was the way she stared at him when no one was looking; she looked at him like he was some sort of monster.

Years later he left for college as did she a few years after him. From then on they only saw each other on the major holidays and after the death of their parents, she cut off contact with him completely. They hadn't seen or spoken to each other in almost four years. He had tried to contact her numerous times, but letters were returned unopened and her phone number became unlisted. It got to a point that he was thinking about hiring a private investigator.

Alan looked down as a soft moan brought him out of his quiet reflection. Slowly Emily began to stir. Groggy at first, but as she slowly realized the situation, she began to panic and fight against her restraints. As she pulled and fought against the fur lined handcuffs (they were ugly and Alan hated them, but they also prevented abrasions to the skin) he sat down beside her on the bed. She recoiled in fear, crying and pleading against the duct tape over her mouth as he reached over and gently caressed her tear-soaked cheek.

"There there, baby, there's nothing to be scared of, I promise," he said as he smiled down at her.

Soon it would all be over and he could show her the true extent of his love for her. Alan pulled the pillow out from under Emily's thrashing head and gently placed it over her face and applied pressure. Emily struggled harder against the fuzzy restraints that held her captive and the more she did, the harder Alan pressed the pillow to her face. After a few moments, her struggles lessened and then ceased. He held the pillow to her face a little longer, just to make sure she had achieved the peace he had promised her.

He pulled the pillow away from her. She looked so beautiful and peaceful as she lay there on the bed. He checked her pulse and her breathing and found nothing. Tenderly he removed the tape from her mouth, careful not to hurt her and then he undid the restraints. He sat silently next to her on that bed for just a few moments waiting. Normally upon death, the body's muscles relax and release the contents of its bowels and bladder. Alan was pleased to see in this case that Emily's body did no such thing. Cleaning up a woman's bodily waste was not something he enjoyed doing.

He undressed Emily, admiring her young beautiful body, her small but firm breasts with their dark areola and small nipples. The smooth skin and toned body of a woman that frequently worked out and took care of herself. He smiled to himself when he saw that she was shaved bare in her most

29

intimate of areas. He neatly folded her clothes and got up and set them on top of the bureau. Hands shaking in anticipation, he undressed and set his clothes next to hers. Slowly he made his way back over to the bed and lay down on the soft white cotton sheets next to her. Emily's body was still warm, but already beginning to cool. Trembling, his hands timidly explored the curves and crevices of her body as his manhood began to harden against her. He turned her face to his and softly kissed her. That night he lost himself to complete bliss and joy with Emily.

*****

Alan found himself wandering in total darkness. The air clung cool and heavy against his bare skin and had a faint sweet smell that was both familiar and unrecognizable at the same time. He wasn't sure for how long or how far he had been walking as he rubbed the rising goose bumps on his arms. Time and distance didn't seem to exist in this void that he found himself wandering aimlessly in. He had a feeling deep down in the pit of his stomach that he should be afraid, but instead he was filled with a sense of peace and comfort that he had never felt before. If this was a dream, he prayed dearly that it would last.

"*Alan Anderson.*"

Alan froze in mid step. The voice seemed to come from nowhere yet was everywhere. Alan looked around, half expecting someone or something to emerge from the darkness, yet he saw no one. He swallowed the lump that had formed in his throat as a sense of dread suddenly filled his body. "Hello? Who's there?"

"*The end is here Alan Anderson. I know of your particular tastes, I know what you desire. Do as I say and all that you dream of shall be yours.*"

Alan wiped away the beads of sweat that were forming on his forehead, the dread he had felt settled like a weight into the pit of his stomach. "Please, I don't know who you are or what you want, but I haven't done anything. I swear."

The void filled with a booming laughter. Alan's hands shot up to cover his ears, to block the sound out, but it was futile. He felt his blood run cold as that booming laughter violated every fiber of his being. It was the laugh of someone who saw through all his lies and deceptions. Someone who knew the monster that hid within him, just out of sight but close to the surface. His soul was laid bare before the voice and he felt frightened and alone.

"You have murdered four innocent young women, smothered the spark of their life while they were in their prime. You desecrated their lithe young bodies over and over before disposing of them when they begin to putrefy. All because your darling sister Elizabeth refused to let you fuck her."

Alan collapsed to his knees, eyes stinging fiercely as the tears flowed like rivers of guilt across his cheeks. He wasn't sure for how long he remained like that, a shaking and sobbing mess trapped in an endless and unforgiving void.

"What do you want from me?" Alan pleaded as he began to slowly recover his composure.

"Humanity is coming to an end and it shall be judged by its dead. There will be those who will stand against the coming tide, who will fight to their last breath to survive, to see humanity redeemed and to see it rebuilt. I want you, Alan Anderson to infiltrate the pockets of resistance you find and to crush them. You will be my wolf among the sheep. You will gain their trust and turn on them and I will see my army grow."

Alan slowly rose to his feet and wiped away the remnants of the tears that had soiled his cheeks. He wasn't sure why, be he felt empowered, like he had a sense of purpose. He was important. "I understand."

"When you awaken, Emily will be there waiting for you. She will be your guide, your protection and shall offer you comfort when you need it. Do well and you shall be greatly rewarded as I promised, but fail me and you will know a punishment that you could never begin to comprehend."

"Are you the Devil?" Alan asked, voice shaking. He was

31

afraid of the answer, but he had to know.

"I am beyond such concepts as Good and Evil, God and the Devil. I am the hunger that shall consume humanity as it turns inwards on itself. But if you insist on naming me, then Devil will suffice. Wake Alan Anderson, wake and swell the ranks of my army."

Alan slowly awoke, confused and unsure of what had happened and where he was. Sweat and the soft white cotton sheets stuck to him. He realized he was in bed, alone. Panic set in. He shouldn't be alone; Emily should be right next to him, cold, and pale blue and beautiful. A faint shuffling sound from the foot of the bed caused him to immediately sit up.

Emily stood at the foot of the bed. She was nude, her bare skin pale as she stared at him with milky white eyes that seemed to see right through him. She took one awkward step towards him, and then another. Alan should have been terrified, but he wasn't. Emily was dead, he had killed her just a few hours before, but here she was, slowly making her way towards him. His mind raced. *Had that dream been real? Was he the Devil's servant?*

Emily sat down on the bed next to him. He wanted to pull away, but the urge to see what happened next was too great. He gasped loudly as Emily's cool soft hand wrapped around his manhood and slowly started to stroke it. He leaned in and kissed her softly on the lips and was surprised when she kissed him back. Not softly like he had done, but hard. He felt her tongue push past his lips into his mouth. More surprise struck when he grabbed her by the hair and returned the kiss in kind.

The recently animated corpse of Emily broke the kiss and pushed him back down onto the bed. For the next hour, Alan was lost in a pleasure he had never known before.

*****

Several long days had passed since that terrifying and wonderful night.

Alan pulled back the heavy curtain and took a peek outside. The view of his little section of the neighborhood didn't reflect the chaos that engulfed the rest of the world. The sun shone, and there were no signs of violence, mayhem or the undead. It looked like a quiet lazy Sunday. He thought about the scenes from the TV as the world spiraled uncontrollably into Hell. No one could explain how or why, but the dead were returning to life and attacking the living. The footage being broadcast was gruesome and brutal. Hordes of the undead were swarming terrified survivors who were either running for their lives or fighting for them. The carnage was unsettling at first for Alan, but after a while he found a certain predatory beauty to it. The undead were an unrelenting force of nature that couldn't be stopped; spreading like wildfire until they would eventually consume everything.

In between the broadcasts of horror and violence, newscasters would pop up on the TV and announce the locations of government and military maintained safe zones, heavily fortified areas full of food, water, medicine and other necessities. Alan wrote down the locations of these safe ones. After all, he had the Devil's work to do. The other night, Alan had dreamt again of that dark awful place and the Devil had told him more of his plans for him and his silent companion. He was to make his way into these groups and at first opportunity, kill one or two survivors in the night. Their corpses would reanimate shortly after and feast on the others as they slept, turning them as well.

That morning Alan had packed up some supplies in an old hiking backpack. Lots of canned food, a few water bottles, his first aid kit, a couple pairs of socks and some other items that he felt would be necessary. Now the pack waited by the front door until he received the sign that it was time for him to leave the safety of his home.

Emily silently followed him everywhere he went. At times he wouldn't even realize that she was nearby until he'd turn around and see her standing there, staring at him with those milky white eyes that seemed to peer into his very soul. Over these past few days, he had learned a few things about the undead just by watching her. She made absolutely no noise.

She didn't make snarling or moaning noises like the undead did in movies. Unless she bumped into something while walking, she was a ninja. Dead Emily also didn't seem to decompose like other dead bodies. Usually by now, a body would be in the beginning stages of putrefaction, but Emily was still just as beautiful as she was that first night. Adam was sure the Devil had something to do with that.

Closing the curtain, he made his way to the kitchen when his stomach growled loudly; reminding him he hadn't eaten yet. Luckily he had gone shopping before everything happened and he had been eating sparingly since. As a result, he had a fair amount of food on hand. The power finally went out last night so he rummaged through the cabinets and got the things he needed to make himself a peanut butter and jelly sandwich. To pass the time he had tried making advances on Emily, but when he slid his hand up her shirt, she just slowly turned her gaze to him and stared at him blankly. Though her expression never changed, he got the feeling that she wasn't in the mood. He couldn't help but chuckle at the memory as he savored the taste of his sandwich. He had to be the only guy in the world who got shot down by a zombie. Zombie; using the word felt silly, but before the power went out, the people on the news were finally calling them that and it did seem to fit.

The silence was shattered by the sound of the kitchen door behind him being violently kicked in.

"Stay where you are mother fucker," boomed a man's voice.

Alan nearly jumped out of his skin as he dropped his sandwich on the counter and turned to see a filth-covered and crazed man leveling a pistol at him. The man wore torn jeans and a light blue t-shirt with some dumb catch phrase on it. His wild and unkempt dark looked like he hadn't showered or slept in days.

"Whoa, easy man, there's no need for the gun," Alan said as he raised his hands in front of him.

The man cleared the distance between himself and Alan in just a few quick steps. He grabbed Alan roughly by the throat and threw him to the kitchen floor, knocking the wind out of him.

"Don't tell me what I need this gun for, asshole. Now shut your hole and stay where you are or I swear to Christ, I will shoot your fucking face off," the man threatened as he waived the gun at Alan.

Alan nodded his head and watched as the man saw the half eaten sandwich on the counter. Without taking his gun off of Alan, he snatched it up and quickly inhaled it. As he finished what might've been the first thing he'd eaten in days, the stranger wiped his mouth off on his forearm.

"Hey asshole, what else do you have to eat in this shithole?"

"There's some more sandwich stuff in the cabinet behind you. I also think there are some chips and crackers as well," Alan told the man, choking back his fear.

The crazy guy slowly backed to the cabinet, keeping his gun on Alan. He let out a low whistle as he opened the cabinet and saw all the food. Turning his back to Alan, he tucked the gun into the back of his pants and began taking the food out and setting it on the counter. Out of the corner of his eye, Alan saw something move. He turned to look and saw Emily silently and slowly making her way towards the man who had invaded their home. Alan felt his pulse quicken. The man didn't know that his death slowly crept up behind him.

Emily bumped into a stool, knocking it over with a loud bang. The man turned quickly, his eyes growing large with fear as she slowly approached.

"Fuck me, it's one of them!" The man cried out as he fumbled around his back for the gun.

Alan didn't know what came over him. As the man brought the gun around to bear on Emily, he launched himself, tackling him to the ground, knocking the gun from his hands. They rolled across the kitchen floor, wrestling for any sort of advantage. Sadly for Alan he wasn't much of a fighter. The stranger quickly got the advantage, rolling on top of him and pinning him down with his knees. Pain exploded in Alan's head and everything went blurry as the stranger's fist came down hard on his skull. All urge to defend himself left his body as several more blows rained down on his head and face.

Barely aware that the man had been pulled off of him, he could hear the sounds of struggling and a sharp cry of pain followed by a wet slurping sound, as if someone ate spaghetti nearby. He tried to shake the cobwebs from his head, but it just made him dizzier. It took a moment, but when his vision and head finally cleared, he saw Emily hunched over the stranger. She tore large chunks of flesh from his throat and shoulder. Alan gagged slightly as the strong coppery smell of blood assaulted his nose. Emily stopped and looked up at him, blood smeared across her face and shirt as she chewed and swallowed the last bit of the stranger that she had in her mouth.

Alan managed to get to his feet and leaned against the counter for support until the room stopped spinning. After a few moments he unsteadily made his way to the bathroom and checked himself out in the mirror. The man had done a number on him. He could see his left eye beginning to swell shut and he had a steady drip of blood running from his nose. He grabbed a towel and did his best to clean himself off. When he was relatively pleased with the results, he turned to see Emily silently standing there staring at him.

"Come here baby, let me clean you up," he said to her as he took her hand and pulled her into the bathroom.

He grabbed the towel again and started cleaning her off. If it wasn't for Emily, his zombie protector, he'd be dead. The Devil said she would protect him, and he had been right. He finished cleaning off her face and tossed the towel onto the counter.

"Thank you Emily," he said to her leaning in to kiss her.

Just before their lips touched, she turned and slowly walked out of the bathroom. Alan hung his head, shot down again. He exited the bathroom after her, just in time to see the stranger begin to twitch. He wanted to grab a knife and drive it through the stranger's head, but that's not what his job was. He was supposed to build the ranks of the Devil's army, not thin it out. Stepping past the animating body, he walked over towards the spot where they struggled earlier and picked the man's pistol up off the floor. The cold and heavy gun made him nervous, but he'd need it in the near future. Just like the stranger earlier, he tucked it into the back of his pants.

A noise from the front of the house caught his attention. Fearing another invasion, Alan bolted out from the kitchen to the front hallway were he heard the noise. He found Emily standing in front of the door, staring at it. She turned her head, those milky white eyes locked on to his for just a moment before her attention turned back towards the door. It was time to go.

Alan grabbed the backpack he loaded up before from its nearby resting place and slung it over his shoulders. He opened the front door, letting the warmth and light of the late morning spill over him. He felt Emily's cool hand slide into his, taking hold of it.

Smiling at her, he held her hand tightly and together they stepped out into the horrible new reality of the world.

Eddie Smith, Part One:
The Truck

Hey kid. You having trouble sleeping tonight? Yeah? Eddie too. It makes my skin crawl to try and sleep out here without two fences between us and whatever is out there. What's that? Thinking too much eh? I think a lot too when I shouldn't. Want me to tell you a story to help you sleep? Well I ain't got no happy stories anymore, but if you want to hear one, I'll tell it to you.

What's that? That's a long story son. How we got to be on the road on this here trip? Okay. 'Spose there's enough time for that. Let's start at the beginning, and try not to skip over the juicy bits.

I've spent a lot of time on the road, sitting behind a big old ring of a steering wheel, and if there's anything that you can achieve sitting behind a steering wheel, it's thinking. I've thought a lot. I used to think behind that steering wheel that when I retired, and stopped driving for a living, I'd find time to do things where I plain old didn't have to think anymore.

Problem is, I like to hunt, and I love to fish, and I'll be damned, but both of those occupations leave you time to do two things: think, and drink. I'll be damned if I spend my retirement sitting in a flat bottomed boat with a rod in one hand and a Bud in the other, thinking about all the thinking I thought while I was driving.

Of course, retirement sort of implies that I'll be done doing my day job, and if you know anything about anything kid then you know no one really has a day job anymore. Some of us

39

work hard still, real hard, but none of us have day jobs anymore. Well, I guess there might be a government office deep inside a bunker somewhere that folks still put a shirt and tie on in, but I can guarantee you they ain't cashing no paycheck.

I bet they're eating good though, and nowadays, that's better than money ever was, amirite?

I am what you may refer to as retired from driving, though I've done a lot of it lately. You see, here we are heading east again, on the road. We've met several folks who have been kind enough to pass along the location of a safe place. A place where some very important people are living. Maybe you've had the dreams too.

But the end of the story comes later kid. We're talking about the beginning right now.

Today's story is about history. Not boring history like how the Louisiana Purchase went down, or the migration of weird and strange folks across some frigging ice bridge in Alaska. History about how I got to where I am right now as I tell this story. We're gonna talk about some regrets, some successes, some mistakes, and maybe when that's all said and done... I'll talk about the place where we're heading. But you gotta be a good listener, and keep your hand away from that revolver on your hip unless you see something coming. Hands on guns makes me all ornery.

When the world first shit the bed back in June of 2010, I was delivering a load of diesel to a handful of my company's gas stations. I worked early hours that day. My boss had called me at home and woke me up to come in four hours early. He'd been watching the news, and knew that people would panic, and he wanted to have all our stations loaded right the hell up so we wouldn't sell out early. Rightfully so, I told him to go fly a kite, but he said he'd pay me double time for the shift, and as I'm sure you can understand, I got bills to pay. I hopped in my truck, and headed down to our operations center.

I left our main facility in North Texas with a full truck of diesel for five of our stores. To be honest, it seemed like a complete waste of time to me. Most of our shops had been refilled that night prior during the overnight shift, and having me make a second round about four hours after Billy finished his run through didn't make no sense to me. But, for double time, I'll drive a truck around full of diesel for twenty solid hours if they let me.

I knew shit was bad when I turned on Sirius. You ever listen to Sirius? Good stuff. I had caught a little of the news before I left my trailer that morning and things were definitely weird overseas. Grade A weird. People biting folks, riots, martial law, Mayan calendar nonsense.

I heard the word "zombie" several times on the boob tube, so I figured I'd listen in to the news on the radio. I started with the British channel, the BBC one, and after listening to that for an hour, I switched over to the CNN one for an hour, then back to the BBC, then back to CNN, and so forth. You probably like zombie movies too, kid your age.

I live in north east Texas outside a small city called Longview. If you can get your hands on a map without it getting bit off, you can find my back yard between Dallas and Shreveport Louisiana right off I20. Closer to the Shreveport side, but really, that ain't no real fact that's important anymore.

I am positive you've heard the stories of how it jumped the pond. Well, I guess more accurately, how it started to… what's the word? Manifest? Appear? Strike like the vengeful hand of God? It all started overseas right around our midnight I guess, and by late morning that day it had reached the eastern seaboard. I did the math. I listened to every single hour on the hour that morning from 3 am on, and I'll be damned if I didn't have the time when it hit east Texas to within an hour.

Right about an hour before noon that day the gas stations were a damned mess, and the sense of me delivering got real apparent, and real stupid, all at the same time. It reminded me of hurricanes. We don't really get nasty hit where Longview is, but I used to live down in Florida, and when a real bad storm is about to come in, everyone and their damn brother runs out and buys all the shelves clean of food and water, and then fills all their damn gas cans, car tanks and whatnot, and if you get

41

in their way, y'all gonna get curbstomped.

Of course, most folks agree to get along, and little curbstomping actually goes down, but that day was different. One little fire here, one little fire there, and the next thing you know, all hell actually breaks loose.

I was in the city of Longview when I saw my first fatality that day. Just off of the 120 exit at our gas station there. The shop is only about three hundred yards from the exit, and by that time of the day, I was getting mighty paranoid. Company rules say we aren't supposed to carry our personal guns on us, but they can kiss my ass. I typically carry my belt piece, which is my .38 snub, and I had that thing carrying heavy in the small of my back. I was glad to have it, but I was feeling the urge to pull it every time some damn fool came close to me or my truck.

I was just putting away the hoses and such after topping off the diesel at the shop when I see a patrol car coming down off the ramp in a real hurry. It makes the curve towards town, hits the main road going a solid seventy, and someone in a dang import station wagon makes a lane change, and the trooper can't stop in time. The cruiser rolled right over there in the middle of the way, and hit another car head on. Another car wound up hitting the ass of that car, and before you know it, there's four cars in the road all crashed up.

I was some ways away, and lot of other folks were right there stopping in, so I stood there and watched with my hands on my hips. No more than ten seconds after the cars in the crash settled, and the first of the folks were getting out their cars to check on the injured, dead or dying, another cruiser came off the ramp like a bat out of hell, and slowed at the accident. He wound up leaving the scene after talking to the officer in the rolled over cruiser. That trooper had a broken arm, but he seemed okay.

I kept watching, and no more than two or three minutes later, one of the injured folk in the car that got hit head on started to flail and try to get out the wreck. You might say that's when the wheels came off for me. I had this... sick feeling

42

down in my gullet when I saw that old guy start twitching and wheeling his arms all about. No one in a car accident does that after they've been passed out for such a time.

Well of course the folks rush over to help the geezer, and wouldn't ya know, when they get to him, he does what you'd least expect him to: bite people. Two arms reached into the car window to help get the door open, and both arms came right the hell back out with big old bite marks on 'em. Now at first I thought maybe they'd cut themselves on the wreck. It happens. You aren't paying enough attention to the twisted metal, and something sharp reaches out and bites ya. Happens all the time with cars and wrecks and stuff. But after the first guy pulled back holding his arm, and then the second, I could see the looks of betrayal on their faces. I mean they looked angry that they'd been hurt, and that's when I knew shit was on. The first dude bitten got the hell back in his car and drove away. He spun around the wreck in his Mustang and floored that sumbitch to the I20 and was gone heading west towards Dallas before you could count to ten. The woman who was bitten sat around, but I didn't see what happened to her.

All I could hear in the back of my head was what that BBC guy had kept saying earlier in the morning, "It seems that the bites are poisonous." He said all British-y, and snooty, but I kept thinking to myself…. Why risk it? With that Mustang fella on the interstate heading who-knows-where, all infected or poisoned or whatever, I figured he'd die and crash, then bite other folks, or maybe even stop, die, and then bite other folks. I mean hell at that point I felt with that one bitten dude free on the interstate, we might as well have been invaded by the Russians. Or the Chinese. We were occupied. Enemies right here on our precious soil.

At that time I truly felt that Jesus Christ was my savior, and for that I am thankful. I surely hope he really is the forgiving type, because I made the decision right then and there that I had to get the hell out of Longview, and get somewhere safe. And I made that decision right then and there because I still had a truck three quarters full of diesel, and if this shit went south as hard as I thought it might, I was in possession of liquid gold. Say what you will, but diesel makes the world go round boy.

I got myself back inside the store, and loaded up my credit card with all the water and food there. I think I got pretty lucky on that end too. Folks wound up rushing to the grocery stores to stock up that day, but no one went to the convenience stores like ours until things got much more desperate. I cleaned it out with my eBay MasterCard, racked up a whole shitload of points for auctions, and headed out. I needed to get my truck full of gas somewhere safe. I needed to get it into the back of my property where it wasn't visible from the road. I also needed to get out and lay low for a day or two. I wanted to treat the world like I treat my women; avoid the crazy for as long as you can.

Getting out of the parking lot and onto the highway was a hassle. The crazy man inside the car that had bitten those folks was flailing around all... well, all crazy like, and you could see the man was dead as can be. He had a dent in face that made his cheek all gone and his neck was split up the middle making it look like a bloody awful hotdog roll. When I saw him trying to pull his dead ass out the car, I knew all this jazz on the radio was the real deal. I didn't stop to help though, forgive me. I knew I had to get out. Of course sitting here tonight I'm starting to see my purpose in all this, and I feel a little better about it.

I live off of 300 north of Longview outside the city, and I did my level best to not think about the jail time I'd have to serve if all this blew over and was nothing. I figured I'd get grand theft auto, and possibly something serious like a felony for stealing the fuel, but I concocted a pretty good story about how I swung back to my place to change my clothes 'cuz I shit myself while I was driving. You see, our trucks have GPS on them, and if they got all nosy and shit and tracked the truck on me, they'd see plain as day it was sitting in my yard. Now if all this had just turned out to be nuthin' I'd need an excuse. I'd like to say I got lucky and that this turned out to be all real, but inheriting the

44

world we're in right now is just about the worst luck anyone can have.

Anyway kid, I live at the end of a dirt road in a 14 by 80 trailer that I paid for with my own money. I worked a lot of overtime, plus when my dad kicked the bucket he left me a small insurance policy so now I live on eight acres well off the road with no mortgage. I drove my truck around the back and parked it behind the trailer so if anyone happened to come down my road, they'd have a hard time seeing the oil tank. Gotta protect what's yours kid. Especially now.

I parked my ass in front of the television as soon as I got all my guns loaded and placed strategically around the house. I'm not a gun nut kid, but I believe in owning firearms for recreational and home defense purposes. I have a couple shotguns -both twelve gauge- a SKS because I like guns and stuff, and a few handguns. I already told ya about my revolver, but I've got me a .357 as well as a 1911 my dad gave me. That day I didn't go quite so far as to slap on the holster and the .45, but I kept it in my lap right up until dinnertime.

Right around then was when things were getting real bad in Texas though. It's kind of silly how bad things got and how fast. Back then we knew nothing, and I'm sure folks responded in as dumb a way as possible. You see, I think the worst thing that we suffered from that day and the first couple days after was indecision. Some folks thought it was nothing. Some folks thought it was just a nasty rabies style thing.

Most folks who saw someone infected, or whatever you want to call it, tried to help them. Cops were bitten while arresting them, paramedics were bitten while rendering aid, and the vast majority of folks were too scared of going to jail for shooting the dead folks to shoot the dead folks. I know the first time I saw a dead guy up close, I knew I had to shoot him, but kid... shooting someone is scary business. No one wants to go to jail, and I am positive a whole lot of folks waited until the absolute last second to shoot a dead guy, and waited too long and got bit as a result. It's the whole... I'll shoot you to defend myself story, but when you're twenty feet away, I'm gonna wait until you're right up on top of me to do it.

It also didn't help that there was a riot in Dallas.

That's what made me realize I had to go out. Right around five in the evening the new blew up with all these reports out of South Dallas. South Oak Cliff to be specific. I guess a few of the locals took it upon themselves to liberate many of the local retail establishments of their goods. Now in retrospect, looking back on it, that's what that means kid, every single business in the whole wide world should've just opened their doors and let everything go for free, but nope folks put up a fight. They couldn't see the writing on the wall just yet. They couldn't just give it away like they should've. Not like their damned insurance wouldn't have covered 'em for it. Greed did a lot of folks in.

You remember those riots after those cops in Los Angeles got off for beating that poor black guy? It was like that. Only the police response was lot heavier handed. Oak Cliff ain't the best neighborhood on a good day, and that day was a lot worse than any day ever before. Dallas cops are Texas cops, and with folks dying all over the place, the law decided to play it safe, and shoot every motherfucker that seemed even a little dangerous. You could say it got ugly kid.

You know how the dead come back right? We know that as a rule now, but back then… they had no idea really what to expect when they gunned down about a hundred looters in the middle of one of the shittiest neighborhoods of South Dallas. I've no idea how many of them sat back up, but if just fifty did, then they bit just fifty folks more…

That's how Dallas fell. Like a house of bloody cards my little friend. I remember watching the news for the next day or two, while it was still on, and then the radio after that for a few more days. Yeah, Dallas hit the fan. Fort Worth and everything in between went with it. Corpses everywhere, up and attacking. Back then we didn't know if it was viral, or fungal, or whatever, so yeah, it was a mess.

Anyway son, I sat there watching the riots break out in Oak Cliff, and I realized I needed to get my ass out of the house, and stock up on some more supplies. I'd been sitting there with my eyes stuck to the television set for a good long time, and when I saw all that shooting and fighting over food already, I knew I'd need to get me some stuff and fast.

I had good food. Lots of it. I poach deer kid, I won't lie. I am not the best person in the world, that's obvious. I put some salt licks out back the trailer and sit on my porch at dusk and dawn until a white tailed deer comes through and then I stock my freezer for some time. Back in… what was it, June? Late June? I'd bagged a deer just a week before, so I had meat. I also keep canned food on hand. Food wasn't the issue. Diesel wasn't either.

I needed my truck back, and I needed more ammo. You see kid, I had just driven my rig back to my house, and left my truck at work, at the distribution facility. I'm not the brightest fella, but I do keep a Polaris ATV on hand in my shed, and my Sportsman 550 was to be my ride for a few hours.

I was so damned worried about carrying my SKS out in the public that day that I left it at home. I was also still scared shitless to arrive at work on my four wheeler with my rifle like that. Again buddy, if this had all blown over, that's a recipe for not only unemployment, but a free ride to the loony bin. I played it a little safe, and left with my 1911, and the three mags I got for it.

The drive to the shop was about an hour, but I went pretty slow, and I kept to the trails. I wasn't entirely sure about the route to take to get there, but I made it safe.

Now let me set the scene for you properly son. I think it was about eight at night when I got there, so the sun was heading downwards like a sinking stone in a pond, and the sun's heat was relaxing a bit. Just a bit though. This is Texas in June remember. You can fry eggs on the hood of my truck at midnight some nights. The facility, hell, you've seen it already, has that big double fence around it, and has all those gates and stuff, and when I got there Greg, the geezer who sits in the security booth, you've met him too kid, was still there, but instead of being inside his little air conditioned hut, he was standing outside, scattergun in his mitts, and the hair on the back of his fat neck standing on edge. Hells, you ain't seen him big, have you? He was a regular heffer before all this happened. Grits and gravy instead of blood and guts I suspect. End of the world makes for a great diet plan kid.

So Greg hears my Polaris coming down the road and he gets his gun all ready and I slow down, and start hollering to him that it's me, and he and I have played poker before, so after a few seconds he lowers his gun, and I putt-putt up to him and he fills me in. The shop is long since empty. You remember Greg is from south Louisiana right? And he's got that New Orleans drawl to him? So he tells me all about how everyone up and left, and half the folks left real early to get their kids out of school, and how none of the drivers have returned with their trucks yet, and he's surprised to even see me.

I told him about the car accident I saw, and the news, and he already knows all about all of it. He's had the radio all day. He may have been a lazy man, but you gotta credit that Greg. He was there all that day and night, and stayed there until we returned a few days later. But that's another story. So I tell him about how I left my truck in the lot, and he says he knew already, so he buzzed me in, and I drove over to it. I drive a Ford Super Duty in diesel, and I keep two loading ramps in the back for my four wheeler, and I drove it right up in the bed, easy as pie.

When I left there and said good day and good luck to Greg, he said good luck to me, and I drove off to North Texas Firearms, where I do all my gun shopping. NTF is two miles as the crow flies from work on the edge of the industrial park in Longview's outskirts. NTF is ran by my good pals Rob and Carline Pastell. Rob and Carline have been friends of mine for about five years now, and they and their two sons run the shop. They've got an indoor shooting range and they sell a lot of stuff to the local hunters, and they're good people.

When I pulled in, the two Pastell boys, Rob Junior and Carl were in the parking lot with some heavy gear. Full on AR guns and body armor, and ballistic glasses and camo. They both looked like the end of the world had hit, and they were right. I think they recognized my truck, and then waved me in. I talked to them before I went inside to see their mom, and they told some tales of crazy folks coming to stock up on guns and ammo, so their dad left to go get more from their home, and to get more of the family's gun collection. They had plans to ride it all out in their shop, which was a great idea. They made it, still alive as far as I know.

Carline was as sweet as ever, though she looked like a long tail cat in a room full of rocking chairs. Nervous in the service. I picked up about five hundred worth of ammo and she wouldn't let me pay for it. I told her if she needed some fuel, to come see me, and I'd let her into the distribution facility for work, and that's a deal we made good on several times. Kid, barter is where it's at now. Have something good to trade for something good, and life is very achievable. Listen to me. I'm your damn elder. And wake up, I haven't even gotten to the good part yet.

I keep a CB in my pickup, and I was jamming with a few of my local chums. I'd kept off the radio almost all day, just listening really. The radio was almost dead now though. A few folks calling out the same accidents over and over, and all the dead folks now wandering the highway and city streets. Mostly in the areas toward Dallas, and right downtown in Longview where that accident had taken place. Well kid, let's be honest, it was starting to get real bad everywhere.

As I was heading home, truck full of 7.62 for my SKS and .45 cal, I heard a radio come out that stopped me cold on the side of the road. It was a guy I'd never heard before, and I could hear pain in his voice kid. You ever hear someone try and talk after they smash a fingernail with a hammer? Or right after they get something real heavy dropped on a toe? How they talk through their teeth instead of with their mouth?

This guy. He sounded like that.

He says, "Is anyone out there not driving that can help me? I can't drive anymore and I need help."

Then he says, "I've been bitten, I'm hurt awful and I've got a

49

box filled with people that need some help. Someone's gotta get them out of here."

Now kid I ain't no coward, but I was afraid to respond. I sat there on the side of the road for a good two minutes waiting for someone else to give him a thumbs up, but no one did. Finally, I nutted up and talked back to him. I said to him, "Where you at dog bite?"

He laughed back at me, and said, "I ain't been bitten by no dog, driver. I had one of them crazy people bite my hand, and my leg too, and I can feel the fever already. I can't see good, and I can't drive no more." Then he says, "I'm on the side of the street heading to Spring Hill Junior High."

Now kid, that was about a mile from where I sat. It was like Jesus himself had reached down and given me the opportunity to deliver people from danger. I can't say what came over me, but I hit my CB again, and I told him I'd be right over. As I pulled back onto the road and turned around, he told me he was driving a short haul trailer, and he'd just left the Dallas area with a load full of people. He was bringing them to the Junior High because he'd heard it was open as a shelter and he lived in the area. No one had driven by since he'd pulled over, and the trailer still had all the folks in it. If I could just get there, and switch out with him for a few minutes, I could drive the truck up the rest of the way to the school, open up the back of the truck, and be off. Folks rescued, driver aided, and I'm the hero. Eddie Smith, hero of Longview right?

Heh.

Well you see kid I had to take a bit of a detour around some Longview cruisers that had been parked to block the road. No one in the cruisers of course, but they were parked there to stop through traffic, clear as day. I looped around the neighborhood, and made my way to the street the driver said his truck was parked on. There it was kid. Unmarked 24 foot pup trailer, no sleeper.

I parked my truck on the side of the road behind his trailer and walked up to the cab of his truck. I was nervous kid, scared. I ain't afraid to admit it friend. I'd seen too many abandoned police cruisers, car accidents, and dead bodies on the news for any normal person to deal with and not be afraid. I could hear the people inside hooting and hollering for help, and I told them, yelled into the trailer to them that I was there to help. They simmered down. Right when I got to the distance where I could holler out to him, my better brain kicked in, not the one in my rick you smartass, and I stopped walking. Two things hit me like a prize fighter from Mexico beating folks up for a green card: one, I'd left my pistol in my truck's cup holder, and two, this guy had said he'd been bitten.

Now kid, by then I knew that the bites were the end of the road, and I knew they killed right quickly. I hadn't even considered that I'd have to plug this guy yet, so while I was thinking about needing to do the deed, I ran back and grabbed my 1911. I thumbed that safety selector down to the kill people setting, and I walked back to the truck's cab again.

I didn't need long to realize the driver had died. I grabbed the door handle of the cab and pulled myself up to the window to look in, and he reached out at me like I was a damned happy meal at the drive through. He was dripping blood, and biting at the air, and I jumped backwards off the truck, and I tell you kid, seatbelts save lives. If it weren't for his, you wouldn't be talking to me right now.

I landed on my asshole hard enough to split my tailbone and lose the air in my lungs. I damn near dropped my piece too, but I held onto it like I was jerking my gherkin. As I got the air back into my lungs I steadied myself on the ground and watched as that poor dead driver tried his level best to get at me. He couldn't get loose of that seatbelt though, and that's about when I knew how smart they were. Kid you already know they ain't that bright. But that night, when it all started, we knew nothing.

As I watched him, I leveled the .45 on him, and I put one through his chest. Gun was loud as a motherfucker I tell you. Shooting a heavy handgun like that in a residential neighborhood is the strangest thing. Normally you shoot at the range, or on your property, or in the middle of the woods hunting, not in someone's front yard, or on the side of the road like this. Plus you usually got plugs in 'yer ears.

Kid you already know the bullet didn't take him out. They're dead. Shooting them in the heart doesn't stop them any more than asking them to does. I shot him again, this time in the head, and that did him in. What was left of his skull flopped forward near the wheel, and as the folks in the back started screaming again, I opened the door and got him out as best I could. I put his body in the grass of the yard right nearby, wiped the blood and sweat off my forehead, and yelled to the folks in the back of the truck that we were on the move.

His truck drove fine, which was good. Though it weren't far. Mile, maybe two. When I pulled up to the Junior High I could tell things were bad there. Something had gone very wrong outside the joint. I saw the bodies of two of the local cops on the ground right at the entrance of the school parking lot. I had to stop or I'd drive over them.

I hopped out the truck to check on 'em, but they was dead. Both shot in the head. I took their service handguns, and their cuffs, and their spare magazines too. Most of which were on the ground. Judging by the direction the spent brass was in, they were shooting down the road away from the school at someone coming up the road. I never did figure out what had happened.

No dead folks around though and I saw a parking lot filled with cars, but no people. There was no one in the windows of the school, or the hallways. It was empty, deserted, and not safe at all. I won't lie. I was worried and a little panicked, so I got the hell back in the truck, and I turned it around. I couldn't stomach leaving those folks there at the school. As I turned the truck around, and drove back, I started thinking about a place I could leave these people. There was no way in hell I was bringing them back to my place right? Not enough food, and the last thing I wanted was twenty strangers in my trailer.

If the Junior High was shitcanned, then the High School would be the same. I ran through about thirty places in town that I might be able to leave them at, when I got back to the spot my truck was. I pulled over to think about what I was doing. Finally, as I stared at my truck, I realized I should ask these people where they wanted to go. Mighty kind of me, don't you think kid?

I hopped out of the truck and went to the rear of the trailer. I banged on it real hard to let them know I was about to open up, and just as I was turning the handle, I heard some folks screaming on the inside. They was yelling help! Help! Loud as they could.

I stopped and hollered again, "What's going on in there?" I asked loud. I heard about ten folks yelling and screaming at the same time, but they all kept saying the same thing over and over again, as loud as they could;

"He's biting us."

I listened to them scream for a second or two more, then I took my hand off the trailer lock. Kid, I couldn't let them out. If they were all being bitten, or had already been bitten, there was no way letting them out was a good idea. I listened to them fight and scream for a solid minute or two before the last of them stopped. I sat there, scared as can be for a bit, but then I went back to my truck, and grabbed a padlock out of the glove box.

I locked the trailer shut with my lock, and wrote in the road dust on the back of the trailer "DO NOT OPEN, INFECTED ARE INSIDE."

I think I spelled inside wrong though. Spelling was never my strong suit kid.

I left in my truck and drove home, straight to the my trailer where I turned off the lights, and stayed up all night long worried to death over whether or not I'd condemned those people to death because I didn't let them out when I first got there.

But you know what kid? I can't ever know for sure. I did what I thought was best at the time, and the price I pay is in my darkest nightmares of the dead, every single night.

Life is about tough decisions kid. Doing what needs to be done, even when it's the hardest thing you can imagine doing.

That's why we're on the road right now. That's why we're heading east. Heading towards a few people that I truly believe can lead us out of this nightmare.

What? Where are we heading?

Why we're heading to a place called Bastion son. The last truly safe place for us, we believe. We'll tell you more about why we believe that as we go I'm sure. Tell you more about a man I'd like to meet.

Maybe I'll tell you another story tomorrow night. Sleep if you can. Rest well, you'll be safe.

I'll be up all night.

No rest for the wicked.

Uncle Martin

Steve Gonzales

Jesse Garcia studied the aging farmhouse. Obviously it had been abandoned long before June 23rd. Haunted by ghosts maybe, but Jesse was pretty sure there were no zombies around. The old home was grayed and weather-beaten, fraying around its edges like a rough sketch in pencil. Several small outbuildings leaned in the overgrown yard like gravestones huddled around a tomb. A single crow stood like a shadow on the roof and plucked a fat grub from a gutter stuffed with dead leaves. It swallowed the meal whole and stared at Jesse before fluttering off with a screech.

"I think it's okay." said Jesse hopefully, ignoring the crow. He had circled the house twice and found it sealed up tight. But was it a fortress or a prison?

Jesse's uncle Martin sat behind him on a crumbling stone wall covered with thick vines. Martin wheezed and forced a smile. "It'll be good to spend a night or two indoors." he replied. Martin had long ago realized that he was too damned old to be sleeping outside.

Jesse nodded and examined the dilapidated structure again. The sun was a sliver of orange melting on the horizon and it was difficult to make out details in the gloom. Someone, long ago, had spray painted the word "haunted" on the sides of the house. Jesse just hoped it was free of the dead. There was a chill in the air, the first whiff of fall. They would have to find real shelter before winter. The cities and towns, infested with zombies, weren't an option. They needed someplace isolated to hole up in and the old farmhouse would be perfect. Jesse's stomach growled a reminder. Maybe there would even be food. They were down to two despised granola bars and Jesse and Martin were trying to see how long they could go before hunger forced them to finally eat the damn things.

Martin hooked a vine with his finger. The creeping plant had the fence in a snug embrace, its tendrils were pulling the stones back into the earth where they belonged. Martin closed his eyes and imagined the vines pulling him down into the moist ground where it would be cool and quiet. There he would be free from the illness and dread that plagued him.

Martin had been sick for weeks. His chest ached from a constant cough. His head pounded and burned and his clothes were soaked with sweat. Martin was sure he was dying.

A flashbulb went off in Martin's head. The image of a white room smashed his bleak fantasy into black shards. The shards turned into crows that winged away, cawing, until they were blotted out by whiteness.

An unseen voice tickled the inside of Martin's head. "There is no solace in death." The refrain was repeated two more times. Angels maybe, whispering warnings in his ear?

Martin didn't need angels to tell him the dead no longer enjoyed the peace of the grave. He could see the damned things walking around. They'd been trying to eat him and Jesse for months. The living dead. Ghouls. Zombies. Martin shuddered. Even worse than the zombies were the dreams. He could sense an intangible evil riding the ether. An arcane presence reflected in the few fitful snatches of sleep he could manage. Unlike the zombies, the evil wasn't interested in Martin's flesh, it wanted his soul.

Jesse mumbled something and Martin opened his eyes.

"Can you make it?" Jesse asked again. Martin coughed harshly and a wad of phlegm flew from his mouth, barely missing Jesse's leg. The sputum was flecked with blood. Jesse's face revealed both concern and disgust.

At sixty-four Martin had been surviving the zombie apocalypse remarkably well. Months of walking and a forced diet had shorn his frame of its flabbiness. Stern eyes were flanked by tangles of long black hair run through with gray. He had cast off the weight of resentment and disappointment that burdened his life and replaced it with a focus on survival. Then he'd gotten sick.

"I'll be fine." Martin said, taking a sip of water from his canteen. "Just need some sleep. Maybe there's a bed in there with a bottle of Jack under the pillow."

Jesse grinned. "Or maybe there's a bottle of that nasty cough syrup mom made me take when I was a kid. How'd you like that?"

"Up yours." grunted Martin.

He stood and leaned on a four foot length of lead pipe that served as both a walking stick and a bludgeon. The grooves on the end of the pipe were caked with dirt and dried blood. Martin had bashed in many a zombie skull with it. He poked Jesse in the ass with the pipe. "After you, chico."

Martin often kidded his nephew about being a boy even though Jesse was thirty-six. It surprised him that Jesse had lasted so long after June 23rd. If Martin had known what was coming he would have bet that Jesse wouldn't have survived the first day. Lots of better men hadn't.

Jesse was soft. Martin knew that. As an only child Jesse had been spoiled by his parents. He was gangling and gentle by nature and was blessed with the traditional dark family hair that made him look like a latino version of the character Shaggy from that famous cartoon. Unlike Shaggy, the monsters would have gotten Jesse long ago were it not for Martin.

Jesse was still regarding the farmhouse and stroking the stubble that covered his face. Despite months of not shaving, the hairs refused to blossom into a full beard. Martin poked him again.

"Ow!" cried Jesse. "That hurt!"

"A bite from one of those things would hurt even more." said Martin. "Now let's get going."

The house was completely boarded up. Even the second floor windows were shuttered. The front door had been replaced with a sheet of plywood reinforced with two-by-fours. Jesse thumped the barrier with the rusty crowbar he carried as a weapon. "Anyone here?" he called.

Jesse and Martin waited a few minutes. Nothing. Jesse shrugged. "Guess no one's home. Probably went to a square dance!"

It was common to find homes full of zombies. Even though the farmhouse was abandoned and probably empty, they had to be careful.

Jesse pulled a hand cranked flashlight from the duffle bag that held their few possessions. Charging the flashlight reminded Jesse of a movie camera he'd seen in a silent film about Egypt. He felt like Howard Carter at the tomb of Tutankhamun. But if there were monsters in the house they wouldn't be mummies.

When the flashlight was charged Jesse ran the light over the sagging porch they were standing on. He saw the outline of a welcome mat, dead leaves and an old wine bottle probably left behind by a transient. Jesse wondered if the man was dead and shuffling out there in the dark, watching them.

Beyond the trees that fringed the yard squatted a barn that Jesse had already explored. The barn was in much worse shape than the house. It was collapsing in on itself, sucked in by the black hole of decrepitude. Salvador Dali couldn't have envisioned a more twisted architecture.

The interior of the barn had smelled of piss and was littered with the boozy detritus of other bums. "We can't stay here." Jesse had said to his uncle Martin. "One sneeze from you and the whole thing will come down!"

"Quit daydreaming and open her up." Martin said with a grimace. He wanted nothing more than to lay down.

Jesse held the flashlight under his chin, illuminating his face. "They're coming to get you, Martin!" he intoned, mimicking a famous horror movie scene.

Martin rolled his eyes. It was good that Jesse still had a sense of humor but sometimes the jokes really grated on his nerves.

A wave of pain washed up in Martin's skull. He wavered on his feet. Phantoms danced in his eyes. A white room spun madly and dark lurching figures reached for him with decayed fingers and gnashing teeth.

The evil loosed on the world had seeped into Martin's very being, poisoning him. Martin knew the cure lay east of them, his fevered dreams told him so. Go east and find redemption. They may have been hallucinations but they gave him hope. Hope that there was still good in the world.

"Quit daydreaming and take the flashlight." laughed Jesse.

Jesse handed the flashlight to Martin and attacked the two-by-fours with his crowbar. The door frame they were nailed to was dry and brittle and gave up the boards without a fight. The plywood proved more difficult to remove as it had been cut to fit within the door frame. Jesse managed to pry one corner loose. He stuck his fingers in the gap and wrenched the barrier free with a shriek of rending nails.

Jesse held the plywood out like a shield as Martin stepped forward and shined the flashlight in the doorway. No zombies came shuffling out. Not even a cat or a bat to startle them with a cheap scare. The house offered nothing more dangerous than raggedy cobwebs and a musty odor that wrinkled their noses.

Jesse kicked at the dust on the floor inside the house. "No one has been here for a long time." he said. They were standing in what had once been a living room. Jesse mulled that over. Empty houses depressed him.

Martin waved the flashlight around the living room like a lighthouse keeper searching for wayward ships. The beam revealed an enormous couch that had likely been considered too big to bother moving. The couch sagged in the middle, mocking them with a fat grin. An empty gun cabinet stood against a wall, a disarmed sentinel left to watch over the house in its years of decline. The front door, more a large pane of intricately embossed glass, lay covered in dust on the moldering carpet. Martin imagined it to be a portal to the underworld. The only thing of promise was a yawning fireplace that beckoned with the promise of crackling warmth.

Three open doorways and a set of stairs called out for further investigation. It was like being on the set of a macabre game show. Behind which door is the flesh-eating zombie?

The first thing they had to do was secure the front entrance. Martin laid the sheet of plywood against the door frame while Jesse dragged the gun cabinet over to hold it in place. "No wonder they left this behind." he said with a chuckle. "It's heavier than your last girlfriend!" Martin ignored him. He didn't like to joke about women.

Martin walked over to the couch and thumped it with his pipe. No critters or unduly large spiders emerged so he sat down. He handed the flashlight to Jesse. "Take a look around." he said. "I need to rest for a bit. I'm really tired." Martin sighed and closed his eyes. "Maybe I'll start a fire and take a nap. Don't let me get eaten."

One door led to a kitchen. Jesse whisked the flashlight beam back and forth. The cheap linoleum that covered the floor was curling with age. An ancient refrigerator squatted in a corner bleeding rust. Jesse saw no point in opening it. The back door, as fortified as the front, looked like a scab on the peeling kitchen wall. Open cupboard doors mocked Jesse by showing off bare shelves. Then his light revealed a single can sitting on a counter littered with fly corpses. Jesse's stomach growled in anticipation. He picked the can up and read the label. Lima beans. He hated lima beans.

People ate much worse than lima beans when they were starving. Jesse moved the flashlight closer and read the expiration date: 4/18/92. He had been eighteen when the beans expired.

Jesse had read that canned food was edible far past the expiration date and the can looked undamaged. Still, if he was going to get food poisoning it may as well come from something he liked. He put the can down and sighed. He knew Martin would want to try them anyway.

Something in the dark shifted and laughed. Jesse could hear his uncle snoring away in the other room so it must have been his imagination. "Don't let your fear get the better of you."

60

Martin had told him. Jesse took a deep breath and decided to finish checking out the rest of the house. Then he noticed the letter.

The can of beans had been holding down a yellowed envelope. The name Charles was scrawled on it in a terse script warped by the rounded impression of the can. Jesse opened it and pulled out a single piece of lined paper.

"Charles,

If you get this letter I thank God you have returned. I am sorry for what passed between us. I should have told you sooner that you weren't my my biological son. Please believe me when I say that in my heart I always felt that you were. I may have treated you harshly but that was not the reason why. Your dear mother went to Heaven last year. I am happy that she is with the Lord but I cannot stand living in this house without her or you. I am going to Texas to live with my brother Robert. I have left the house in your name. Mr. Evans at the bank has all the details as well as some money for you. Please take some flowers to your mother's grave and say goodbye to her.

Your loving father, James"

The letter also included a black and white picture of a family of three. The photo reminded Jesse of the painting American Gothic with the pitchfork replaced by a young boy. In the bottom of the envelope was an obituary notice for an Ada Martins that left Jesse's fingers smudged with ink.

Jesse felt an ineffable sense of sadness. Apparently Charles had never returned. He and his father were likely dead, their differences never resolved. What was the point in going on? Life on earth had been reduced to a mad scrabble for survival. Every day was a trial of hunger and despair. Every road led to death. Why not just give in? Everyone Jesse knew was dead. Except for uncle Martin and Adrian.

What? Where had that come from?

Jesse hadn't thought of Adrian Ring in years. Adrian was a boy Jesse had known in elementary school back east. He remembered playing dodgeball and smear the queer with

Adrian and some other boys during fourth grade recess. The faces of those other boys flickered in his head like images in a faded Super 8 film but Adrian's was crystal clear. Weird.

Jesse left the letter and the can of lima beans on the kitchen counter and checked the other two rooms on the ground floor. One was a bathroom boasting an antique clawfoot bathtub and an empty medicine cabinet that was hung slightly crooked. The other room was a study lined with bookshelves that offered Jesse a set of dusty encyclopedias dating back to 1968. A beat to hell Davenport desk sat dejectedly in the center of the room, its drawers empty save for pencil stubs and mouse droppings.

Jesse rumbled upstairs, the rotting steps crying out with every footfall. A hallway separated the stairwell from two bedrooms. One was empty. In the other was a bed covered in plastic sheeting. A dresser stood in one corner. In the top drawer was a bible. Written on the inside of its front cover were the words "To Charles from mom and dad."

Jesse put the bible back and closed the drawer. The second and third drawers held bed covers and pillows that reeked of mothballs. Jesse shrugged. At least uncle Martin had his bed. No Jack Daniels though.

Jesse tromped downstairs. "That you?" asked Martin. The couch had all but swallowed him. Jesse turned the flashlight on his uncle. Martin was flushed and sweat beaded on his forehead. He wheezed and his chest rattled. "I'm in a bad way, kid."

Jesse nodded. "Found you a bed upstairs." he said. "But no Jack."

Martin pushed himself up and out of the couch. Spittle hung from one corner of his mouth. He wiped it on a sleeve in disgust. "Never wanted to go out like this." he thought to himself.

"Come on, gramps!" laughed Jesse. "I'll help you up the stairs!"

It bothered Martin that he was now weaker than Jesse. And that made him ashamed. He pushed Jesse's outstretched hand away. "I can manage." he grunted angrily. "You worry about yourself."

"How is it?" asked Jesse. Martin was lying on the bed. The climb up the stairs had worn him out. His body ached so badly that it was a struggle to find a comfortable position.

"Beats sleeping under a bush." Martin replied, tucking a pillow under his head. "Plus I always wanted to die in a bed that stunk of mothballs."

Jesse frowned and sat down next to his uncle. "You're not gonna die here." he said. The thought of his uncle dying scared Jesse more than anything.

Martin made a fist and thumped Jesse's back. "I think it'll be better if you sleep in the other room." Jesse understood what his uncle meant but protested anyway.

"Don't argue with me." Martin told Jesse. "If I die the last thing I want to do is take a bite out of your skinny ass."

Jesse nodded. He was glad the darkness hid his tears.

"Lock the door on your way out." said Martin with a grin. "I don't want you sneaking back in here after I'm asleep!"

Jesse locked the door and went into the other bedroom. He tried to get comfortable but his duffle bag made an uncomfortable pillow and the dusty carpet aggravated his allergies. His stomach rumbled. He thought of the lima beans down in the kitchen but he was saving them as a surprise breakfast for his uncle and he wasn't quite famished enough for another granola bar. Oh well, it wouldn't be the first time he went to sleep on an empty stomach. Sometimes Jesse envied the zombies. At least they got fresh meat every once in a while.

Jesse could hear his uncle coughing through the wall. Martin was all Jesse had left. Without him what would he do? It was Martin who had saved Jesse in the days after June 23rd. That had been the first day of the end of the world.

Jesse had been working in the comic book store. Stocking comics, listening to Cream on the radio and flirting with Maddie, his favorite customer. Maddie was young, petite and perky. She had striking green eyes that sparkled behind her over-sized glasses. A delightful package topped off with a pixie cut.

Maddie was polite and had listened as Jesse told her all about a Mustang convertible he had his eye on. His old beater had finally went to the junkyard in the sky and he was saving for a new one. Then the music had been replaced with a frantic news report. Some crazy story about the dead returning to life. Jesse had switched to another station but it was reporting the same ridiculous story. Maddie had left after that. Jesse remembered her saying something about a dream she'd had the night before.

Jesse was sure the news reports were some sort of hoax or exaggeration. He had also hoped that sales of his zombie comics would skyrocket. No such luck. Maddie had been his last customer.

By the end of the day the stories had been confirmed by government sources. His mother and father hadn't answered their phone so Jesse had locked up the store and walked to their house. When he got there, his uncle Martin had been standing on the porch with a funny look on his face.

"They're not here." Martin had said. "Come on, let's go to my place. I left them a note to join us."

Martin owned a bar and lived in an apartment on the second floor. The only value in the place as a sanctuary were the barred windows and solid doors. Unfortunately the streets were packed with cars, many of them wrecked. Fights were breaking out. A disaster movie come to life. That was when Jesse and Martin saw their first zombie.

Jesse closed his eyes as his recollection sped up. A kaleidoscope of horrors marching by in fast forward.

A man trapped in a smashed pickup truck, his chest crushed. A passerby reaching in to help and getting bitten on the arm for his trouble. The good Samaritan screaming and another man blowing his head off with a shotgun. The man with the shotgun killing the thing in the truck.

Uncle Martin pulling Jesse from his car and pushing him through the crowd. Running with him through a field and into a stand of woods.

Standing on a corner and watching Martin's bar burn to the

ground. With it went Martin's invaluable gun collection.

Wandering the countryside, scavenging what food and supplies they could. Martin killing the dead they ran across. He called them abominations. They occasionally crossed paths with other survivors but they were either mad and useless or predatory fiends as void of empathy as the zombies.

Walking through a small village and seeing a mountain of burned bodies in an empty lot. A single arm sticking out, fingers clawing the air.

Zombies pulling at a chain link fence crowned with barbed wire. In-A-Gadda-Da-Vida booming from loudspeakers. Crazy-looking men behind the fence laughing and shooting the zombies.

Martin had done all the killing and most of the scavenging. Jesse had felt useless. He'd never known any hardship. Didn't have any survival skills. He was something less than a man. He could see that in his uncle Martin's eyes.

Jesse's visions slowed. Adrian Ring floated in front of him and disappeared.

The last time Jesse had seen Adrian was in the summer between fourth and fifth grades. Jesse's father had announced they were moving to Ohio where he'd gotten a job as a factory foreman. Jesse and his mother had went to K-Mart for moving supplies. They'd been in the checkout lane when Jesse spied Adrian walking through the doors with his mother and little sister. Adrian hadn't seen him and kept on walking. Jesse wondered what Adrian looked like now, if he was still alive.

"He killed them you know."

The hairs on Jesse's nape stood up. Something was in the room with him.

"He loved and hated your mother for what she did. Why do you think he followed her to Ohio?"

Jesse played the flashlight around the room. Nothing.

"Your uncle is a murderer. He used the chaos to hide his crime."

A vision formed in front of Jesse's eyes. His uncle was standing over his parents holding a bloody knife. The same knife Jesse carried in his duffle bag. The one Martin insisted that Jesse carry.

"Why do you think he never wanted to look for them?"

Jesse hated the nightmares. He'd been having strange visions ever since the apocalypse. He sensed uncle Martin was having them too but they hadn't discussed it. Neither wanted to admit they were probably crazy.

"He's not your uncle."

Jesse closed his eyes tightly. A white room appeared in the distance. Then it winked out.

"Adrian." whispered Jesse.

"Forget Adrian! He's rotting in the ground!"

A cold vise squeezed Jesse's heart and he gasped for breath.

"Your father just died!"

Thump!

The sound had come from the other bedroom. Something was pounding on the door.

"Uncle Martin?" called Jesse. He was fully awake now and standing in front of Martin's bedroom door. The visions had receded.

Thump! Scratch! The door rattled in its frame.

Jesse knew his uncle must have died. His reanimated corpse was trying to force its way through the door. Trying to get at him. Trying to eat him. Jesse retreated to his bedroom and closed the door. He was holding Martin's knife in his hand.

Maddie coalesced in front of Jesse. "Come with me." she said with a smile.

Something whispered in the darkness, too faint for Jesse to hear. "There is no solace in death."

Martin woke up with a start. Sunlight poked through the shutters that blocked the window. He felt his forehead, finding it cool to the touch. His fever had broken in the night and his skull no longer throbbed. He was still alive. Martin coughed and a clotted piece of sputum landed on his shirt. He probed it with a finger. It was dry and sticky, a sign that his lungs were clearing up.

Martin recalled the night. The visions had come again in his sleep. The white room with three indistinct faces beckoning to him. A mohawked man Martin didn't know was killing zombies. Then Jesse screamed. A murder of crows was lifting him into a darkening sky.

Martin sat up. "Jesse!" he screamed. "Answer me!"

All of a sudden Martin was freezing. He felt light-headed. Something awful had happened. He needed to find Jesse. He needed to know it had all been a bad dream. Martin swung his feet over the edge of the bed. His stomach was knotted in a tight ball. "Jesse!" he called again.

There was no reply save for a faint tittering from the eaves. Scurrying mice or perhaps the whispers of baleful ghosts? Martin didn't care for the sound either way. He closed his eyes and focused on the white room. When he opened his eyes the black thoughts had retreated. Feeling a little better, Martin put his shoes on, picked up his lead pipe and went looking for his nephew.

Martin's first stop was Jesse's bedroom. He rapped on the door with his pipe. "Jesse? You in there? Come on buddy, talk to me!"

Martin turned the knob and found it unlocked. The door shrieked in protest as he pushed it open. Outside a crow cackled in anticipation. Darkness whirled around Martin's soul, plucking at it with talons. Then it was ripped away entirely.

Jesse was standing in the middle of the room in a pool of blood, bathed in sunlight that streamed through the window. Flies and dust motes danced around him in the light. The shutters had been opened and were hanging limp with age from the window frame. Perhaps Jesse had wanted to see one last sunrise before he did it?

Jesse was dead. He had slit his wrists with Martin's knife and still clutched it in one red-speckled hand tinged blue in death.

The zombie that had been Jesse Garcia lifted its head and looked at Martin with hollow eyes. It clacked its teeth and took a step forward, its shoes sticking in the drying blood. It offered the knife to Martin and moaned.

Something whispered in Martin's ear. "Join us."

"You bastards!" cried Martin. "It was me you wanted! Why didn't you just take me?"

Martin swung the pipe and hit his dead nephew in the side of his head. Bone crunched and an eye squirted out of its socket and plopped on the floor. The thing that had been Jesse continued its advance, comically slipping when it stepped on the eye. Martin held the pipe over his head and brought it down squarely on the zombie's skull, splitting it open with a dull crack. The zombie dropped the knife and keeled over, thudding on the floor. It twitched once and was still. Martin hit it again just to be sure.

The zombie was officially dead. Jesse was dead, gone forever.

Martin held the pipe up in front of his face and looked at it in disgust. Pieces of brain were clinging to it like fat slugs. He tossed the pipe away, the clatter of its landing not even registering. He no longer wanted it. He would have to find another weapon to kill the dead.

A trail of blood led from the center of the room to a wall. On the wall, in his own blood, Jesse had written the name "Adrian" and the word "east." Martin studied the words and nodded. He understood what they meant and what he had to do. Now it was time to go and do it. But first he had to take care of Jesse.

Martin covered the corpse of his nephew with the plastic sheeting from his bed but the flies just crawled under it. He would have to do something about that. He wouldn't leave Jesse for the bugs.

The smoke rising from the farmhouse hung over the sun like a shroud of gauze. Martin sat on the stone wall and watched Jesse's funeral pyre burn. He picked at the vines that ensnared the stones. Death no longer had any appeal for him. He was sick of death.

Perched on the fence on the other side of the yard was a crow, likely the one from the night before. It cawed angrily and fluttered off into the sky, becoming one with the smoke.

Martin drank long from his canteen. He had a quite a haul

in front of him, heading far to the east as he was. Still, he stayed put and watched for a time as a blanket of somber clouds lumbered after the sun like a fleet of warships heavy with cannon. Martin half expected them to disgorge a rain of pestilence to bar his path. He watched the tall grass in the untended yard sway to the rhythm of the fire like a sea of penitents. He watched until the farmhouse was nothing more than a heap of embers glowing dull orange. He knew then that it was time to go.

Jesse's duffle bag and crowbar lay beside Martin. He stood up and ran through the contents of the bag in his head. Flashlight, knife, dirty clothes, comic books, first aid kit, the two granola bars, matches and an empty tin of lighter fluid. Tucked away in a side pocket was a wrinkled photograph of Jesse and his parents that Martin had almost thrown into the fire. There was also a can of lima beans he'd found in the kitchen. It wasn't much to travel with but at least the beans would make a good lunch.

A Girl Alone

Lee Smallwood

Kim woke to the sound of an axe hitting timber... It was the same sound she heard every day. Her Father George was outside splitting logs again, it had become an obsession.

"We'll need more wood for the winter. Remember how cold it was last year?" was all he kept saying every time Kim asked him to stop.

She worried about her Dad since her Mom had taken ill early winter. Her death had been hard on both of them but her Father had taken it the worse. He feared that his daughter would be left alone out here in the wilderness and wanted to make sure she was ready if he passed away. George had a heart condition that the doctors said was brought on by being overweight and unfit. That wasn't a problem anymore. His frame was now that of a much younger man and his body carried almost no fat as he swung the axe down again. However the heart condition would not repair itself, it was permanent and that was what scared him the most.

Kim dropped into her sweats and walked towards the door of her room. She paused to remove the thick timber locking bar from the hangers mounted on the frame before stepping out into the day. Squinting against the strong northern sun she waved as her Fathers eyes came round to meet hers. He nodded a good morning before going back to his work. Time was running out was the only thought running through his head.

"Want me to check the traps?" Kim asked as she pulled on

her boots that had been sitting on the covered deck of the cabin.

"Done it. You can start preparing for jerky if you want," George said as he swung the axe again.

"Do we need more? We have sacks of the stuff," Kim said trying to cover the fact that she hated the taste.

"We can never have too much. You never know what's around the corner," George said pausing a few seconds to check the blisters on his hands. He would stop just before the skin broke to avoid an infection if possible. "Besides the meat will only go to waste if we don't dry it."

"Ok.," Kim said smiling. It would stop her getting bored anyway.

There wasn't much else to do out here in the woods, there never had been. She had been coming up here with her Mom and Dad for years as a child and it was the perfect place to run when the dead came calling. They had been on a visit to the ski resort to stock up on ammunition and fishing supplies for her Father while her and her Mom had stocked up on white wine and glossy trash magazines filled with celeb gossip along with before and after surgery photos. Her mother Kerri was not one for the outdoor life but she loved her husband so would spend the days lounging by the lake while George fished. The cabin itself was miles from the nearest hard road, the only way to access was via a dirt track that ran for miles through the trees of the forest that surrounded the small town high up in the hills. The family had inherited the cabin and the surrounding acres of woodland from George's Father who had been a forest guide most of his life. In winter it was different, deep snow and traitorous weather meant they only had access during the summer this fact had saved their lives... Her mother had passed away during the winter after falling through the ice on the lake during an ill judged fishing trip and developing pneumonia. Her father still blamed himself.

As George was placing the last of their supplies into the back of the old blazer he kept at a friend's house in the town he heard the first of the gun shots. He contemplated grabbing his rifle from the back of the truck and heading over to lend a hand only to lock eyes with his beloved Kerri. She knew him well and knew he wanted to do the right thing. But she had also seen the news that day and knew they needed to get out of there. There were screams coming from down the street now as George stood thinking. By the door to the store he had been visiting his whole life were two large mesh bins filled with hiking meals, the type you just added water to. Two-for-one deal of the day, the label read. He took a breath and opened the back of the truck, Kerri's head dropped as she thought he was reaching for his rifle case. He wasn't.

The next sound she heard was the sound of dried food packets cascading into the rear of the truck followed by anything else that was placed by the door to the store. The trunk slammed shut and George climbed in. A flurry of gravel announced their departure as totally out of character George gunned the motor and fled the scene of his first-ever theft.

As they drove away George looked in his mirror to see the shop's owner standing on the steps of the shop. He was smiling and his hand was raised in a friendly wave. Stanley the owner of the store was in his seventies and had known George his whole life. He was pleased George had put family first. Stanley wouldn't leave, though he would have given George more if he'd asked.

The town had been out of bounds since that day, at first it was the dead that kept watch over the shops and taverns, now it was the living.. George had gone into town twice since that day in June, twice he had returned saddened by what he saw. Militia now ran the town and anyone not with them were now used for sex or dead. George wouldn't let that happen to his eighteen year old daughter. He had spent the time since the dead rose teaching Kim everything he had learned about the land, she was a fast learner and good at almost everything. Now here she was, skinning and removing meat from carcasses that her father had provided.

Kim was just getting to the end when she noticed the sound of wood being split had stopped. She was pleased because it meant her ever working Father could rest for a while. She wiped the blood and gore from her hands before walking back towards the cabin from the lean too they used to prepare the meat. She stopped a few meters short when she saw the axe lying on the ground with a timber block still wedge onto the blade. It was their only axe and her father wouldn't have left it that way. After it was used it was always cleaned and sharpened before being returned to its resting place inside the cabin. Her eyes scanned around but she couldn't see him anywhere.

"Dad," she shouted but got no reply. She was worried now as she had left the safety of her room without the old revolver her father had given her soon after they had arrived. She looked around again before heading for her room, she figured he'd either gone after something with his rifle or been taken by someone who had sneaked up to the place. She stepped into the dark cabin and headed straight for her room. The door was open as she reached it and standing in the doorway was her father. She stopped and stood staring at his back before speaking. "Are you ok..?"

Her father's head had been leaning slightly to the left twitched and his body turned. Her heart sank as the death in his eyes came into view. The white eyes, devoid of life gazed upon her as she stood frozen to the spot.

As George took his first step towards her she turned and ran. Getting out into the bright light was the first stage of her survival. The second meant grabbing the once-cherished axe and splitting the timber from its blade. It took her two tries to clear the blade and as she raised it for the last time, her father stepped into range.

"Ok Dad... just like you told me..." Kim said with determined tears streaming down her cheeks. "Single blow to the head."

As she said the words her father's now dead but animated body crumpled and fell to the floor.

She stood confused as the body lay before her. How did this happen, why did this happen. She stood motionless holding the axe high as her arms filled with pain. Was it a trick, had she

74

missed the sound of a shot? Was it safe for her to say goodbye...

Eventually her strength waned and the axe slid from her grasp falling noisily to the ground. The body of her father didn't move at all. She slumped to her knees and sobbed for over an hour before gritting her teeth and taking deep breaths through her nose. They had talked about this. Dad knew it would happen someday and he got you ready for it. *Now it's up to you.* She told herself.

Later Kim spent some time piling rocks on top of the grave she had laid her father to rest in. it was next to her mother's grave... She was pleased they were now together as she wrote the date on his head stone. March 3rd... She was glad she hadn't had to finish him.

She couldn't stay up in the mountains alone. All her life she had been a social animal and she craved other people's company. What she didn't want was to go into town. Her and her father had spent many an evening going through plans to get back to Westfield using old trails and logging tracks that ran south, now she would be taking them alone. She started out by packing light, if it didn't protect her or provide food it would be left behind. Her father's clothing was too big for her but it made her look more like a man from a distance and a final sacrifice of her hair completed the look she was after. Sitting at the mirror where her mother had spent hours combing her long golden locks Kim took the scissors from the kitchen and removed her own. Her fingers now ran through the cropped golden hair and she smiled to herself. Picking up her backpack and her father's rifle she heaved the heavy wooden door of the cabin closed and walked to the grave of her parents. She would return one day to place better headstones she told herself. Then turning for the trees she said goodbye to the land that had saved her life.

She placed her Father's hat on her head, and checked the guns on her hips before setting off towards the lean to. As she passed she took the reins of the old mule her father had picked up from a neighbor's cabin a few miles away. The neighbors were long dead and the mule had survived by eating the grass and weed that grew along the lake side, her father didn't say how they had died but she knew they had killed themselves shortly after the 23rd of June.

Loaded with the dried meat she hated and the tools she would need to survive she took the first step.

Alone now she would head south, she was going home...

Thirty Thousand Feet
Tracy Wilson

June 23rd, 2010

Eighty souls occupied the Boeing 737 on a nonstop red-eye from Dallas to New York, departing five minutes after midnight. United Flight 1269 climbed rapidly, passed through a thin layer of clouds and turned to the northeast. A full moon hung from the heavens, escorting a long string of stars that spread out as far as the eye could see.

Seat number C-34 in coach was right next to the window and six rows from first class. It gave the passenger sitting in it an excellent view of the night sky and he stared out at the dark; watching as thousands of lights twinkled and surged, slowly fading away when the plane shot up through more clouds. The man was above average looking and didn't raise any suspicions with cropped dark hair and a day's growth of beard. Blue jeans and a black dress shirt hid a well toned body and black boots finished off the look. A low profile was something he had perfected over the years, confident no one would even pay him any attention. However, if anyone dared to take a longer look would realize this was a man you didn't want to mess with.

Elliot Bane loved the job, but despised the hours. It had been a tedious transition and the change of hours had been rough. Considering the fiasco in Barcelona two months ago, things were on the upswing. Regardless, the loss had taken its toll and no matter how hard he tried, Elliot couldn't shake it. *That had been a complete mess,* he mused …shaking away the thoughts. Bad dreams had kept him up for days. But it was what it was and Elliot had to deal with it on his own terms-to the chagrin of his supervisor. To set his mind right, he looked over the rows of seats, counting the steps between his spot and the front- calculating how quickly it would take him to get to the pilot. At thirty thousand feet, reaction time was critical. There was no room for mistakes.

At thirty four, he felt on top of the game. It wasn't perfect of course. Nothing was in this day and age. However, life had been decent enough that he really couldn't find any complaint. Other than the fact that he was still single… under the circumstances it was hard to keep a serious relationship. Not that he had any issues with the opposite sex. It was just the fact that most times it ended too quickly and more times than not, too messy. Elliot chewed on his lip in thought, trying to rationalize his past mistakes with women. It wasn't the fact that he didn't try. He had always given more than a hundred percent…

Perhaps he thought, that right there was the problem. Always trying too hard to make the relationship work. But with his type of work schedule, maybe things went too fast. Elliot's mind wandered for a moment, turning each memory over for a closer look, examining every success and mistake. Which according to him, the mistakes outnumbered the successes seven to three. Each one of their names etched into his soul so that he wouldn't forget.

He eyed the flight attendant's reflection and immediately recognized her. A cute red-head. Petite with a great bubble-butt. He always had a weakness for red-heads and glanced at his watch. She was busy with another passenger just ahead of him. He focused in on her, watching each subtle move she made. Each smile that curved her lips as she chatted with the older man until she broke away and walked toward the front.

He was half tempted to stop her, but froze. It had been almost two years since the last time he had seen her... and now. Now he couldn't even think straight. Two years since a broken promise had ended something that could have been. Even with the age difference... his mind calculating that she would be twenty three by now.

Bad thoughts came crashing back and he stood, making a beeline to the bathroom. With the door secured, he stared at the reflection. Flipping through the what if's and should haves that could have happened between them. Too many circumstances that threatened to drive him crazy. Elliot quickly relieved himself and turned to the sink, washing his face and hands vigorously, trying to forget. He nearly freaked out when he looked up and saw someone else in the mirror.

"Thomas?" he said.

It had to be an hallucination. Too many hours and not enough sleep.

"Hello buddy," the apparition replied. "And no, you're not seeing things.

"Bullshit," Elliot said. Rubbing his eyes. "I'm just tired. That's all."

"Elliot, you goofy bastard. Did you forget last night already?"

The words of his dead partner froze him with a chill. "It was only a dream." Elliot said, staring at the mirror.

"Not just a dream, my friend. If you had only met me half way, I would have been able to tell you. But you wouldn't open up and be receptive."

"You're dead, brother. This can't be... it's impossible. I don't believe in ghosts."

"Nothing is impossible, Elliot. No matter what your brain says, this is very real and you have to listen. I don't have a lot of time, okay? You have to pay attention and not screw this up. Your life depends on it."

Elliot shook his head. Unable to believe. This didn't make sense.

"There's something coming. I don't know exactly what it is

brother... but it's some serious shit. You have to get the Captain to land this plane at the nearest runway. Get everyone out."

"Is it a bomb?" Elliot asked.

"No, something worse."

"What can be worse than a bomb?" Elliot asked, raising his voice to no one in the tiny room. "Seriously... if I'm going to risk my neck over some kind of messed up mind fuck... I have to have something for God's sake."

"I don't have all the details and my time is running out. I wish I had more for you... I really do. No matter what you have to trust me. Get this plane on the ground, okay? And be ready. Get your balls screwed on tight, cause the shit is about to hit the fan."

And like that, Elliot was staring at his own reflection. Confusion muddling his brain as he tried to shake the uneasy feeling. Uncertainty played tricks on his mind as he made his way back to the seat. The face of his partner haunting him as he scanned each passenger. He wondered if any could pose a serious threat, but none had met the criteria that would have raised the alarm, so he dismissed that idea. He stomped out the absurdity of the whole encounter that just occurred and filed it under stress. It was nothing more than a brief lapse of reality and he had to get his mind right. No distractions. But despite his best efforts, it took a brief glimpse of red hair to make him forget. The image flipped a switch in his brain.

Elliot pushed away the negativity of his relationship with her as if it were a persistent fly. *No, not this time.* He would make things right with her. He would correct the old mistake and... the thought died as quickly as it had formed. What if she was seeing someone else? Maybe even married now? Kids? He hadn't noticed a ring on her finger when she passed.

His mind floated back to that night they had met. Caught between flights, she had been aggressively negotiating an ATM when he happened by. The colorful language she used had caught his attention and he made the first move. Engaging her in a brief yet interesting conversation, she had reluctantly agreed to a cup of coffee. And slowly, very slowly... he had cracked her shell open just enough to see the real her. The bright, funny and so full of life version that made him weak in the knees. They parted with the intentions of meeting in Chicago in two weeks and this time he promised it would be more than just coffee. With a smile, she handed him a piece of paper- one that he didn't look at until she had been gone for a full ten minutes.

Anna Bishop. She had even dotted the i with a small heart along with her phone number and email. She got right to the point when she underlined <u>Don't leave me hanging.</u>

He smiled at that memory.

He looked around the cabin. Most of the passengers were either occupied with books or settling in for the three hour and forty minute flight. The cabin lights were dimmed and Elliot debated on what to do. He had one of his favorite books stashed away in the carry-on bag -which he had yet to even crack open in a month- or... his mind drifted for a second until he heard a commotion that put him on alert.

She -Anna- passed him, leading a middle aged man by the arm. He wore a business suit and held a white cloth to his mouth that was stained red. Powers of observation. Years of training taught him to take in every aspect of his surroundings. Elliot could see the concern on the flight attendant's young face, but he knew they were trained to handle any emergency, so he didn't worry. It didn't look too bad from what he saw anyway. Elliot casually leaned to the side and hazarded a look back, catching the sway of her hips and trying to imagine what she looked like naked. *Twenty three was a good age,* he thought with a grin.

The cell phone vibrated with a text message, interrupting the moment of appreciation and forcing Elliot to twist and fish it out of his jeans.

*****

Israel Dajovic could feel it. Something wasn't right and as he took a deep breath to stop the panic... It was an excruciating pain. Starting deep within the stomach. At first, he thought it was merely a reaction from the food. But the longer he sat, the worse it got. Sweat beaded across his forehead. He reached for the call button, doubling over and gasping for breath. He pushed the button again. Hands shaking, trying to wipe away the sweat. The first cough sent a bolt of pain throughout his chest. And then another. He reached for a handkerchief, coughing violently and praying that he wouldn't throw up. That would not be very dignified. He caught a child staring at him from across the aisle and wiped his mouth.

"Something's coming." the child said to him.

"Sorry?" Israel said, staring at the boy.

"Be ready."

"What?" the man demanded, blinking as his vision blurred. "Sergey? Is that you?"

The young boy only laughed.

"No, no, no… this was impossible." Israel said. His son had been dead for ten years.

"Sir? Are you okay?" the flight attendant said, pushing back a strand of her red hair.

He stared at the woman, confused and frustrated. "That child…"

"What child?" she asked.

Israel looked at the empty seat. Fear reaching into his thoughts as he began to think it was a heart attack. He started to stand.

"Do you need help, sir?." Anna asked, using her hand to steady him when he stood.

"Yes. Yes, please. I'm not feeling well," he replied, holding a cloth to his lips.

After walking to the lavatory he thanked the young flight attendant and locked the bathroom door behind him. He bent forward and spit up blood into the sink. After a moment, he splashed cold water onto this face as the feeling faded. In his fifty years of life, Israel had never been this sick and it worried him. Another coughing fit and this time he threw up a lot more blood. The pain inside him felt unbearable and it drove him to his knees. He gasped.

Mind racing with panic, Israel's body began to shake. He recalled the young woman from last night. She had been a high-end escort. Very beautiful. Very young. Curves in all the right places. His assistant Caesar had picked the young woman personally and there had been no doubt it had been an excellent choice. Even the hefty price had been well worth it, though he had tired easily after an hour or so. But there had been something strange about her behavior. Some of the things she wanted to do and experiment had been interesting to say the least. He tried to wrap his mind around all that had occurred when his body started to shut down. The world closed in, faded into nothing and Israel Dajovic died at thirty thousand feet very much alone. His body slumped to the floor and fell against the door.

*****

Captain William Kennedy wasn't sure as to what he had heard. The words had been mixed in with static and loud pops that came from the headset. He adjusted the earpiece and double checked the radar. So far, there were no signs of any bad weather and this lead him to believe he may have been hearing things.

"Did you say something, Alex?" he asked, looking at the co-pilot

"Hmm?" the other man answered.

"Did you say something?"

"No, sir," the co-pilot said.

"Must have been radio static," William replied, tapping the headset and setting the auto-pilot.

The radio popped again, alternating between traffic from other planes and something odd. With nearly twenty years of service, William had experienced many strange occurrences that he couldn't rationally explain. He had simply put it away, never dwelling on it much as if it were nothing. However...

"William." The voice cracked and fizzed from the headset.

Catching him off guard.

He turned again to the co-pilot. "Stop playing games, Richard."

"He can't hear you," the female voice said. This time it was familiar. The same one he had heard two nights ago.

"Please stop," he begged as he tried to close his mind from the pain.

"You know I can't. They won't let me."

"I don't..." he started when the sting hit him in the chest. "Elizabeth, please..."

"I thought you loved me."

"I do. And I always will."

"Is that what you thought when you were with that whore two nights ago? Is that how you show your love?"

"You've been gone a very long time," he said, gaining confidence while wondering if he was losing his mind. The co-pilot sitting beside him didn't seem to hear or realize anyone else was talking, yet he was. They were.

"I'm sorry my love," the voice replied. "I suppose it's hard to see you with someone else. We were together for so many years. I won't lie when I say it hurts. But... I can understand."

"Then I must suffer your ghost?" he asked.

"You know why I've come to you, William. We spoke in your dreams, remember?"

How could he forget? It had been one of the most terrifying experiences. So realistic that it had forced him to miss a day of work. And now by mentioning it, the details came flooding back. "I don't know if I can," he whispered. Hesitant. Praying she would go away.

It took a few seconds before the voice came back. "They are very clear and precise."

"I won't."

"You'll leave me here to suffer for eternity then? Is that how you want to remember me?"

Her words started to break his heart and he wiped at the tears. "There are too many innocent souls on this plane, Elizabeth. What you're asking me to do..."

84

The radio crackled again and for a moment, he thought the ordeal was over.

"William... please. I'm begging you. And you know in all the years we were married... I never asked or begged of you for anything."

"Okay," he agreed. "I will do as you ask."

"Thank you, William. Don't worry about what is coming. While there will be loss and the world will suffer... you're doing the right thing."

"What if someone sees me?"

"Your actions will be concealed. But do not hesitate; it will be only for a few minutes."

"Then you will leave me in peace?" he asked.

"Yes, my love. I will be set free and you will only be left of memories of what we had."

William swallowed hard, knowing the decision to follow through would be the end. "I will always love you."

There was no reply when he stood and excused himself from the cockpit. He counted each seat as it had been instructed to him in the dream. He removed the pen knife from his jacket and carefully placed it in the lap of a sleeping woman. Not even taking the time to look at her. He was too afraid. Afraid of what would happen. With a last minute burst of clarity, William pivoted and returned to the cockpit. He locked the door and promptly released the fire extinguisher from the wall mount. He struck the co-pilot in the head from behind. It took three vicious swings before William stopped; sickened at what he had done. There was no rationalizing it, he thought. No going back. But at least the other man wouldn't have to suffer once the events started.

William quietly settled into his chair and closed his mind to every thought. Every nerve that ached and throbbed from the center of his core. Without a doubt, he would pay for taking this path, but at least he would finally find peace and quiet.

*****

Elliot couldn't quite make out the text message and he re-read it three times. There had been an incident at one of those ritzy Dallas hotels and the local police had called in the FBI. It was a mess from what he could tell; within an hour the media was all over it like sharks. He got up, stretched and headed towards the back of the plane, stopping at the curtain that blocked off the flight attendants area. Nervously scratching his face, he parted the curtain. A male steward was sipping a bottle of water, quietly conversing with a female co-worker. Elliot was about to speak when another text came through. This one had a name and photo on it and the suspect was on board. All efforts to secure the person would have to be taken. Authorities would be waiting on them in New York.

The woman looked up. "May I help you Marshal?"

"Can you please check the manifest for a Nora Grant for me?"

"Of course," she replied and pulled out an electronic device. "Is there a problem?"

"I don't think there will be," he lied.

The woman scrolled down the list of passengers. "Here you go. First class, seat A-6."

He eyed a glimpse of her bare leg. "Thank you."

"Anytime," she replied with a cozy and inviting smile. "Anything else you need help with?"

He returned the smile, catching her subtle wink. And then it hit him. *Becky...*

His stomach dropped and those deep, sea green eyes bore into him. She had chatted him up roughly eight months ago. His brain stumbled over itself as he dredged up memories... They had coffee and an hour later, she had him in her apartment.

"You don't remember, do you?" she asked with another toothy grin.

"Uh-oh," the steward with the water added.

"Cat got your tongue, Elliot?" she purred.

"Becky... I..." he stammered, heart thumping in his chest.

"What? Please, entertain me with one of your excuses.

Between me, Miranda and Heidi...I would love to add it to my book of useless information."

"Miranda?" he asked, flustered.

"And Heidi," the male said.

"You're not helping," Elliot replied.

"Shut up, Russell," Becky said and stood quickly, closing the gap. She pressed against his body. "Water under the bridge, Elliot...But I know about you and Anna. And as far as I'm concerned, you best not fuck things up again with her, understand? You broke her heart... but she still cares about you. So keep that in mind when you two talk. I would really hate it if I have to cut your balls off."

"Understood."

"You better. She's a good kid... don't screw it up."

Elliot turned and was halfway down the aisle when he was stopped by a hand catching his arm. Surprise flared over his face when he saw her.

Anna's eyes lit up when she spoke. "Is there a problem sir?"

"Nothing serious, ma'am," he said with a relaxed tone. "Just routine business.

No need to alarm the passengers."

"As usual?" she asked. Green eyes that had a hurt look.

"Anna," he tried, afraid to say the wrong thing. He stared at his feet, thankful that for the most part, no one was paying attention to them.

"You don't have to say anything," she started quietly. "Not that it matters really."

"It matters," he replied, taking in her expression.

"Two years is a long time," Anna replied, taking a step forward this time and lowering her voice further. "A long fucking time. Never hearing from you again. What am I supposed to do?"

Elliot glanced around the spot they were in and guided her to an empty seat.

"Saying sorry won't cut it," he started, sitting next to her. "So I won't because I can see you're pissed. And you have every right. I screwed up, Anna. Big time."

"Yes you did." She crossed her arms in defiance, waiting until he continued.

There was a mix of anger and pain in her eyes that he couldn't even think.

"Anna... "

"I'm listening."

"I take full responsibility for what happened. Every part of it. What I did was wrong... and I know you probably will never forgive me."

"Two years," she responded. "And I won't tell you how much that hurt."

"I know."

"Not even once did you try to call or email me."

"I know," he said. The growing anxiety was starting to reach its limit, but Elliot didn't move. "I'll do anything to make it up to you," he finally said.

"Anything?" she asked.

"Of course."

"Then ask for forgiveness."

He didn't even hesitate. "Please forgive me. I'm sorry for what happened."

The sting of the slap was sudden.

"That's for making me wait," she said, leaning in closer. "And this…"

She pressed her lips against his in a hungry kiss- pulling with her teeth. "That's for apologizing."

"Maybe I need to apologize more often," he said with a teenager's smile.

"Smartass," she said with a giggle. "So. What's up with you asking Becky about the passenger list? Or can you say?"

"Dallas PD had some kind of incident at a hotel. I really don't have all the details yet... but one of the passengers may have been involved."

"Is it serious?"

"Must not be too bad.. they're letting us fly on to New York where the authorities will pick this person up for questioning. They want me to make sure she doesn't do anything stupid."

"So that's good news," she said, touching his hand. "And... that means it can wait for a bit?"

"Well..." Elliot hesitated, not sure. "I suppose it could. Not like she can go anywhere, right?"

Anna nodded, biting her lip.

"What?" he asked, finally catching when he saw her look in her eyes.

Her eyes darted toward bathroom and her body language changed drastically.

"Ten minutes of your time is all I really need." She almost pleaded as she touched his cheek. "Or I can get us a blanket so we can cover up... Becky and Russell won't make their rounds for at least another thirty.

"Right here?" he said almost with a squeak.

"Why not? This spot is empty and no one is paying us attention," Anna said. A wicked smile played across her lips. "I mean, after all. Why not pick up where we left off? Of course, if you're not interested I could go back to what I was doing. Either way-"

He stopped her with his hand. "No...it's not that. I just didn't want you to think..."

"That I'm just a piece of ass?" she snorted. "Give me some credit. I know we-"

Hesitation brought her to a quick stop and for a moment, Elliot thought she would shut down and walk away. Leaving him there with nothing.

Anna cleared her throat. "I know it's more than a physical thing really. At least that's the vibe I got when we first met. That month and a half was amazing and more than I could have asked for... so yeah, I think we've moved past that. At least I have. Like I said, two years is a long time."

"I won't disappoint you again," he said, kissing her palm.

Anna exhaled. "You better not. I don't have many pieces left to mend."

"Then perhaps we can move somewhere that's less open? I'm not one to show and tell."

Anna giggled. "If it makes you feel any better. Give me a

few minutes so I can have a head start and make sure we won't be bothered. I'll be in the one on the right. Don't leave me hanging."

*****

Whispers. Buzzing and burning her ears. Growing louder until it forced her from sleep.

Nora Grant turned her head toward the aisle, locking eyes with another passenger. It took a moment before she realized where she was and who was watching her. The man was attractive -at least in her eyes- with neatly combed dark hair. He had a smooth face and the most intoxicating pale blue eyes. Eyes that penetrated her soul. Nora stared back and smiled.

"Are you ready?" he asked.

Nora's smile widened. "I am. More than ever."

"Excellent. You are our most trusted agent, Nora. You and no one else will have this opportunity to start the fire. Do you understand? This will be your time to shine."

"I will do whatever it takes," she said. "When do I start?"

"Soon, Nora. You will know the exact time to act. Just remember… let no one stand in your way. All you have to do is open the door and let history take its course. Then you will be free."

His words wrapped her in a warm and comforting feeling. Sending tremors throughout her body. Emotions ran like a fever, mixing and turning with a building desire.

"I will not hesitate," Nora replied and closed her eyes. Waiting as she held the pen knife.

"Good, Nora. You will not fail. We will not fail."

*****

Elliot watched Anna leave, focusing intently on the perfect sway of her hips. A few passengers stirred in their sleep, unaware of what was going on around them. *Sometimes,* he

90

thought, *the perks of being on a red-eye flight were really good.* Not that this would be the first time... but it would definitely be one to remember and perhaps... Elliot caught his breath in a deep seated hope. Perhaps this was something that would rekindle a lost relationship. He leaned back in the seat, staring at the curved plane ceiling with a smile. He ticked off the seconds and devised a plan on what he would do to her. Or what she would do to him. She had been extremely talented the more he thought about it...

*****

Anna sat on the toilet seat, fighting the demons and tears that were telling her this was wrong. Her mind raced so fast that she couldn't keep up. Worry expanded and dug deep into her body, coiling around her chest. Too many thoughts to keep track of, and too many desires that wouldn't stay dormant. She stood, hand touching the handle. And then sat down. Repeating the action at least six times before she decided to sit there and wait on him, hoping this wasn't a mistake. She shut her eyes, whispering a small prayer that she would have the strength to follow through and give him another chance. Two years had been a really long time.

But there was doubt. Could she allow him back into her already complicated life? She nervously bit her lip again, staring at the door. "You can do this. This isn't a mistake... so grow up and deal with it. As long as you tell him about Sam. Surely the news won't upset him, right? Good grief... why do I do this to myself?"

Doubt started to fill her again and she balled her fists, squeezing and digging fingernails into skin until the pain was too much. She swallowed the fear. God, she loved him and there couldn't be anything else she wanted. Even after all that time and heartache, she still had the same feelings. Regardless of what had happened.

"Let's hope I don't fuck this up," she said, wiping her face.

Anna almost didn't hear it. Three knocks, quick and light. She pushed open the door, trying to hide her emotions. It was overwhelming and the temptation had taken over. No looking back now.

She yanked him into the bathroom, locking the door and engulfing him with wild kisses. Elliot's hands pulled at her uniform top, stopping for a moment to take in the quick view of her black lace bra. She promptly removed the bra, exposing small, freckled breasts that he gingerly cupped.

"Boobs." Elliot muttered before she attacked with more desperate kisses.

"Shut up," she replied, pushing him against the sink and tracing a hand across his chest. She gave him a wicked grin and lowered to her knees.

"You don't have to do…"

"Be quiet," she admonished him, stopping in mid-zip. "I know what I want. So relax."

It only took a few moments of pleasure to drag Elliot into a fog. He couldn't even focus as the sensation started to become too much- and as much as he wanted this, it wasn't his intentions. Instead, he pulled her up which caused her to elicit a confused look.

"As tempting as it is, I'd rather do something else," he said, lifting her onto the edge of the sink.

"Oh really?" she asked, toying with his shirt. "What do you have in mind?"

He parted her legs and pressed against her, kissing her hard.

"Ouch!"

"What?" Elliot asked.

"Something's poking me," Anna said, trying not to laugh. "Ow! What the hell? Something hard."

"Well…"

"Ha ha, asshole. Not that… at least I hope not!" she giggled, putting her hand along the top of his pants and removing his belt.

"That's my gun," he replied, carefully removing it from the

concealed holster. "And my baton too. Sorry."

Anna wiggled out of her pants and then wrapped her legs around his waist. "Always on duty."

Elliot shrugged, taking in the beauty that was before him. "Always."

Anna gave him a hungry look and smiled. "That means you have handcuffs?"

"I never leave home without them."

She lifted her arms and pulled him to her, feeling him press against her thigh. "Cuff me."

"Sorry?"

"I won't ask again..." she breathed into his ear and nuzzled his neck.

Elliot didn't hesitate, managing to put the steel bracelets on her without losing too much concentration. Now she was all stretched out, hands cuffed above her head.

"I'm all yours." she whispered, closing her eyes when his lips touched her body.

Anna whimpered, relenting to the building excitement that followed his touch against her chest, down her stomach and between her thighs where he vigorous efforts were met with elated sighs. She bucked against him until she couldn't take it any longer.

*****

"Now."

Nora sat up, palming the pen knife and concealing it from view. Intently focused on the weapon and feeling power surge inside her. It was a strange but satisfying urging, giving her resolve. A smile played across her lips as she got closer. Surprised at how calm she was. She moved with grace and purpose, coming to momentary halt.

"May I help you?" The flight attendant stood just before the bathroom. Very pretty. Black hair pulled back and looking genuinely professional. Too bad she had to die.

"Yes… sorry," Nora said, holding onto one of the seats. "I wasn't feeling too good…"

Faking an unsteady look, Nora lurched forward. The flight attendant moved to help, which opened up the chance to strike. It was quick and well executed with the knife finding its mark before anyone could react. Nora pushed with every inch of her strength, burying the weapon in the woman's neck as they fell against the bathroom door. Blood -hot and metallic- squirted across her face.

Gasping for breath, Becky the flight attendant was shocked at the brutal attack. Trying to stop the bleeding as it gushed between her fingers. But it was too late. Her eyes rolled back into her head, bleeding out as her attacker pushed her out of the way.

Nora heard thumping from inside the small bathroom enclosure. Over and over with urgency.

Voices swirled in and out of her conscious. Let me out. Let me out!

Nora relieved the emergency key from the dead flight attendant and clicked open the bathroom door. Nothing could have prepared her for what she saw and her resolve wavered.

Fear jolted her and a scream began to build, racing forward from the depths of her soul.

*****

At first, the thumping sounds didn't register in Elliot's brain. He was too much into the moment as her curious mouth found his in another deep kiss. That was until the noise got louder. At first he thought someone else was getting lucky in the other bathroom like he was, and he dismissed it.

Anna broke the kiss, taking hold of him with her legs again. "Do you have a condom?" she asked, eyes filled with anticipation.

"No…" Elliot said. "I thought you may have been on the pill."

94

Anna sighed. "Yes, I am.. but that doesn't mean... Oh for fuck sake. Just do it."

He was inches from her, intoxicated by her playful smile. Moving closer and covering her mouth with his. Forgetting everything but the sight of her- filling him with overwhelming passion. He yielded and pressed forward. Every sound the plane made. Every knock and bump that resonated throughout the metal. Nothing mattered but her as she closed in and squeezed around him.

"Elliot..." she whispered into his ear. His lips grazing the side of her neck. "Elliot...."

Overwhelming memories came flooding back and she leaned into him- just like riding a bike. You never forget and she moved and relaxed, mirroring what he did. Their first time had been hurried and awkward- but after several attempts, things had moved into a more comfortable engagement.

"Wait," Elliot said, listening.

"What is it?" she asked, perturbed at the interruption. "Don't tell me you're chickening out. Really? What the hell..."

He put a finger to her lips and pushed away, pulling up his pants. A heart-stopping scream in the bathroom beside them sent a chill down his spine. A hundred thoughts shot through his mind as Anna squirmed against her restraints and Elliot had to forcefully pull away.

"Sit here and wait, got it? Let me look first."

"Like I have a choice?" she replied. "But that sounded pretty serious."

"I know, that's why I'm going to look before I leap."

"Passenger safety is my concern. At least give me the key before you do something stupid and get us all sued by some lawsuit happy jerk off."

"Here," Elliot responded, putting the key in her hand and unlocking the door.

He turned just as Anna removed the handcuffs.

"What?" she asked. "Don't give me that look. This isn't the first time I've been handcuffed."

He shook his head and retrieved his gun, wisely keeping his

mouth shut, filing it for later conversation. Apparently there was more to her than he had even imagined.

With the door cracked slightly, he held the Sig Sauer P226 handgun in one hand, slowly pushing with the other. At first what he saw didn't make any sense; his brain unable to comprehend it all. He locked onto the dead flight attendant's body in the corridor and took a step. Another body was laying prone half way into the second bathroom, the door ajar. At least the lower half looked normal. The upper half was a different story and it nearly made him gag. He had seen a lot of carnage overseas but this was... The shell of what was once a man hovered over the second body, making a meal from blood and sinewy cartilage. He looked up at him with dead eyes.

"Elliot?" Anna spoke quietly behind him.

"Stay here," was all he could muster as he pointed his service weapon.

Other passengers were starting to stir from the initial scream, not quite registering what was going on mere feet from their seats. For the moment, things were still under control.

"What's going on?" Anna asked again, pushing against him.

"Stay here," Elliot hissed over his shoulder, and took a step forward, directing his voice to the man. "Air Marshal! Sir, step away from the body and raise your hands. Do it now, sir!"

By now the commotion had drawn the male flight attendant Russell. Surprise filled Russell's eyes.

"Sir... stay back!" Elliot ordered in a commanding voice to him.

"But..." Russell started. "Becky may need medical attention, sir. I have a duty..." The flight attendant's eyes fell to the other body.

"Becky is dead... now please sit your ass down and shut your mouth."

Elliot's heart was racing when the feasting man stood. Out of the corner of his vision, he could see a handful of passengers move out of the way.

What was once Israel Dajovic took an uneasy step. Gore

covered his face and shirt.

"Show me your hands!" Elliot ordered him, aiming for the man's chest, recognizing him as the one Anna had escorted to the bathroom.

Another shuffle and the man made a lunge. Elliot fired dead center twice, intent on stopping the threat. The man fell on his face just inches away from Elliot's feet.

The close quarters didn't absorb the loud boom, and Elliot's ears were still ringing as he slowly approached the body. He ignored the passengers as the scrambled for cover. By now everyone was awake, peering over the tops of their seats, watching the event unfold with fear and curiosity. Unable to look away like watching a horrible car accident.

The man's body twitched as he sat up, sending Elliot scrambling backwards. Elliot fired again. Three quick pops again didn't even stop the man as he got to his feet, shrugging off the effects of clearly lethal gunshot wounds. Within seconds, the body of the dead flight attended shook and sat up in the same way. Her neck had been ripped open and fresh blood was oozing down her ripped shirt.

"What the fuck?" Elliot said. Eleven bullets left in the fifteen round magazine.

Those that were close enough started to panic. Panic in an airplane nearly seven miles from the ground was not a good thing. Any hopes of retaining order faded when someone made the mistake of screaming. It drew the attention of the two 'dead people' away from Elliot and he took that moment to quickly herd those in coach to first class. The task was nearly impossible. One man doing his best to direct nearly eighty bodies and rushing them like sheep to safety. Instead, it felt more like leading them to a slaughter.

Add to the mix a severe case of mass confusion. Not everyone understood what was going on. He didn't either. Elliot pushed and prodded, urging them on as he watched the first two maul Russell flight attendant.

"Come on, people! Move it! Move it" Elliot urged them, glancing over his shoulder and wished he hadn't. The two undead were tearing at Russell's flesh, ripping and gnawing in a gruesome feast. Russell's screams and pleas echoed throughout the plane. Another problem would soon be at hand, Elliot surmised. If they died and kept on, he could too. The mass of bodies huddled together in first class with nowhere else to go. All his options running out, Elliot quickly picked up the wall phone that would ring into where the cockpit. After the second ring, someone picked up.

"This is the Captain."

It didn't even register that the Captain's voice was oddly monotone. "This is Marshal Elliot Bane. Sir, we have a serious issue out here and shots have been fired. The crew has been compromised and the passengers are at risk. We need to make an immediate emergency landing. Notify the authorities th-" He never finished the sentence when the Captain disconnected the call. "Seriously?" Elliot said, leaving the phone to dangle against the wall.

Too many bodies pressed together and too many questions all at once. All overwhelming his thought process as they were hurled at him. Most looked upset over being moved. Only a few appeared scared.

"What's going on?"

"Is there a bomb?"

"Are there terrorists on board?"

"Marshal? What can we do to help?"

"Listen up people!" Elliot raised his voice. "Listen! Everyone needs to stay put right here! We have a situation in the rear area… but the crew has it under control."

"We heard gunshots."

"And a scream."

He soothed them. "I'm going back there to find out. Until then, everyone stay right here! Understand? I don't need everyone causing a mass panic." Another scream came from the back, which made the people press closer. Elliot turned, pushing through. "Find some seats, people. Find some seats and stay put."

Then his mind clicked. Anna was still in the bathroom. Or at least he hoped and parted the blue curtain. Hope faded quickly when he saw them. Four zombie? The word died at the tip of his nightmarish idea. *Hell, what else could they be? They sure as hell wasn't sparkly vampires.* They were now munching on what had been a well dressed man. Business suit and the whole nine yards. But now, their feast had turned the whole nine yards into a kibbles and bits -all you can eat- zombie buffet. And they were really going to town with gruesome effect.

"Holy shit," was all he could say as he walked closer, gun raised and pointed toward the feeding frenzy. This wasn't something you learned in the academy. Nothing in the text books or on the job prepared you for an incident like this.

"What in God's name is that?"

Elliot turned and nearly collided with a curious passenger. Behind him were several other peering faces, hiding behind the curtain.

"Marshal?" one of the asked.

Three let their curiosity get the best of them and were pushing forward, straining to see.

"Get back!" he ordered the passengers, causing them to scramble out of the way.

Two of the undead looked up at the commotion, forgetting their human meal and starting to make their way towards them. Slow, uneasy baby steps as if they had forgotten how to walk.

*****

Anna held the door shut, praying, using every ounce of strength. Under normal circumstances, the urge to pray would have fallen to the side and been forgotten. Not that she didn't believe.

The initial shock had faded and the training had kicked in.

"Open your eyes." She forced her muscles to respond.

She cracked the door open and she saw blood. So much of it smeared across the walls and tracked along the floor. More than she had seen in her life. Anna repressed the urge to vomit and eased the door open, carefully looking to the left. She could make out the forms of her former co-workers as they kneeled over a body. Her brain tried to process what her eyes witnessed. Two more people were walking toward the front.

Her heart sank when she saw Elliot.

*****

Eleven bullets. Elliot remembered the extra ammunition was in the compartment above his seat, almost to where the walking bodies had reached. He walked off a few paces, calculating his next shots. No room for mistakes. Center mass didn't work the first time. Elliot took aim at the man he shot at the start.

Breathe in. Breathe out. Hold it and squeeze.

The first bullet struck the man's throat, sending him flailing backward. Deep breath. Hold it again and acquire the next threat. The next shot struck the woman right in the head. Zombie goo and blood splattered the ceiling and walls as she fell, sliding down one of the seats. Elliot took a step, pausing and then taking a few more that closed the gap. He checked the woman, kicking her to make sure she was actually dead. He nearly pissed himself when the man rose no more than five feet away again. His panicked shot struck home, entering right between his dead eyes, blowing out a healthy chunk of dark blood and brain.

The dead flight attendants had now taken notice of the noise and were getting to their feet. Elliot was ten feet from them and was taking aim when Anna's blurred shape came into view.

"Get back into the bathroom and lock the door!" He waved her back, trying to get her to move out of the way.

Anna nodded and retreated to the safety of the enclosed room.

Elliot had the first zombie in his sights, ignoring the streaks of flesh that hung from her body. He focused on her bloody lips. He hesitated for a heartbeat as her white eyes stared back. Eyes that had been so green and full of life were now full of hunger. This wasn't the Becky he remembered from the galley. *Simple and easy. Headshots is all it takes...* The round missed as he fell, tossed to the side at the sudden and violent dissent of the aircraft. The plane jerked and shook, causing the living to scream from fear and panic. The movement had only been a one-time thing, but it was enough to cause several injuries. Broken bones mostly but one with a broken neck. It would only take a few moments for the more seriously injured person to succumb, adding fuel to the fire.

Anna held onto the door handle when the plane bucked. The movement threw her hard to the floor, causing her head to strike metal. The resulting connection tore a gash into her forehead causing her to emit a tirade of expertly placed cuss words. Shortly she was able to stand, holding onto the sink and rising to her feet. With a free hand against the wound, she grabbed rolls and rolls of toilet paper, trying to halt the blood. There was a lot and she soon felt light headed. Anna leaned against the door frame, listening. No sound was heard since the last gunshots. Which made her wonder if whatever had happened had come to an end. To make certain, she pressed her ear against the door. Straining to hear any signal that would indicate an all clear. Nothing but the sounds of the engines.

Washing away most of the blood with cold water, she applied more toilet paper; pressing it hard against the gash and opening the door slowly, daring another peek to the left. She took a brave step out and a glimpse to the right nearly made her vomit. Pools of blood and body parts were left as evidence to what happened. It took all of her will to fight the gag reflex.

Gathering her wits as best she could, Anna turned toward the cabin. One. Two. Three bodies were laid out. Anna stopped at the first; recognizing the clothing of the man she had helped earlier. She sidestepped his body and paused at the next. She could make out the back of her friend and co-workers who were kneeling over someone. As she got closer, the sickening sound of biting and chewing -like that of a rabid dog- made her freeze. All she could see was the other woman's head going up and down, and then her eyes fell on the man's legs and the edges of his black shirt. Anna recognized him immediately and her heart stopped.

This can't be real. This can't be... the dead aren't supposed to come back and start eating people. Come on, Anna.. wake up! Wake up! You're going to wake up and be in the bed...

A handgun was at her feet. She grabbed it. "Get the fuck away from him!" she hollered.

Her dead friend turned, snarling with a mouthful of flesh. Dark blood oozed from the zombie's mouth when it stood up. Anna raised the gun, but her fingers wouldn't respond. The image wasn't registering and her already frayed nerves had twisted her insides. Making her doubt what was really going on. The second flight attendant slowly got up, forgetting what it had been doing and now locked onto this new treat. Anna took a step back as the two approached, her heart sputtering and turning cold. This wasn't a dream. This wasn't something out of the movies cither. That oh-so tiny voice in the back of her head finally woke up and started to scream.

The reality of what was happening cut across her conscious. Anna stopped near the last row of seats, planting her stance with determination.

"I'm sorry, Becky. Russell... God forgive me please." The shots weren't perfect, but at that distance it wouldn't matter. Anna didn't even hear the gun go off, amazed at how easy it was to pull the trigger until there were no more bullets. The immediate threat had ended when the gun clicked in her shaking hands. The last bullet had embedded into Becky's head, knocking the body over to the side as if it were merely resting. Russell's body lay crumpled in a butchered mess.

Anna dropped the gun and was at Elliot's side in two steps, trying to find the most severe wound. It was impossible to tell with all the blood. She had been trained for emergencies and terrorists. Nothing had prepared her for this. The training

102

manual didn't cover dead people coming back to life. She did her best, trying to stop the flow of blood even though she knew he was dying. Tears streamed down her face as some of the passengers slowly approached; uncertain if it was safe or not. She cried and yelled, beating his chest in frustration. This wasn't supposed to happen. Her body shook with sobs as she collapsed beside him, exhausted and frustrated from the overload of what was happening.

It was too much. Anna kissed his cheek and closed her eyes, shutting off her mind to those that dared to move closer, unable to even muster the strength for another prayer. She knew it was a moot point now. No last minute miracles. Not even the grace of God would save them. She exhaled slowly and sat up, watching him take his last breath.

"I'm sorry," Anna said, touching his cheek. "I'm sorry I didn't tell you sooner, but you had to leave and I couldn't tell you, I had no way after... Elliot... I wanted give you the news that you're a dad. You stupid, stupid, beautiful man."

A distant scream from the front jolted her, but she didn't move. Even as more yelling came rolling down the aisles, Anna refused to leave.

"His name is Sam," she said, running her fingers through his hair. "And he looks just like you. Of course, Mom wasn't happy when I told her... But you had to be the hero, didn't you?"

"Lady? Ma'am? You need to move! Please? Is there more ammunition? Another gun perhaps? We need help in first class. Please? Ma'am? Can you hear me?" The words fell short and Anna curled up against the man she loved. The world she knew was gone; flipped upside down and then flushed down the toilet. The gory and violent images played over and over in her head. Things like this didn't happen. Wasn't supposed to happen. But here she was.

Focusing on her blood-covered hands, Anna didn't feel him move. It was a quick and decisive attack; his teeth locking onto her arm. She screamed, sending those who were close climbing over chairs and each other to get away. Anna pulled back, tearing the hole that Elliot had started. He grabbed her leg, sinking teeth into the flesh and pulling out long strips of muscle with a hard yank. Pain shot through her body as if she had been struck by lightning. His grip was strong and he tore into her again, dragging out the muscle and exposing bone. Anna pulled free when his hand slipped. She tried to push away from his gaping mouth but the bleeding was too much and her body slipped into shock.

Black shapes started to fill the corners of her eyesight and she tried to focus on his boots. Elliot was now on his feet, shuffling away toward the screams. All of it started to fade away like a bad nightmare after waking, but this wasn't a dream. Another set of feet passed by her head, leading another toward the rest of the living that were scrambling to find an exit. Some fighting to get away. Others putting up a fight as best they could.

Funny, she thought. *No one can hear you scream at thirty thousand feet. Not* that it mattered. Her world tilted to the side when the plane nosed toward the Earth, intentionally heading to the ground to crash.

The impact killed all aboard, and left nothing but a broken metal shell full of the undead.

It took thirty minutes for first responders to reach the crash site.

They had no idea what they were walking into.

Eddie Smith, Part Two:
When Work Becomes Life

Well hell. Three of ya can't sleep tonight eh? Strange that insomnia seems to be catching since I started telling you stories, son. Hm? You want to hear more about how we made it through up until now? Hm.

Well I got first shift, and I know I won't sleep well out here without those two fences around us, so I might as well tuck you little shits in with a story or three. Make sure you get all stuffed into those sleeping bags. These aren't the happiest stories, and there's gonna be a chill in the air tonight. We aren't in Texas anymore.

What story to tell? What was the last thing I told ya?

Oh. The truck. Yeah that was dirty work. I still dream about those people. Some of them are angry with me still, but most are thankful I didn't set them free to hurt other folks. Might weird how we only dream of the dead now huh? I miss dreaming about lots of folk. I certainly miss dreaming about pretty ladies.

Alrighty then. Late June of ought ten. The world has more problems then there are fleas on a farm dog. It's all bad everywhere. I laid mighty low after I got my pickup and ATV back to the trailer, but I knew I couldn't stay there forever. No one is ever quite prepared enough for when all hell breaks loose. Like I told ya before, no matter how much food and drink you set aside, it never lasts as long as you want it to.

So I was sitting on that big fat truck of diesel in my backyard when I realized that I needed to get connected to stay alive. I knew I'd make it quite some time on my own, but I didn't just want to survive, I wanted to be ready to thrive, if you get my meaning. If the world was going to get flipped over, I wanted to upgrade my station in life, and I knew just how to do it.

I went to Church.

What? I'm an idiot? Child are you insinuating that our lord and savior Jesus Christ is a joke? Because I do beg to differ. Heading to that church that day was the best thing I have ever done in my life, and I've done... well... Okay maybe not the best comparison, but going to that church was a good idea.

I'm not a big church goer. I pray, and I do my best to be a good person, and I go at least once a month, but with all the death and dying and walking dead folk, I knew I needed to get my fat body to inside a place of worship. Nearest my place is a church I don't normally go to. It's a Baptist Church, and I usually go to the Methodist church, but in an apocalypse I think it's more important that you have faith in something than faith in nothing. My old county road was empty, and when I geared myself up and drove down to the church that day, I made sure I had enough stuff to last me a few days in case I couldn't get home quick. That was the first day I left home with my SKS over my shoulder. I remember now feeling like it was all post-Katrina New Orleans with the neighborhood watch people wandering about protecting homes with their personal weapons. Later on in that the military and Blackwater people showed up to help, but that day, it was Eddie Smith with his SKS.

Man I miss that gun. But that's another story for another cold sleepless night.

I was heading to the Methodist, happy to be out on the road, even though I was ripe to fill my britches with a load of turd. I didn't see none of the dead people for some time and when I saw the parking lot of the Baptist church and all the cars and trucks in it, for some reason I said, 'might as well,' and pulled in.

The church -you've seen it kids I'm sure- is a pretty old white building with a tall and proud steeple. I would say there's something special about that steeple, seeing as how long it's managed to dodge tornados, but I am not the suspicious type.

Well that ain't true at all. I got lucky socks, and I will NEVER wash them on Cowboys game day. But that's probably not a problem I'm gonna have ever again, I'm sad to say. There might still be cowboys out there, but they ain't playing no football.

So aside from that pretty white steeple, the rest of the church looked like it was ready for a hurricane to blow in. Heavy sheets of plywood across all the stained glass windows, and the front door had a big old handmade barricade at the top of the steps. The house of Christ was invite only now, and I figured I'd try and see what was happening.

I knocked on the 2x4 and plywood entryway barricade and I hooted and hollered to let the folks inside know who I was. It wasn't two shakes of a bull's tail before I could see the actual church's door open inside. It was a heavy door, a good door, and it swung inwards and out come two people I had never laid eyes on before.

Your daddy and his friend Ray. Adam and Ray got twelve gauges on me as soon as that door let the sunlight in, and they're all serious and taking no chances and that's smart. Your daddy is a smart man, boy. He has helped keep me alive, as well as you and your mother. All of us.

So your daddy says, "Sir, we don't have any food or batteries spare to give away, but we'll share some clean water if you need it."

And I thanked him kindly, and said I was simply looking for a place of Christ to take a knee for a bit, and possibly talk to other sensible living souls while there was still some left in the world.

We stood there on the porch talking, hot as Hades for near an hour. I still remember the taste of the sweat that ran down my face. I was so dang well soaked in it that day I had to wring out my bandana just to smear more sweat around. Made me thankful for my cap, and even more thankful after they let me in.

I drank almost an entire bottle of water right off the bat, which gave me some cramps, but also brought me right back to life. It was then that I made my way past the forty eight souls in that church to say my prayers at the foot of Jesus. I think I was there for the better part of another hour, asking for forgiveness, and praying for the safety of friends and what I knew of my family. Huh? No, I never really met my momma. She died right after I was born in a car accident. Daddy told me she was on her way back from the store with food for dinner. But that ain't the point.

When I got done praying for all that I needed to pray for, I sat down with Ray, and Adam, and Bob, and Clayton and Colton, and Sally, and Lauren, and Gerald, and Michelle and Cailie and all the folks who are with us tonight, as well as a whole slew of folks that didn't make it this far. It's a troubled world kids.

If you can remember, your daddy Adam was the manager at a Home Depot, and he was smart enough to shut the store down, lock up, and load a flatbed up with lumber the afternoon of the 23rd. He also grabbed up screws, nails, a handful of generators, water filtration gear, everything a smart person needs to survive the end of times. Thank you, orange smock wearing hero. I hope he can't hear me, he's apt to smack me for making fun of him, and I like your daddy too much to shoot him in the foot.

So one hour of talk turned into two, and then two hours of talk turned into six, and before you know it, we were formulating a plan for not just that night, but that summer, and potentially that whole year. We were on to something that night. Ten reasonably bright folk, all willing to share their possessions and ideas, and all with the get up and go attitude that could get stuff done. Some old dude said that if we don't hang together, we'll all hang separate, and times could not reflect that more.

That very next day we all set out to achieve what we'd planned.

Now boys, it's important to remember that what we wanted to do was dangerous. Very dangerous.

Colton worked at a kitchen supply company. Specifically, one that sold deli equipment and butcher's equipment. That was our first stop. No son we didn't need aprons. Well that's not true, we did want some aprons, but not the cloth kind. You see, real industrial meat cutters use gloves that are like medieval chainmail, and wear aprons that are the same. It's pretty light, and is knife resistant. Knife resistant means bite resistant, and we knew that these unholy abominations liked to bite to spread their evil. Bites are always lethal kids. We also had the idea that with some chicken wire, and some dirt biking gear, and the great enabler of invention herself, duct tape, we'd be able to fashion us up some anti-zombie armor.

Man I hate that word. Zombie. It sounds uneducated. A cop out. Skipping the full day of work if you know what I mean. Doesn't do 'em justice. You know who calls offa work? People who don't get nowhere.

So that next day we got our trucks rigged up, and we headed out to Colton's place of business. That was easy. No one there you see. Nothing worth stealing out of a business that sells nothing but aprons and packaging materials right? Well boo to them is what we said.

Butcher's gloves, and cut resistant aprons rescued from the clutches of a dark and dirty warehouse rack, we returned back to that Baptist church and sent out a few more cars to scoop up some chicken wire off a farm down the road from my trailer. I remember hearing back that day when they had to put down old man Keller at the farm. He'd cut himself some bad on the leg and bled out, and of course when we got there, he was all kinds of dead and ornery, walking down his driveway looking for something to bite, and they had to shoot him. We said prayers for him that nigh as we made our first sets of armor from chicken wire and duct tape. It worked good, really. Small rings of wire about three quarters your width of whatever body part cut to size, then covered in strips of that good old gray tape, then buttons were sewn on so you could fasten yourself in. The tape only covered maybe half of the wire, so your skin could breathe, but no teeth could get through to you. I took some wood stripping from my shed and made slats of more reinforced armor just like the stuff I'm wearing right now. See, small strips of wood under the tape? Yep, its light, and it helps protect against the worst bites. Some of the others have taken to using soccer shin pads too, but I don't like how they make my shins sweat in the heat.

So we made real simple stuff that night and the next day. Just forearm guards, and shin guards, and Colton made himself a knightly breastplate out of the wire and tape too. That didn't last. Especially after we started to pick up cop vests. Day after that arts and crafts session we buckled in, and we took that flatbed and three pickups back to Greg's Home Depot to get some more lumber.

You see, I'd told them all about the diesel yard, and how it'd be perfect to move to. We just needed some lumber to make it all happen.

Now I done told ya these aren't the happiest of stories. I drove the flatbed due to my experience behind the wheel of all vehicles commercial, and that suited me just fine. There's no need to put lipstick on this pig, I know my role. Some of them we'd brought with us were veterans, and they were well armed with semi-automatic weapons, and they knew how to shoot them too. It was a good feeling. We felt safe. As safe as we could be I suppose.

We weren't of course. Now son, don't be scared, your daddy made it back with us that day, he's here tonight with us. Smile. These are stories of brave men and women creating a new world, despite fear and danger.

When we arrived at the Home Depot it was being looted.

Now we'd made the plan ahead of time to leave any other looters be. We were not the police, nor did we want to involve ourselves in the activities of others. We would have enough trouble atoning for our own actions, let alone the actions of others.

All that is well and good, but when we drove up into the contractor's access, and Adam hopped out the truck, someone over at the regular entrance across the way started shooting at us. I do not consider myself a particularly brave fellow, but I threw the truck's brakes, killed the motor and got out with my SKS. I didn't even know who was shooting at who, but I had the distinctly poor feeling someone else was shooting at us, and when all our other brothers got out and started to shoot at the other entrance, I knew where to point my weapon.

I didn't fire one round. But the time I had figured out which end of the rifle was up, and which way I needed to be pointing it, our people had gotten off about fifteen shots, and sent whoever it was right back into the store. Course that's when we saw that our girl Diane had gotten in the way of a bullet. We didn't even realize we'd lost someone she'd gone down so fast. Clayton had come back to the Dodge to get some of our extra flashlights, and there she was, flat on her back on the ground, her head pretty much missing. It's a strange fortune when you get killed like that boys. No need to worry about coming back and harming those you're with. Of course it's stomach turning. No one is ever meant to see the insides of someone like that. 'Cept maybe doctors and surgeons, and even then I don't understand how they keep their dinners inside 'em.

It just ain't right kids. You know that though. I know you all have seen too much already in your young lives. It speaks volumes that half of you kids are just barely into your teens and you're all veteran carriers of handguns. Heck, I can see the lumps under your sleeping bags where your guns are right now.

Cold out isn't it?

Mighty cold. Almost 40 degrees.

Diane was dead, and we all said our words over her body

quick. The other guys knew that the folks that had killed her were still about, and we needed to get what we'd gone there to do done before they started shooting again.

I was tasked with the admirable job of holding down the fort outside. I took me some cover next to the flatbed, and I put my head on a swivel like a lawn sprinkler. Now I can tell you all the nitty-gritty details of the inside shooting in the store, but I'm sure you've heard most of the details from your daddy, or someone else who went inside. I can tell you that they had to fight, aisle to aisle inside that big building, taking down some crazy assholes that thought they had to kill us to keep their haul. We would've gladly let them walk out with whatever they wanted, so long as they kept the peace. But they didn't, and we had to protect ourselves.

We left three of their dead inside that Home Depot that day, and it was with heavy hearts we loaded the trucks up with all of what we wanted. We'd made so much noise though that by the time we were half loaded with our supplies we needed to start peeling off people to cover us. We'd drawn in about ten of the dead folk just while everyone had been inside, and I'd been able to send them to a resting place with some squinting and a few missed shots. Well, a few is being mighty generous. Shooting at a moving target a few hundred yards out that's the size of a paper plate is actually a pretty steep feat. I think I spent a whole 30 round mag plugging away at those poor guys. Remember kids, head shots are the only thing that counts against the dead. Gotta wreck that rotten melon to put them back to sleep for good.

It took us the entire afternoon just to keep the crowd of the dead out of the parking lot and get the trucks loaded and strapped down. I'll say this though; we left that parking lot with nearly everything we've ever needed. We planned smart, worked quick, and did Diane justice. She did not die in vain.

Saying words like that doesn't make her any less dead though kids. Big words are meant for impressing small minds my daddy said.

No, jackass that wasn't meant as an insult.

112

When we left the store we went back to the Baptist church. It was fortified enough in case anyone followed us, and we certainly didn't want to lead anyone to where we really wanted to go. Folks was hard to trust back then, more than now I think. Now we all know there's nothing left to fight over. But back then, with such a ripe basket of things to pick over, it was easy to get violent. Lord knows we had our fair share of shootouts with people over what's left. Man you guys remember when everyone started to get sick? When the water all went bad? Those were hard times.

Anyway, the fuel farm. My work. You remember when we moved in there right? Before we built the whole place up and started calling it The Fort? Can you believe one of those idiots wanted to call it The Alamo at first? The Fort's a kick ass name, and doesn't have all that negativity and such associated with it. Man, those were dicey days. Scared of making all that noise, and we was cutting lumber all day and night to get that place built up and fortified. Truth be told, we couldn't have found a much better place. All that fuel may have made us a target, but it surely kept us in food and supplies.

The next day after we was sure that we hadn't been followed a bunch of us set out in our trucks over to the fuel facility. My good man Greg was still sitting there. He's the one I told you lost all that weight? From not eating and whatnot? He was still sitting guard, right there in the heat of the day, hiding down in his security booth at the gate. When we pulled up he drew down with his shotgun on us, using the booth wall as cover. I dropped out of my truck and as soon as he saw me waving, he lowered the gun. It should be noted he did not put the gun away. Greg's a smart fella.

I offered him a bottle of water, and as he drank it down in three gulps I told him we aimed to be moving into the place. Permanent like.

See kids, it makes a lot of sense to set up shop in a place that has resources at it. If it has some kind of security too, well then that's icing on your cake. Greg needed some cajoling though. It was his sworn duty to ensure that none of that fuel was stolen, and no one trespassed on company property. After thirty solid minutes of us explaining to him that the world had indeed gone sour, and it was every man for himself out there, he agreed to let us in. Agreed to join us.

That first day all we did was scout the buildings. You ever go into a new shopping store? One that's new to town that you ain't never been in before? And each and every aisle, even though it's got the same shit as ever other store you ever been in, is exciting and new?

That was how I felt. How we all felt I suspect. When I brought the crew around to each building and we decided on what was going to go where, it was thrilling stuff. Like how we went to the driver's locker room and decided it'd be our armory. All those steel cages for clothes doubled perfectly for gun safes. The main office building was just about perfect for living quarters for the whole lot of us, and all we had to do was finish our plan on how to make sure no one got into the place, and how we were going to find enough beds for us to sleep in.

I headed back to my trailer that night, and started moving stuff in while everyone else headed back to the Baptist church and kept on planning and getting rest.

I moved my home into a back workshop near the rear of the Fort. Originally it was a machine shop for tool repair and our own company use. I knew the office would be a good bedroom, and it was a sturdy building that was right next to the fences, and about a stone's toss from the back exit. That was part of the good stuff about the Fort kids. Two twelve foot tall chain link fences topped with that coiled up concertina wire. Plus, all those Jersey barriers around the exterior meant driving through the fences was a real bad idea.

I was almost fully moved in by the time I fell asleep in my new machine shop home right before dawn. Two hours of sleep later and we were back at it.

A smart move was deciding that getting all our beds from home was a bad idea. Too much driving, and too much exposure. It was decided that we'd head to a mattress store, and just take a truck load of beds. The local mattress place was on the edge of town, nowhere near anything, and our crew loaded it all up in less than four hours. Mattresses, box springs, frames, and even some dressers and bureaus. Right next door to the shop was a batteries and car parts shop, and we emptied that place of what we could. A few of us know enough about car repair that parts would be useful, and we also knew that car batteries themselves would soon be in short supply. A pickup truck full of that stuff was money in the bank. That voyage to the strips on the frontage roads near Longview was pretty mundane. No stores in that neck of the woods that drew in looters that day, and there were only a few of the dead about. Thankfully someone who is a far better than I am was able to do the trigger pulling for us. Saved us quite a few rounds, and quite a bit of adrenaline. Life is easier when they stay far away.

It took us the rest of the daylight to drive back and get the offices emptied of cubicles and filing cabinets and shit desktop computers that weren't any good to anyone without the internet no more. Besides, that was the day the kids said the internet died. One of 'em was searching through the Google for news when it all just stopped working.

Man I'm tired. You kids tired yet? No? Alright I'll keep talking. Where was I? Uh, yeah, moving stuff out and in. That day was beds. The next week, was food and personal stuff, from home. Well, for the folks that dared risk going home. Over that week things became much worse. The violence in the city from the living folk got much worse as the food inside stores dwindled away. Larger cities and towns I suppose had worse problems with it. Many more folks trying to go after the same food, and everyone is starving and scared and desperate, and it's Texas, so we're all armed in five ways or more.

We spent a lot of nights sitting in the darkness, listening to distant gunfire that week. One of the worst feelings it was. Some of you remember it I'm sure. Nerves frayed, blood boiling. Wanting to either run and hide, or go help. No win to be had in either direction truth be told. Just sadness, and praying that the evil didn't reach us.

We started cutting the Home Depot lumber when the

gunfire died down in the following weeks. Our perimeter was damn well secure from the two fences and the concrete barriers, but we needed elevated firing positions, according to our National Guard fellas. We weren't real scared of being bombed by airplanes no more, so the option of guard towers was our best. On each corner of the Fort's fence and at each gate we built ourselves a thirty foot tall tower. Large ladder leading up the top with a retractable portion so folks couldn't climb up it easily. We lined each tower's floor and walls with sandbags and some cinderblocks for protection against being shot at, and we mounted some spotlights up on the top that we rigged to run off those car batteries. When we put everyone to work cutting and bolting and nailing we were able to put up a tower every four days. Mind you kids, that's eleven hour days for about six adults who know what they're doing, plus time for the concrete to set.

Once each tower was completed, we sent up a shooter with a rifle with a scope so we could keep eyes on the roads and neighborhoods leading up the Fort. We were able to shoot at just about anything and anyone who came at us if they was uninvited.

And we certainly did some shooting. A few weeks later, well hell, I think might've been a month or two later, September I think, we had a three truck convoy roll up on the Fort and try to ram their way through the front gate. No slowing down, no stopping, just driving like a maniac straight in. We figured out later they was trying to get at the fuel, and they weren't the last.

Theo in the tower on the corner called out that they was coming, and we all grabbed our guns and headed to our muster spots. Theo was the first to shoot. He had himself a hella deer rifle and could shoot the wings off a fly at a hundred paces while chewing gum. I listened as he put two through the windshield where the driver was, stopping the first truck cold. It drifted off the road and into a bit of a flat where the passenger got out. He shot at the tower a few times using the truck as cover, but Theo's deer rifle did work on him too.

The second and third trucks made it all the way to the first

116

gate, but didn't get to ram it. A whole bunch of us were either in towers or on the other side of the fences when they got close, and not one of us wanted to, but we lit 'em up. I put a half magazine from my SKS through the engine block and windshield of the second truck myself.

Helluva mess to clean up. We learned a lot that day. Salvage the vehicles as best we can for parts, and the company wrecker was worth its weight in cowboy boots. We towed all them cars to the back near where my new house was, and I was able to strip 'em down and salvage what I could. Good way to pass the time kids.

And that's how the Fort came to be. There's plenty more story after this, but I'm tired, and it's chilly, and I wanna put my head down now. I'll tell you more about the attacks on the Fort, and how we met some new friends soon. Sleep well kids.

Someone's out there right now fighting to keep us safe.

Amy's Daycare

Sherry Knight

Groaning softly, Amy hit the snooze button and tried to settle into her pillow again. Knowing that going back to sleep would be not be possible, she slowly opened one eye and as it focused on the clock, she saw that it read 4:30am and she cursed softly under her breath.

Suddenly warm, friendly arms wrapped around her and pulled her close. Amy heard a tiny moan leave her lips as she felt Andy's lips touch the nape of her neck softly. Smiling as she turned in her husband's arms Amy whispered, "Happy anniversary my love." She found his lips and felt herself giving into his kiss and eventually his morning salute.

Afterward, smiling as she heard Andy sing in the shower, Amy moved her hand down and softly caressed her lower abdomen. "So when are we gonna tell Daddy that you're on the way little one?"

Amy knew that the news would be a shock for Andy. Hell, it had been a shock to her too. Only yesterday Dr. Howard confirmed the little stick with the plus sign for her. Amy had been told going on five years ago that having a baby was no longer an option for her. Not since the afternoon the drunk hit her while she was jogging.

After the initial shock of learning the sad news, Amy and Andy decided to use the insurance settlement from the accident to build this house and the daycare business she now ran. Since it would only be the two of them, they decided to have their 'house' upstairs. That meant they had a cozy 2 bed/2 bath with a full kitchen and living room built above the daycare Amy had always wanted to own.

Downstairs, there was a full kitchen and a craft room. What would have been a living room in a normal house was made into a media room. There were also two classrooms and three half baths, two of them with size appropriate fixtures for kids. And the best room of all, the baby room. The basement had a closed in laundry and the rest of the area was finished off as a baby nursery. It held four cribs, two rockers and changing tables. Everything was as cute as could be.

Andy was on duty today. As a Paramedic his schedule could not have been more perfect. He was on duty for 24 hours and then off for 48 hours. This allowed him time to help out downstairs. A lot of 'her kids' came from broken homes so having a father figure around to play with, talk to or just hang with really made a difference.

Even though Andy was on duty today, the guys at the station had worked it out so that Amy and he could go out for dinner, and that was where she was planning to tell him about the baby. She was nervous, but oh so excited.

As Amy was heading into the bathroom, Andy was heading out pausing just long enough to kiss her deeply and massage her breasts. Amy pulled back and laughed as she swatted him on the ass. "Go on mister; go save people." She knew that she would be hearing from him during the day.

He had bought her an emergency radio and had one of the dispatchers hook it up so that Amy could listen to his calls as they came in.

Every time the radio would go off all of the little boys and even a couple of the little girls would all grab a toy fire truck and go racing around the room and it sometimes got a bit loud. Amy loved it, because she knew how much Andy meant to the little ones and how much they meant to him.

Amy finished her shower, dressed and headed downstairs to get the day started. Seeing her two younger employees Jessica and Kelly outside, Amy unlocked the door and everyone went about their normal morning activities. Amy started breakfast for the early arrivals, while the two teens made sure the changing tables had diapers, etc and that all the toys were put away.

Then the triplets arrived. These three boys were demons from hell. Four years old, each red headed and with tempers like nothing else. They could never enter a room quietly; they had to make sure that everyone knew that they had arrived. They came three days a week, and the only reason Amy continued to accept them was because their mother had basically begged her. Apparently they were banned from other daycares. Amy got them settled and got them some oatmeal to keep their mouths busy. Normally, they had four infants, and thirteen toddlers up to age five. Today, however they would have Mattie, a seven-year-old sister of one of the babies who had trouble during the night with her asthma. Mom decided to keep her out of school.

The morning went smoothly, first breakfast, then Sesame Street while the kitchen was cleaned. Then school as the little ones called it. The three women divided the kids and everyone worked on their ABC's and 1-2-3's.

Just as Amy was finishing up a rather nasty poopy-filled diaper, her phone rang with Andy's ring tone. Amy laughed and rubbed noses with Scotty and handed him off to Jessica. She had barely got a 'hello' out before Andy was rattling off orders to her, she could tell from the tone of his voice that he was serious, and scared.

Amy motioned to Jess that she was going upstairs and then tried to get Andy to slow down so she could understand him. Sitting on their bed she finally got him to stop and start over more slowly this time. As he talked, Amy could feel the color drain from her face.

"Amy, Babe, you need to listen to me. Listen good ok Hun? I need you to get all the kids down in the basement take diapers, food, water, bottles, formula, use the fridge that is down there. Take some toys too and you better take bedding, take their nap pads and grab some clothes and pillows for yourself and also food for you and who's there with you today?'

"Jessica and Kelly," she heard herself whisper.

"Ok good," he continued, "Get them to get the kids downstairs, take a TV and DVD player and some of their DVDs. DO NOT turn on the TV to the news, please, I am begging you, you do not want the kids to see what's on it right now. I am on my way home. Make sure you have everything down there when I get there. I can't stay long, Betty is riding with me today and we'll have to get back to the station. Amy, I love you Babe, please do what I say and I will see you in a few."

The click as he hung up seemed to echo in her ears. Amy sat there for a minute just staring at the phone and then sprung into action. Running down the stairs, she called for the teens to meet her in the kitchen. "I need you two to say nothing, just listen to me and do what I say. We need to pretend we are going on an adventure for the kids. Kelly, help me move two of the cribs down to the basement. Then we'll grab pillows, blankets, and the kids nap mats. While we are doing that, Jess, I need you to move the small TV out of the kitchen and the DVD player downstairs, also take a couple of Dora the Explorer DVDs. You know which ones they'll watch better than anything else."

Jess started to say something when Amy held a hand up. "Girls all I know is that Andy called and something is going down, he wouldn't say what it was. He just wanted us to get the kids down to the basement and make them comfortable and make it fun. While you two are doing what I've asked, I'll be getting stuff out of the kitchen and down there. Once we are set then we move the kids. Oh and one more thing; Andy said to make sure that NO ONE turned the TV on. He said there was some bad stuff on the news. So until he gets here, we do what we need to do to keep these babies all safe and happy." The three of them then moved out.

None of them said anything that was out of the ordinary. Kelly decided to fold up the two pack-&-plays that they used for the infants. She placed all four of the tiny babies that they had there today in one of the big cribs. Just as she had finished folding the portables, three year old Tammy started yelling, "Miss kewy, the babies are eating each other's hands." Of course this strange comment captured the attention of all the kids as they crowded around the crib and watched.

Amy was glad that they had this distraction for a few minutes as she grabbed a laundry basket and started filling it with everything she thought they might need. She had no idea how long they would be down there, so she put everything her hands could grab in the basket.

Just as she finished delivering the fifth basket downstairs she heard Andy come in the door. All but a couple kids had given up watching the fist sucking competition and were playing with their favorite toys. As always when the first child saw Andy everyone else heard about it. Someone called out his name, and everyone rushed to try to be the first to grab a leg. Laughing like he always did, Andy placed his hands on little heads and ruffled hair. As his eyes met Amy's she noticed that the laughter was not in them, they seemed wild and scared. And that scared her more than anything ever had before.

"Ok guys, let's let Mister Andy have a quiet minute with Miss Amy." Jess said as she shooed everyone back into the playroom. She winked at Amy as she led the kids out. Grabbing Amy's hand, Andy almost pulled her upstairs, taking two at a time.

Once inside their bedroom, he pulled her into a hug, a very strong hug. "Baby, something is going on. People are acting crazy, going around biting others and I don't just mean biting, I mean taking chunks of flesh and eating it. I haven't seen it personally, but it's all over the news. Our radios have been going off all morning." Amy nodded her head as he continued. "I have to get back to the station but I need to make sure you and the kids are all safe, so I have a plan. I have Betty calling all the parents, letting them know that their kids are safe here, and that they need to make sure their homes are safe enough and then they can come pick them up. She's telling them where we keep the spare key so they can get inside and then they are to put it back for the next parent."

The nodding Amy had started earlier suddenly stopped. "Why don't I just let them in when they get here?" She asked quietly.

His reply was the one that started her tears. "Because Baby, am locking you guys in the basement, so no one can get you," he said, and then he kissed her passionately.

As he broke the kiss, Amy remembered what she had been waiting to tell him. "Honey, I have something I have to tell you..."

"Not now babe, we got to get moving," he said and then Andy was off back downstairs. As Amy stood in their bedroom trying her tears, she could hear him talking to the kids. "Hey troop, here's the deal; we are having a game. It's time to hide from Mom and Dad ok? We're going to go to the basement and when they get here, they'll have to say 'yooo hooo where are you?' and then when they come downstairs, you can all say HERE WE ARE! Sound like fun guys?" She listened to them screaming their approval. Amy knew that anything Andy suggested the kids would agree with. Within minutes, they were all heading downstairs. Kelly stayed upstairs with the babies until the other three adults got all of the toddlers into the basement. The three women then each grabbed up a baby with Amy taking two and then she handed one off to Andy who was waiting at the top of the stairs.

After everyone was settled on mats or chairs or in bed, Jess started handing out snacks and drinks. Kelly looked at Amy and with her eyes begging harder than her words were, asked Amy if she would mind if she left. Apparently her boyfriend Bobby was getting ready to leave work and wanted her to go with him out of town. Amy kissed Kelly's cheek and told her to go.

Andy started back up the stairs with Amy behind him the whole way, watching as he went to the laundry room and pulled out his toolbox. Turning, he noticed Amy has confused look and he started to explain.

"I'm going to take the handle off the door. Then I am going to push the bookcase in front of the door, that way, unless you know the door is there, no one will think of looking for you. Just in case you need to get out, I grabbed some large eyehooks from the station and some rope, come on and I'll show you what I'm planning."

As they made it back into the kitchen, Amy stood frozen as she watched her husband, her mind reeling from everything she'd heard in the last fifteen minutes. After the door knob was removed he grabbed a wrench and took one of the eyehooks and on the bottom left side as she faced it, screwed it into the wood. As it got harder to turn, he switched to the wrench. When he finished there, he moved down the wall to the door jamb and attached the other eyehook. He then took the rope and tied it securely to the bookcase. He ran the length of rope to the second hook and pulled it through.

He started to explain, "I'll push the bookcase in front of the door. Just far enough from the wall so that the rope can slide behind it. You will have the end of it with you downstairs. I'll slide it under the door. If and only IF you need to get out of there before someone comes to push it open for you, all you have to do is pull on the rope slowly so that the traction of it being through the second hook will slowly pull it away from the door. If you try to go too fast, it might break the rope or topple the bookcase and then you'll be trapped." Amy wrapped her arms around herself and nodded at Andy. He finished his work, stood up, and hugged her again. "When this is over and it will be over, the police are on this big time. We'll go out for that anniversary dinner ok babe?" Andy kissed his wife, holding on to her for dear life. He had not told her that there were rumors out there that the people who were bitten usually died. Just as their kiss ended his alarm went off.

Units 4, please respond to Moore's sporting goods store. PD request, gunshots fired. One reported victim. Over.

"Hurry Honey, get downstairs, I have got to run. I love you Amy." He kissed her forehead and she walked down the stairs.

She stood there as Andy shut the door and she saw the rope snake under the jamb. She heard the scraping sound as Andy pushed the bookcase in front of the door, hiding them. Then he was gone with Betty heading downtown to the shooting at Moore's.

For the first two hours things went smoothly, the kids had their snacks and then laid down for naps. Amy was visibly shaken the whole time, especially after hearing on the EMS scanner that was still on in the kitchen that something bad was going on down at Moore's. The sound was too muffled for her to hear clearly though, so she decided to put the TV on and turn it away from the kids so she and Jess could see what was going on.

The images popping up on the screen could have been from a horror movie. The two women looked at each other and with tears in their eyes looked beyond the TV at the fifteen little souls sleeping like angels. Even the redheaded triplets looked precious right now.

Amy whispered to Jess, "We have to keep them safe." Jess nodded quietly then grasped Amy's arm and pointed to one of the ground level windows.

Outside, there was two pair of feet walking around, just moving back and forth. Slowly and unsteady. Amy moved towards the window, looking up. One of the babies woke up and Jess checked his diaper, pulling him up into her arms. The crying woke the oldest child there today, the seven year old named Mattie. The girl whose asthma had been acting up all night.

Sitting up and rubbing her eyes, she watched Miss Amy go towards the window. Suddenly, the dog from down the street ran past the window barking and growling. Mattie watched as one of the people outside reached for the dog. Abruptly, the second person walking outside lunged forward, falling on the dog. Amy was close enough to see the horrible face of the person who fell, or what was left of their face.

All Mattie could concentrate on was the dog. The animal cried as the two people outside both pulled in it. Her eyes widened as she watched them bite the dog, its red blood splattering all over the window. Amy turned away fast her hand over her mouth and her eyes met Mattie's. Then all hell broke loose.

Mattie started screaming, waking everyone else who in turn started screaming or crying. Amy rushed to Mattie to try and calm her but nothing worked. Mattie started wheezing. Amy hollered to Jess to grab her inhaler.

Jess looked in the baskets they brought to the basement but couldn't find the inhaler. Fighting panic she asked, "Where did you put it Amy?"

Amy felt the blood drain from her face when she realized that she hadn't grabbed Mattie's inhaler or any medications for that matter. Mattie's wheezing soon turned into gasps for air. Amy called for Jess to come hold Mattie and try to get her to calm down and breathe slowly so that Amy could try to get that damn door open.

Suddenly other kids started screaming even louder. Looking up, Amy saw that the two men outside were peering into the basement and pressing on the glass trying to break it. Jessica started yelling for Amy who was at the top of the stairs pulling on the rope, but not feeling it give any. When she glanced back down the stairs Amy saw Jessica lay Mattie down and cover her up with a blanket. Their eyes met and Jess just shook her head and started crying. The chaos in the basement seemed to settle a bit when the men left the window. Jess, sitting next to Mattie gasped when she felt movement coming from the little girl. Uncovering the child, Jess leaned over to caress Mattie's face. Suddenly the little one's eyes opened and what had previously been a beautiful blue were now a milky white.

"Mattie, baby can you hear me?" Jess whispered.

The child reacted by turning her head and biting deeply into Jess' wrist, crunching bone and pulling muscle into her mouth.

Screams filled the room, not just from Jess but also from all of the children. Mattie sat up and bit Jess again, this time in the neck rupturing her carotid. Soon Jess had fallen backwards lying across Mattie, pinning her down. A pool of blood surrounded both of them.

Amy felt herself move as if in slow motion as she raced down the stairs to gather up the kids and herd them under the stairs. She begged them to stop crying and screaming. Suddenly, the triplets all pointed behind Amy and let out blood curdling screams. Amy turned and saw that Jess had sat up. Her head hung at an angle because of the muscle damage to her neck. Jess no longer atop her, Mattie was getting to her feet as well.

Mattie headed over to the pack-&-plays and fell into one while reaching for one of the babies. Soon there was blood sprayed across the wall and the most nightmarish chewing sound as the seven year old tore into all four of the tiny babies. As this carnage took place, Jess was slowly trying to make her way over to the stairs where Amy and the toddlers were. Amy picked up a chair and tried to fend her off, like a lion tamer only without a whip.

"Jess, please stop. You're going to hurt someone. You don't want to hurt anyone do you? Hon, please just get back and leave the kids alone," Amy begged her young assistant. Seeing Andy's golf clubs in the corner she grabbed one and swung. She wasn't going to wait for an answer.

Her hit knocked Jess down. Amy raced up the stairs and pulled with all her might on the rope, praying that it would pull that damn bookcase away from the door so she could get these kids out of here. "Please God, help me!" She prayed and gave one last hard tug. She felt the rope break just a split second before she felt herself fall backwards off the stairs. She landed hard on her back, hearing a loud snap. She closed her eyes and tried to move her legs.

The kids under the stairs were rooting her on. "Come on Miss Amy, get up please." Amy tried to move her arms to push herself up and it was then that she realized that she had broken her back, high up. She could still move her head so she tried hushing the little ones.

Hearing a sound to her left, she turned her head and saw Jess getting back up. Jess moved right past her and started grabbing the kids. Amy heard the children beg for help, them not understanding that she could not help them, and then hearing them become silent one by one.

It was then that Amy knew she was in Hell. All she could do was close her eyes and not watch as they were slaughtered one by one by the young woman who used to work for her, used to care for the kids with her. All the children dead, Jess turned and looked at Amy, realizing that she was still there. She moved to Amy's side carefully, as if she would approach a startled animal. Just as Jess's face dipped towards Amy's stomach, Amy saw the toddlers start to move and she knew that they would be hungry like Jess was.

The only thing that kept her from losing her mind was the fact that she could not feel anything from her shoulders down. Her body shook as Jess ate her way inside her. Then Amy saw tiny hands pulling on her, ripping her open. Surrounded, she never screamed, not once, until she saw the triplets pull out her uterus and she knew that her baby -Andy's baby- was dead.

Then she screamed until death quieted her.

Peace

Shane Hershey

Peace Defined.

By definition the word holds many delightful connotations. It has been given a defined set of parameters by the tribes, nations and people who encounter its balming embrace. Yet peace is inconsistent. It is elusive. Long sought after. Rarely attained. Redefined by each passing generation. Altered by every new circumstance.

Peace Out.

In the 1960's, peace was defined not just by an anti-war movement, but the infusion of sex, drugs and rock music. Found in the escape of reality into the coma-induced hallucinations of drug highs and gyrating rock concerts. Peace was exhibited through the long braids and stoned eyes of random hippies. Peace was seen through photographic icons of rainbow prints and daisies sticking from the ends of military rifles. Two raised fingers exhibited the betrothing of peace from one man to another. Today, bullets have replaced flowers to attempt the stability of peace. The concerts of orgiastic proportions are not in muddied fields of farmland, but in the feeding fields of the asphalt streets of Manhattan.

I was unfortunate enough to have had my flight cancelled the day the dead came. I had tried renting a car to drive my way out, but the airport staff was overwhelmed with angry passengers, and the rental car companies were vacant wastelands; emptied of their wares hours before. I resigned myself to the fact that I would be stuck in the city until help came, and decided to head to the Plaza to see if I could check in. I figured if I was going to be stuck there my boss was certainly going to pay for that expense.

The first sign of brotherly love I encountered was on the train heading back to the hotel. Two bloodied and disheveled gang bangers, pants held up by air, crowded their way into the overcrowded subway car. From my position I could barely see them through the mass. I only noticed them because of the loud rhythmic bass that emanated from their ear buds. The shorter of the two busied himself wrapping a tattered shirt around a wound in his arm. I remember thinking it was just my luck to be confined to a space with two guys who most likely had just 'peacefully' finished business with rival gang members.

At each stop, people would press in and out, and the remaining passengers jostled and reconfigured, pushing the two closer to my direction. Each minute that passed saw more blood ooze through the fabric that encased the short one's arm. Each minute saw his pallor become more ashen. Seconds before reaching my stop, the taller one started shaking his friend by the shoulders. Shock encompassed me when I realized that the short one wasn't responding. His body held up only by the press of passengers.

As the train slowed, I stood and maneuvered my way towards the doors. I wanted to get out of there as fast I could. The doors opened, and I glanced a look back as the short one's milky white eyes made their appearance. The friend in front of him moved his hand upwards to run it in relief over his cornrows. His hand moved past the open mouth of his companion. Bared teeth found flesh, and as panic set in and fleeing passengers pushed me up the stairs from the platform, I saw the two fingers used to inscribe peace ripped from their joints. The feast began.

I ran.

Nature of Peace.

Among every city in every land, peace had been ascribed its place. Grassy knolls and quiet lakes. The serenity of nature provided in the midst of urban sprawl. The chirp of birds as couples caressed their way through quiet paths. The sounds of children's laughter echoed from playgrounds of wood and metal. Fruitful trees and spring blossoms provided escape from mindless routine. Today the real estate of peaceful greens and soft breezes has been replaced with the quiet of dark shadows and bolted doors.

I never made it to the Plaza. The swarm of living that escaped the confines of the tunnels pressed northward, surrounded on all sides by melee. The military arrived and declared martial law. Safe zones were set up, and survivors fought their way to them through a minefield of blood and bodies. Gnashing hands and teeth denied them the solace of escape. Tanks crushed skulls as they rolled through city streets patrolling for survivors, fighting for an end to the combat.

Two days passed before I was fortunate enough to be rescued huddling in a second floor abandoned store off 62nd street. The sound of gun fire outside lifted my spirits, gave me hope for respite. As the thunder of the humvee rolled through, I embraced the daylight, and called out through the window, tossing whatever my hands could find to gain attention.

Hours later, I was in the Sheep's Meadow nestled in the center of Central Park. Cement road blocks created our new boundaries. Bullets blasted endlessly into the night. Survivors settled into a comatose state of existence. Fortify. Eat. Sleep. We worked mindlessly trying to nullify our fear through persistence. Four days later, a breach, not peace, came when the guns fell silent. Cement tons were forced inward opening crevices for the attack. Emaciated bodies pushed through. Sheer numbers overwhelmed the defenses as eviscerated intestines emptied themselves as quickly as they were filled. The press of death pursued as lines of blood were drawn in the dirt. The siege continued. I ran.

Peace Treaty.

Centuries of treaties collecting dust among the halls of museums attest to the hundreds of accords that prescribed peace as the end of armed conflict. Paintings showcase the moment when warring nations put down their weapons and traded them for plowshares. Archeological finds tell the tale of border disputes that ended when pen was set to paper and the rules by which peace would be held were defined. These artifacts enshrine the rules set forth; the means through which Death was denied. Today, humanity defines the peace of warring factions not through pen, but through blade. A blood soaked dagger ends confrontation, not ink and papyrus.

I never knew how many escaped through the brambles with us. Our numbers diminished with every step. Sticks not guns, rocks not bullets served as ammunition for the living. An opening appeared in front of us as the Metropolitan Museum of Art came into view. The remaining handful of us pushed our way through the doors left unguarded by absent curators. The incessant pounding of our pursuers forced us further into the recesses of the empty halls adorned with representations of past civilizations. The only remains of once dominant societies.

Sanity stretched thin through the waning hours of daylight. We armed ourselves with centuries old weaponry. Daggers and spears. Blades and armor. A mocking characterization of warriors of old. As night entombed us in the museum, we huddled around an empty entrance. A lone young woman sat in a corner. A shivering puppy protected in her embrace.

The silence of the endless night was interrupted frequently by pounding and scratching every time a whine escaped from the damned dog. I stared venomously at the woman. I wasn't alone. She desperately tried to stifle the cries of the creature in her arms. Her hands clamped forcefully against its muzzle. Finally, just before dawn, permanent silence ensued as the puppy lay limp in her lap. Tears streaked her face. Sleep overcame me.

A scream interrupted my brief, fitful slumber, and I

134

awakened as the young woman with the dog tore another strip of flesh from one of the men closest to where she'd sat. Her milky white eyes engorged as the blood dripped down her chin. Her wrists were laid open and drained. A bloody dagger sat dormant near the dead puppy. A silent tale to the story of her death. The screams continued as the rest of us stared in horror. The doors bulged. Glass and wood cracked loudly, before exploding inwards. I took one last look before my feet took flight. My eyes locked on the creature in the corner. Clarity breathed momentarily. It moved. It wasn't her dog. My stomach seized. My soul cried out.

I ran.

Inner Peace.

Millennia old religions have espoused the value of peace within. Clarity of mind, body and soul. A peace that passes all understanding. A peace founded in forgiveness. Absolution from wrong doing. It didn't matter what religion, faith or creed, each spiritual advisor provided soothing words that would salve the wounded spirit. Offer sanctuary for the weary. Give a hope of things to come. Today, inner peace is the absence of thought. The loss of self. Mindless abandon. There is no forgiveness. Trespasses are numbered. Sins lack atonement. Sanctuary comes at a terrible price.

I don't know how I ended up there; staring up at the tall spires outside St. Patrick's Cathedral. Time became meaningless. Days were counted not by hours and minutes, but blocks and buildings. My mind was frantic. My clothing was tattered and caked in feces, blood, and fluids. I couldn't scrub it away. Each noise in the city shredded against what remained of my soul. I demanded peace. Quiet. Calm. Living or undead. It didn't matter. Whoever had the audacity to interrupt my temporary sanctuaries paid. Some with their life, some with their body. Usually both. Feral physical comforts consumed me. Food, release. sleep. I was dirty. I couldn't concentrate. I couldn't feel. I needed to clean it off; the blood, the filth, the stains of humanity.

I climbed the steps and pushed open the doors. The draw of this building held an appeal I was unable to focus on. I knew I'd drawn attention. That thought no longer held consequence. My days and nights were spent killing. Re-killing. Surviving, barely. None of it held distinction. Instinctually I dipped my hands in the small bowl at the entrance. I looked at my hands. I had only bloodied the water. Nothing came away refreshed. Nothing was clean.

My feet echoed through the emptiness. I passed pews filled with truly dead. Self-inflicted head wounds. Lucky bastards found salvation. I drew close to the altar. A priest came up behind me. I smashed his head in with a crucifix. I thought he said something. They don't speak. They noiselessly proclaim their blind judgment from the shadows. Had he said something? I looked at the body. It didn't matter. Words were useless. Senseless searches for absolution that would never come. I turned. The mass of pierced flesh entered before me. Pierced hands, wounded feet. Ribs shattering their sides. Mutilated flesh on their backs, their faces. The congregation presented itself. Resurrection stood before me. Judgment day had arrived. I wasn't clean. I ran.

Rest in Peace.

Shuffling off the mortal coil. Eternal rest. Kicking the bucket. Riding the pale horse. Passing away. The absence of care and concern. Worldly worries permanently suppressed. Euphemisms for the final peace. The origination of such terminology was founded in magical beliefs that to speak the word is to invite Death. Something to be feared. Something to fight against. Something to avoid. Today Heaven and Hell have been denied and emptied. A world of grim reapers invade every hiding place of man. Death mocks. Rest in peace a comical refrain. Bite the Big One remains the most honest among the long list of expressions to describe the absence of mortality.

I am in a room with cold smooth surfaces. It's small. Darkened. My shoulder hurts. I think one of the Reapers touched me. I flick my lighter. I'm not alone. Envy crowds my thoughts. I stare at the tombs. I crave their rest. I wonder if I can open one. Crawl inside. Interrupt their peace in a search for my own. Noises above me. I'm still in the cathedral. It must be the crypt. I'm so tired. I want to rest. I want to be clean. I want to forget.

I'm hungry. The darkness is stifling. It's time to leave. I see him as I exit. He isn't like them. He's faster. Movements more defined. He's a survivor. He's my savior. I near him, quietly. He turns. My teeth bare. He raises his weapon. I run.

Peace...at last.

THE ONLY THING THAT MATTERS

ALAN MACRAFFEN

"Duke! Go get it, boy! Come on, Duke!" Sam cried.

Why doesn't he understand, Duke thought. *Why can't he smell the intruder?*

Sam was Duke's best friend. Family. Duke struggled to resist the temptation to run and grab the ball. He almost turned and ran for it at the boy's latest urging, but there was something more important to be done. Duke turned back to the fence, following the scent of the intruder. He stopped and sniffed at one of the small stones lining the edge of the garden.

The intruder had stopped here, rubbed his scent glands on the stone. Rich and musky, it reminded Duke of another dog's scent, but much more pungent. A fox. Male. Duke considered the danger to his family and then continued along the scent trail, despite Sam's protests. Finally he found what he was looking for. The fox had left the yard through the small gap in the fence boards here. Before it left, it had urinated, attempting to mark the territory as its own. Duke sniffed intently, taking in as much information as he could. The fox was an adult, but still somewhat young; healthy and well fed on small game and scavenged trash, without any significant injuries or disease. Duke relaxed visibly. The fox was not a threat to his family.

He took a moment to urinate over the fox's mark,

139

reestablishing the yard incontrovertibly as his territory. The fox would get the message — the yard and house were under Duke's protection.

"Aww, Duke," Sam said as he approached. "Don't pee near mom's garden. She hates that." Sam grabbed Duke's collar in his small hand and pulled him toward the middle of the yard. Duke allowed it, his work now done, but again wondered at Sam's inability to smell the intruder or to understand the seriousness of Duke's work.

The boy was only seven years old — still a young pup by human standards — but he and his parents should be more aware of danger. Duke was constantly on the alert for it, and constantly alarmed by how much they seemed to miss or ignore.

Many animals frequently passed through the woods near the house. Duke knew perfectly well that most foxes and coyotes weren't a threat to his family, but bears and strange dogs could be. Yet the humans seemed utterly unaware of their presence, even when they were just beyond the fence.

One morning a year ago, when the toaster had caught fire, Duke had spent almost ten terrifying minutes trying desperately to alert his family. He had noticed the scent of smoke while sleeping on Sam's dirty and pleasantly stinky clothes in the boy's bedroom upstairs. The family had been in the living room the whole time, right next to the kitchen, and still hadn't noticed. If Duke hadn't rushed down and yowled as if he were dying, they might never have noticed it in time to put the fire out.

Sam stopped tugging Duke's collar when they reached the center of the yard, then lifted the well-chewed tennis ball. Duke's musings stopped abruptly as he focused on the beloved toy.

"Okay, ready?" Sam asked. He held the ball aloft for a few moments, building suspense like a master storyteller, then hurled the ball across the yard with all his tiny strength. "*Go get it, Duke!*"

Duke exploded into action. His work patrolling was done

for now. Now was the time for *play*.

He bolted across the yard with frantic energy. Cool wind rippled his face as his legs pounded against the dry grass and patchy snow, until he felt like he was almost *flying* across the yard, his paws barely touching the surface. With a gleeful rush of adrenaline, Duke focused on the rolling ball in front of him, rapidly gaining on it, then spinning in a perfect turn as he reached out and clamped his teeth securely around its fuzzy shape.

The moment he had secured the ball, Duke steadied himself, finishing his turn and now pointed directly back at Sam. He took off again with huge, bounding leaps of triumph as the boy laughed and cheered.

Nothing could be better. At least not until he reached Sam and dropped the ball, leaping into the boy's open arms and rolling across the dry grass as Sam scratched and petted his thick fur. It was an absolutely perfect moment, like so many moments with his family.

At that point, Duke couldn't have cared less about his family's dim senses or lack of caution. He loved them absolutely, and knew that they loved him just as much. That love was the only thing that mattered.

As always, Duke was the one who first noticed when everything started to fall apart.

*****

Early the next morning, Duke woke from a nap with a start, smelling a very faint but strange burning scent. He quickly got up from Sam's pile of dirty clothes — bless the boy for always rebuilding the pile after one of his parents stole it — and hurried downstairs, his feet and claws clicking and thumping on the steps. He checked the kitchen first.

No fire.

Next he checked the living room. Nothing. The dining room. Nothing. The front hall. *Almost* nothing.

141

The mail slot in the front door allowed just a small trickle of outside air to flow through. From it, Duke could smell the odor of a distant fire. Acrid and noxious, like the stinky gasoline they put in the car. Another scent mingled in, even fainter, making the fur on Duke's back bristle slightly. The scent was so distant and diluted that Duke couldn't identify it, but something about it was wrong.

The distance of the odors didn't indicate any immediate danger to the family, but they left Duke feeling uneasy. He paced around the house a few more times, checking windows and under furniture, all the while waiting for the family to wake up.

After what felt like ages, they did. The one Duke thought of as Mom-Janelle came downstairs first.

Duke ran to the bottom of the stairs, whimpering slightly and informing Janelle with his voice and body language that something wasn't quite right. She smiled and scruffed the top of his head, which felt wonderful and slightly calming, but then she ignored him and continued into the kitchen to begin her routine of coffee-making.

Duke continued to voice his worries, but Janelle just dumped some food and water in his dishes.

"Relax Duke, I won't forget your breakfast," she said. "There ya go—all better."

Overwhelmed by habit and food-smells, Duke gobbled three large mouthfuls of kibble before regaining his focus and resuming his warnings. By then, Janelle was busily watching the TV.

Duke made several more attempts to gain her attention, but she steadily ignored him in favor of the strange, flickering series of blurry pictures that so often hypnotized the whole family.

When Dad-Ted came downstairs, Duke made the same attempts. Ted offered some very nice and distracting petting at the foot of the stairs, saying wonderful, reassuring things like "Good morning Duke," and "Who's a good dog?" but then ignored Duke completely when Janelle began speaking.

"Ted, did you turn on the TV in the bedroom?" she asked. He shook his head no and poured himself a cup of coffee.

"Why? Something good on?"

She shook her head. "No. I mean—it's really weird. There was an accident out at the gas station next to Bobby's place. Somebody must have been drunk or texting or something, because they drove right into the pumps. Just before dawn. The whole place went up."

"Shit, that's terrible," Ted said. "These things happen, though. If people aren't careful…"

Janelle shook her head. "But there's also a lot of other weird stuff on the news. Not here. I mean, it just seems to be everywhere. People are killing each other, Ted. People are actually *biting* each other! It's kind of freaking me out, a little bit."

Ted rubbed her shoulders and planted a kiss on top of her head. "You know the news is all sensationalized. That's why I hardly watch it. It's all spun out of proportion to get everyone scared and constantly tuned-in. That's why I just stick with the sports and weather. All I need." He turned and headed toward the hall, putting his tie in place as he went.

Upstairs, Duke heard the sounds of Sam jumping out of bed and thumping around his room. He made another whining plea to either of the adults. Surely they must have noticed something odd by now.

Ted scratched Duke's shoulders as he walked by. "Don't worry, boy. Sam'll be up soon. Then you guys can play."

When Sam came downstairs for breakfast, Duke tried desperately and failed again to alert his family to the unknown danger. As Ted was getting ready to leave for work, Duke tried yet again. His frantic efforts gained him more scratches and petting, which were delightful, but did little to put him at ease or bring his family any closer to safety.

"Don't worry boy, I'll see you tonight," Ted said.

"Maybe you should call in sick today," Janelle said. "All that weird stuff…"

Ted kissed her cheek. "Really, Honey, I'll be fine. Turn that

TV off and relax, alright?"

She smiled, but didn't relax.

*****

Duke became more distressed as the day wore on. More convinced that something wasn't right. Janelle got Sam ready for school and nearly out the door to the school bus, and then told him that he didn't have to go after all. She helped him take his coat and boots off, then set him up with a coloring book and went back to watching the TV. Duke looked back and forth at his two oblivious family members, whining softly. Janelle stared at the strange rushing flutter of TV images. Sam colored a dinosaur with a gray crayon.

Duke was absolutely certain that something was wrong now. Twice since waking this morning he had heard very loud, distant banging noises. Like the sounds he heard in the woods in the fall. At one point, a strange car had raced down the road at an unusually high speed. Even in the thin trickle of air flowing through the mail slot, Duke had smelled the scent of blood and human urine passing by.

*****

At noon, Duke made a very bad mistake.

He had taken up residence at the front door, monitoring the series of distant but alarming odors trickling through the mail slot. Things seemed to calm down a bit by midday, and Duke drifted into a light, nervous sleep. His dreams were deep enough to allow the approaching intruder to come all the way across the front yard and up to the door without Duke noticing. When he rang the doorbell, Duke snapped awake, panicking, and began barking furiously.

Janelle came running from the kitchen. "Duke! No! Bad boy!"she hissed. She pushed him back as she peered through the curtain and then opened the front door. The intruder reached in. Janelle made no move to avoid his reaching arm. Duke lunged.

He knew something was wrong even as his bared fangs sank through the man's coat, piercing the skin beneath. The scent was not an enemy scent. It was familiar. Not a threat.

The man screamed hoarsely in surprise. Janelle screamed as well, both of them startling Sam and making him scream in the other room. As man tried to yank his arm backward, a large brown package fell to the floor with a heavy thud. Duke tried to release the man, but the screaming frightened him, and he nipped one last time, reflexively, before dropping back into the hallway, his tail tucked between his legs.

"Jeee-*zus!*" the mailman shouted. "Sorry!" He blushed brightly, clearly embarrassed by his scream and curse. "God *dammit* that hurts! Sorry! Jeez… Oh man. What's got into that dog?"

"Sorry!" Janelle said. "Oh God, I'm so sorry! He's not like this!"

"Don't I know it!" the mailman said, clutching his injured arm. "I've been coming to this house and seeing that dog for years and he never said a peep about it!" He backed away. "He'd damn well better have all his rabies shots up to date!"

Janelle leaned out after him. "I'm so sorry, Dave! Yes—he's totally up to date! No rabies! I just don't know what to say. Can I get you a bandage for that arm?"

"No thank you," Dave said. "You wanna do me a favor, get a leash for that dog!" He rushed back to his mail truck as if Duke were hot on his heels.

Janelle stepped back inside and shut the door. "Fuck." Her foot hit the side of the box on the floor. "Oh goodie. My book's here," she muttered sarcastically.

"Mom?" Sam said, standing next to Duke. Both seemed to be clinging protectively to the other. "Is somebody gonna kill Duke now?"

"Oh honey, no," she said, pulling Sam close. "You've been watching too much TV." She glanced at the television in the kitchen. "Maybe we've all been watching too much TV. He's just scared. But I think maybe it's a good idea for him to have a little break, okay? Let's take him outside for a while."

Duke submitted silently to Janelle's hand as she took his collar and led him toward the back door and the leash hanging there. His eyes darted sheepishly from side to side. He knew now that he would be put in the back yard, practically a world away from the family he so desperately wanted to protect.

*****

Looking in through the windows from the spot where his leash was tied, things seemed calm inside the house. Janelle had finally turned off the TV and was now attempting to keep Sam occupied and distracted. They played cards, a board game, read a book together, but always Sam would come to the window to look mournfully out at Duke. Duke wanted to go to him and reassure him so badly it hurt.

Things were worse outside.

With nothing between his nose and the drifting breeze, Duke was now aware of a great many alarming things.

Smoke from multiple fires hung in the air. The sharp stink of gunpowder drifted past more than once. Blood. Human blood. Its smell rich, coppery, and laden with fear.

Worst of all, Duke scented the growing odor of death.

With no walls and windows to filter it out, Duke's keen ears could hear the distant pops of guns. The squeals of tires. The sirens and the screaming. At one point he could hear Janelle talking on her phone, her voice full of fear.

And he saw. Through the small, fox-sized hole in the fence, he saw the neighbors' house. Saw the car that drove with glacial slowness down the street, then veered up onto the curb and into the neighbors' yard before coming to a stop against a concrete bird-bath. Saw the human shape inside move against the door, then spill awkwardly out the driver's side window. Saw it stand up on crooked, unsteady legs and begin limping toward the neighbors' front door, even though it smelled of nothing alive—nothing but blood and fear and tainted death.

The fox's escape route proved the perfect vantage point. Duke watched, whining fearfully and then barking furiously, as the dead thing moved into the house. As the shouts of the humans inside reached his quivering ears. As one neighbor emerged from the patio door in back, falling onto his back with a bloodied leg and a fireplace poker in his hand. As the dead thing approached with its relentless limp, not stopping until the man pushed the poker into its eye and straight to the back of its head. His attacker vanquished, the neighbor collapsed from loss of blood.

When the freshly dead man began to get up again, smelling of nothing but shit, dried blood and death, Duke's barking reached a furious, fearful crescendo.

Janelle was at the back door, about to open it, but then moved away as lights illuminated the front yard. Duke heard the familiar sound of the family car pulling into the driveway.

He ran to the end of his leash, jerking himself right off of his feet, barking desperate warnings to his entire family.

Duke heard the sound of the car door opening and closing. Heard Ted fumbling with the latch on the gate into the back yard. He also heard the dead neighbor steadily shuffling its way from next door, toward that same gate.

Duke jerked his leash again, then again, snapping it loose on the third pull. As Ted opened the gate and came through, Duke barked like a Hound of Hell at the approaching silhouette of the dead neighbor behind Dad-Ted.

Ted turned just in time to see the reaching shape, and somehow managed to jump back and swing the door shut quickly enough to prevent it from slipping inside. Duke's charge carried him forward, and he slammed against the wooden gate even as the dead thing leaned against it from the other side.

"Son of a bitch!" Ted gasped. "That's Bill! *They got Bill!*" He grabbed Duke's collar and pulled him away from the gate with great difficulty, then guided him in through the back door where Mom-Janelle and Sam were waiting, both in tears.

"What's happening?" Janelle cried. "I only got part of your call. Are you okay?"

Ted nodded, guiding Janelle and Sam away from the windows, toward the middle of the kitchen.

"What's going on out there?" Janelle said.

"It's…" Ted fumbled. "It's bad. It's real bad."

Duke took up position between the three humans and the door, listening for any sounds of immediate danger. His nostrils flared, checking the air as well. He could sense almost immediately that Dad-Ted was not well. He smelled of many alarming things, but worst of all were the smells of blood, pain, and death coming from him. The same smells the neighbor had before he died and rose again.

*****

An hour later, Dad-Ted closed his eyes for the last time in life.

The family was gathered in the den, still watching the useless flickers of the TV. Duke ignored the annoying strobe, glad of anything that made them feel better. Sam snuggled up between Duke and Janelle, and Ted slumped against her other shoulder, breathing long, slow breaths.

Duke could smell Dad-Ted getting worse. With every minute he smelled less like Ted and more like something… wrong. Something *broken*.

At first, Duke had tried to sit next to Ted, tried to lick his hand like he always had and comfort him. But the smell had become too upsetting. Instead, Duke focused on the boy, who was terrified. Duke could sense Sam's fear lessen just a little when he pressed up against him.

The process was so gradual, even Duke's sharp ears almost didn't notice when Ted's breathing dipped from slow—to nothing at all.

Duke softened his own breathing, listening intently for the sound of Ted's breath to resume.

It didn't. But he did begin to move.

Duke smelled the change vividly. The last vestiges of Ted's scent were overwhelmed by the odor of illness, death and that horrible, gut-wrenching *broken* smell. Duke let out a low warning growl as Dad-Ted began twitching, then lurching into a more upright position.

Janelle roused from near sleep and stared at the shell of her husband beside her, blinking glazed, whitish eyes.

"Ted?" She tried to sidle away from him, but the weight of Sam and Duke prevented her.

Duke began barking ferociously. The thing that had been Ted ignored him, locking its dead gaze on Mom-Janelle. Duke let out a deep, threatening growl, but he didn't lunge—not yet. He did not want to hurt this thing, as horrible as it was. A moment ago it had been family. It smelled wrong, and he almost always trusted his nose, but it still *looked* like Ted, and that was enough to make him pause. He continued growling, throwing several short, vicious sounding barks in for good measure. Any living thing would sense that he was at his limits, and not to be pushed, but the thing animating Ted's body was not living, and did not acknowledge the rules of nature. It lunged forward, jaws snapping so hard that the teeth *clacked* together with a sound like wooden boards.

Duke lunged across Janelle's lap, and she reeled back, pushing herself and Sam farther away from the thing. Duke's body collided with Ted's corpse powerfully, knocking it back and tumbling it off of the couch. Janelle was pushing at it with both arms, and she screamed as the body pulled away with a wet ripping sound.

Duke continued pushing, forcing the corpse-Ted onto its back and snapping at its thrashing head and shoulders. He could smell Janelle's freshly spilled blood, and see it on the monster's mouth and chest. He continued to press with his paws and snap menacingly, but did not want to bite—not so much because the thing looked like Ted now, but because the smell of wrongness emanating from it was so overpowering.

Suddenly Janelle was up from the couch, her shadow

149

looming over them both. Duke jumped back just as she swung down with the large glass candle holder she had grabbed from a nearby shelf. The heavy glass cracked brutally against the Ted-thing's head once, twice. The thing's arms continued to thrash and grab at the air, until a third blow landed with a snapping crunch, staving in Ted's skull.

Duke leapt up onto the couch, shielding Sam with his body. On the floor, Mom-Janelle continued wailing with fear and grief. Her head was bent over Ted's ruined body as if to embrace him, even as her fist continued to rise and fall, pounding his chest with impotent desperation. After a moment, she turned her tear-streaked face toward Sam and Duke.

"*Sam!*" she sobbed. "Sam… I'm so sorry." She rose to her feet shakily. Blood was continuing to pour from her left wrist in a steady stream, and her skin was growing ashen. Sam could only cry in answer, his sobs shaking Duke's body.

"I had to protect you, Sam!" Janelle said. She swayed, then took a step forward, reaching out for her son.

Duke now understood what was happening, and what was at stake. He rose, blocking Janelle from reaching Sam, and let out another threatening growl. At Janelle. Janelle who was still living. Janelle who was his own family. But the smell was there. Growing stronger with each pulse of blood that flowed from her ragged wrist. Soon she would not be Janelle. She would not be family. There was nothing Duke could do to stop it. Nothing he could do but protect the only family he had left. He must not allow Sam to come to harm, no matter what. It was the only thing that mattered now.

"Duke?" Janelle wheezed. Her face was a mixture of fear and betrayal. She took another, shakier step forward. "Sam? I'm going to take care of you Sam, I…"

Duke barked like a wild beast, fur bristling. Janelle faltered. She lost her balance and fell to her knees on the carpet.

"Duke?" Her eyes began to cloud over. "Sam? *Sam… I love…*" Her eyes rolled back, and she slumped limply to the floor, her breath stopping moments later.

"Mommy!" Sam screamed. He pushed at Duke, trying to move around him. Duke would not budge. He could smell the last of her scent fading, smell the death and corruption pouring out of her. Her undamaged arm twitched.

Duke spun and grabbed Sam's sleeve firmly in his teeth. He began pulling the boy off of the couch, leading him forcefully toward the hall.

"No! No, Mommy!" Sam screamed. "Duke, no! Mommy!" Duke continued to pull the boy toward the front door. Behind them, Janelle sat up.

Duke growled around the mouthful of sweater and continued dragging Sam away. Corpse-Janelle was now rising to her feet with a series of terrible, awkward jerks.

"No! No!" Sam screamed. His cries were heartbreaking in Duke's ears. "Mommy! *Mommy!*" Deperate and terrified, the boy reached out and grabbed a hold of a small lamp on the little table in the hallway. He pulled it off of the table and swung it around, smacking Duke soundly on the back with it. It did no serious damage, but Duke cringed, horrified by the boy's fear and anger, and nearly lost his grip on the sweater.

With slow, lurching steps, corpse-Janelle followed them into the hallway. Duke pulled harder. Sam, crying inarticulately now, flailed out with the lamp again. This time it connected with Duke's sensitive nose. The pain was sharp and more than a little dizzying. Duke yelped pitifully and lost his grip on the sweater.

Sam darted away, running with his hands thrust out toward his mother. She continued her approach with arms open and eyes lifeless.

Duke howled in pain and terror, bolting after Sam. His legs were much faster than the boy's, but the distance was small, and corpse-Janelle's stiff arms were almost around Sam by the time he reached him. Duke lunged, trying to grab a secure mouthful of sleeve. He did that, but in the process also nipped painfully through the skin of Sam's arm. Sam screamed shrilly, terrified and now in pain as well, but Duke could not release him. He pulled back with all of his strength and speed, pulling

Sam away just as his mother's fingers brushed through his tousled hair, seeking a grip.

Duke ran with everything he had in him, dragging Sam roughly to the door, his teeth continuing to hurt Sam even as he saved him. The boy's cries were like knives in Duke's heart.

He reached the front door, crashing into it, and slapped desperately at the lever-style handle. Ted had talked for months about swapping it out for a knob after they'd first discovered that Duke could operate it, but Ted's home improvement drive was no match for his procrastination, and it remained unchanged. Ted's laziness saved his son in that moment, as Duke hammered repeatedly on the handle until it unlatched. He pulled the door open with his paw, still gripping Sam's arm in his mouth, and then pulled the boy outside and across the front lawn.

Sam's cries rose to become shrill shrieks as he reached for his mother, who now stood stiffly in the open doorway. She shuffled down one step, then tripped on the second, falling hard on her face on the concrete walk with a crunch. When she stood up again, her face was covered in abrasions and several of her teeth were gone.

Sam wailed, caught between terror at the sight and the powerful need to run to his mother. He continued to pull against Duke. Duke whined pathetically. He could taste Sam's blood in his mouth. The wound wasn't severe, but it was getting worse with every tug. He desperately wanted to release the boy, but couldn't allow him to run to his dead mother. Whatever happened, he *must protect the boy.*

A wash of bright light shone over them as engines revved at the end of the street. A car and two large trucks approached, smelling of gas, oil, metal and live human beings.

Several bright spotlights swung about, causing sharp-edged shadows to leap all around. One beam focused on Janelle's corpse as it limped toward Duke and Sam. Duke heard a sudden sharp bang and the smell of gunpowder, and Janelle's skull spurted blood. She toppled like a pile of rags to the grass as Sam screamed louder than he ever had before.

Just as Duke began to relax his jaw, ready to release Sam to his now harmless mother, another beam washed over the two of them, followed by another sharp bang.

Duke yelped and flipped to the side as the force of the bullet knocked him off his feet. The movement pulled Sam over, and he immediately began to cling to Duke, screaming "*No!* Don't kill him! Don't kill him!"

Several living men rushed over, converging on Duke and Sam. Duke immediately smelled that they were healthy and untainted by the corruption that had taken Janelle, Ted and the neighbor. He tried to sit up, then felt a searing pain in his side and slumped back to the pavement. Sam took his paw in his tiny hand, tears spilling everywhere. Duke's breathing was becoming quite painful, and more difficult with every breath. But the living men were taking hold of Sam now. They would protect him. He would live. Duke began to relax, even as Sam was pulled away, crying pitifully, his little hand slipping free of Duke's now limp paw.

The boy would be alright. The boy would live.

Another man approached and examined Sam's arm, then sent them back toward the trucks. "I'll need to bandage it, but he'll be fine."

One of the men standing nearby with a rifle was wiping tears from his eye. "Aw shit, man. I thought it was attacking him. I didn't know it was the kid's dog. Can you do anything for him, Arnold?"

The man who had checked Sam turned and kneeled next to Duke. "Lemme take a look. Head back to the truck. You just did what you thought was right." The crying gunman moved away as the man named Arnold examined Duke's wound. The injury didn't look too bad on the entry side, but when he rolled Duke over the dog yelped in agony.

"Oh, fuck. What a mess." Arnold shook his head. "I'm sorry, boy. You did real good. What a fucking day…"

Duke panted in short little wheezes from the pain, then took several sharp sniffs. He could smell something coming from Arnold's ankle. It was the smell of a wound. It smelled of cotton, adhesive, blood, antiseptic, and… death. Corruption. It smelled *broken*. Duke growled, faintly.

The man didn't know. He would rejoin the others. He would die. He would kill.

Every breath was agony now. All Duke wanted to do was relax and slip into sweet sleep. But his job wasn't done. Not yet.

He eyed the man, waited until Arnold looked back at the others to shake his head regretfully. Then he lunged upward. The effort of movement tore through his side like razors. He felt something strain, then rip inside him. He kept pushing, sinking his teeth into Arnold's throat and clamping down until his jaws clicked shut. Then he relaxed, pulling most of the man's throat away with him. One of the other men spotted this, and screamed, opening fire. The bullets went wild, most hitting the street, but one bore into Arnold's skull, dropping him to the street like a stringless puppet.

Another hit Duke. It dug deep, puncturing his heart. He jerked, and felt the pain, but didn't care anymore.

Now his job was done.

Now the boy would live.

Duke loved his family. It was the only thing that mattered.

Eddie Smith, Part Three:
Chasing Hope

Kids, y'all realizing we need to move at first light right? Your momma is gonna tan my behind if she finds out you stayed up to the wee hours listening to me rant and rave about things that done past.

Oh? Is that so? You're gonna take the fall for Eddie? Jump right on top of that grenade for me? You're a crew of kind critters aren't ya? Ha. I suspect your momma is gonna accept your tale of woe and good intentions and tan my behind anyways. Mothers are like that.

What's the story tonight? What is it you simply must hear about to keep yourselves warm as we head stupidly north and east to our destination away from the warm embrace of the Lone Star state?

Why? You wanna know why we're doing this?

Hm. That's a bit of a complicated one kids. It's like explaining how you know the sun's gonna rise in a few hours. Sometimes, things in life are just decided for you, and your job in it all is to accept that decision and do your part. God's will, as it were.

Well you probably recall the Fort and how we was all set up inside it, selling and trading fuel to the locals who wanted peace, and shooting up the ones who didn't. Dark times that first winter was. None of us inside the fences of the distribution facility had much in the way of a green thumb, so we had a bit of a 'being hungry' problem. Fortunate for us, we had a lot of fuel to burn to run generators to keep warm, and to trade to the people who had food spare. That wasn't much.

I lost something in the way of fifteen pounds that winter, and of all forty of us back then, I had it easier than some. We never ate each other like some did -barbeque style Texan- but we did share a few too many one-spoon meals.

What's a 'one-spoon meal?' That's a deeee-licious sit down dinner where you crack open a single can of something barely edible and each person gets a single spoonful. If there's enough for a second spoon, then it goes to the children. If I never sit down in front of a bowl of beans, corned beef hash or chicken noodle soup I'll be a happy man. Perhaps a happier man. I don't know if true happiness is attainable anymore, but that's part of why we're on this road trip. You probably don't remember the times we only had one spoon because you never had just one spoon. I'm good with that.

Right. Where was I going with this?

So the winter of ought ten into ought eleven was a tough one. Cold and hungry. We didn't lose anyone to starvation, and we had enough rain for water, plus we just had plenty of water in general, so that was good. We did lose a few people protecting the fuel depot though. Theo bought the farm in a shootout over a gasoline sale, and we lost Max and AJ the same day. AJ's wife Danielle shuffled off this mortal coil by her own hand just a few days after that, and then the twins Ivy and Violet left with their mother to head home on the gulf. That incident directly led us to dropping down to just thirty left. Barely enough to protect the fuel.

When the weather turned warmer in late February things got better. Local gardens were making a comeback and we were able to do some plucking and replanting to get some food growing, and we took in that group of Masons we'd been working with on the other side of Longview. They were down to eleven, and we had good relations with them, so it made sense to have one safer home than two. Brad that's how you got to us. Your momma and daddy are good friends of mine now.

That summer was an un-blessed mess. It was a good thing we had another eight adults with us. We took on attacker after attacker every week pretty much. People wanting fuel and thinking it'd be easier to take it by force than simply trade for it. We had to kill off thirty and nine that summer.

How do I know that number?

Because I kept count as I prayed for them over every grave I helped dig.

You can't just take a life and walk away from it kids. That person, a strange though they might be is still a human being with life, love, dreams and family and when their life is taken from them, by you or those who you stand beside, you must do what is right and see to it they are given peace.

If you can't see the inherent good in doing that deed on its own merit, then maybe you'll do it so they won't haunt your sleep each and every night, begging for a proper burial.

I had that experience. Once.

Despite the death and fighting, our fuel and diesel supply kept us warm and fed, which is more than we had any right to ask for with the dead wandering the world, and the living doing their best to kill each other off. We made it to about August, when the heat was right about insufferable without the juice to power the air conditioning at full blast when the McCoy family made their way to us.

Pete and Emma McCoy came to town from the east coast with their two little girls Patience and Katie. They were traveling to California taking as many back roads as possible to stay far off the zombie jams of the interstates, and smelled our meat cooking as they rode their horses and begged for some shelter and rest. We couldn't say no to the kids and they offered to leave one of their two spare horses with us for payment. They had good timing, as we'd been stocking up on horses for when the diesel ran out. That's why we brought the horse trailers. Eight isn't enough for all of us to ride, but it's a good start, and we got a good pair of studs. In a few years with proper care we'll have enough for all of us to ride and then some.

So Pete and Emma are telling us this tale as we sit around eating some wild hog that night. They explaining that up north there's this man who it all rides on, and two more people are coming to him, and they form a trinity, like the holy trinity from the Bible.

Of course in Texas you do not worship false idols, but they way they explained it, and the way our dreams were being, we all knew the Lord's hand was in the mix. Their story made as much sense as any, and like a seed planted in a fertile field, the words the McCoy family shared with us that night took root, and bore fruit.

Many of us knew that when the fuel ran dry, there was little reason to stay in Longview, especially no good reason to stay at the fuel plant. Other than the tanks in the ground, it had nothing to offer us besides good fences. And you know what boys? Fences can be built around anything.

The McCoys told us about their meeting two people up north who had met this man. A girl named Angie, and a man named Raef. Raef didn't much care for this man, the one the McCoys said was important, but Angie liked him a good deal, and they couldn't argue with the dreams.

No one can, once you have one.

So a few days and more than one conversation later Pete and Emma left with their four horses and their two kids for the west coast. I sure do hope they made it. Doesn't make much sense for us to head north here in the late winter, but we're hoping we'll get to Bastion as it warms up.

What's Bastion? It's a place. It's where we're going.

Oh right. Why?

Well the McCoy family took their Irish blood west and we stewed. More dreams came, and in those dreams we saw and heard more of the Lord's truth. He had chosen a new path for us, and we had to walk together as one or fall together. And this man, this Adrian... He was the one to lead us. He and the other two in the trinity of man.

So we spent the next few months fighting off the locals, and shooting hogs, and putting down the stray dead that walked their way to the edge of town, and generally just getting through the winter. All the while debating what's real, what's fake, what's right and wrong and what to do. Was it enough to just survive? Or did we need to do more.

Some of us prayed. Some of us laughed at it all. Some of us drank. Those of us who could get their hands on booze, that is. Had a lot of fighting back then. I guess that's to be expected when confused, scared people piss through bottles of whisky and vodka left and right. In all this I think one of the greatest blessings is we're running out of liquor.

It all came to a head two months ago in our town meeting in the cafeteria. Right before Christmas.

Your daddy -Adam- says this to the group. He says, "I believe our time here has come to an end. Longview has treated us as well as we could've hoped and prayed for, but with our fuel supplies dwindling, and the news that salvation is possibly within reach, I would like to speak of the idea of relocating to this place called Bastion."

He said it real polite. People lost their minds anyway. Most of us have never stepped foot outside of Gregg and Harrison county, let alone Texas aside from those that served, so the idea that our leader tabled seemed like insanity. Absolute insanity. Think of it kids; why would you leave a secured, safe place and drive halfway across God's country to try and track down some dang crack head that likes winter claiming to be the second coming struck everyone as a bit insane. Now if you're clever you'll be thinking of the wasted fuel, the foreign roads we'd be driving on, and the fact that the world is littered with a hundred million of the feisty dead.

Maybe two hundred million. It's real hard to get a handle on the population since the census bureau was eaten alive. God rest their souls, amen.

As you can imagine, there was a lot of arguing. That's what adults do, after all. Some folks used that moment to confess that they was thinking of leaving to go find relatives or friends in other places, and some folks said they had no interest at all in going anyway. Only a few of us were thinking real hard about the reality of our situation, and the idea that leaving was a good idea, and that this stranger in a strange land was a good enough reason to.

One night we was sitting around a small bonfire outside, and like it always seemed to, the subject of the man and the three came up.

Casey -that pretty lady we lost in Missouri- says as the fires crackled in our barrels, "I wanna go. I wanna go north and find that man."

Dentley and Greg were sitting there with me and her, and Dentley says in his Arkansas drawl back to her, "What's this man going to do for you? Assuming he's real at all? He gonna turn your water into wine? He gonna make things safer? You thinkin' he's got a force field that keeps all the dead folks away? More'n likely he's surrounded up to the gills with disease, bandits, the living dead, and people lining up to kiss his ass, whether he's worth it or not."

Then the funniest thing happened. Casey just smiles with her dimples and looks over at Dentley like he's the biggest damn fool in the whole world -and let's be honest, she wouldn't be too wrong in that assumption kids- and she shakes her head. Then she says, "Dentley you old dog I don't care about any of that. What I can't stop thinking about since the McCoy family came along is that for the first time since June, I have a reason to live. Just thinking about this man and the two others gives me hope. And I haven't had hope in a long time, and I'm thinking that's enough for me to head north."

That shut him up. Shut Greg and I up too, and you know what? She was right. Hearing about this stranger gave us all purpose. There had been a certain sense of life since we'd heard of him, and with our grapes withering on the vine in Longview, I knew Casey was right.

I stood up, looked at 'em and said, "I'm going to start getting ready to leave. I need to find this man and decide for myself."

And I left. I had welding to do. Casey left too, and that left Greg and Dentley there talking it over.

The next day I met up with your daddy, and told him I'd assembled some parts and gotten some work done on the flatbed so it was mobile. I had some hinges and some plate steel I welded over the tires, and I had started work on the wedge that's now on the grill. He was happy.

"This is the pilgrimage of our time," he said unsure. "I don't understand it, but I know we should do this."

"Adam we've got so little here now. Only a few tankers left of good fuel, another hot summer headed our way next year, and the people here get hungrier and angrier with each passing day. The dead aren't getting thinner either, and one way or the other, change is upon us. Real or not, there's something in the air, and it's coming from the north."

He looked at me, and to this night I can't tell if I saw love and hope, or desperation in his face. No matter how you cut it, we set on our path to get it done that day.

Of the thirty two of us at that time twelve wanted to leave to go elsewhere. Family in Oklahoma, or San Antonio, et cetera. Six wanted to stay. That left fourteen of us to make the trip. The trip we're in the middle of right now.

So yeah. Kids. That's why. Because we decided it was better to chase hope on the road than sit and stew, waiting to die.

Time for bed. We only got a couple hours before we need to get the horses out and looking for supplies before we head back on the road. If we're lucky, we'll find more water. I'm sick of boiling snow. At least it's not yellow snow.

Maybe next time I'll tell you about that time we was attacked on the road in Tennessee near Bristol.

161

Meanwhile in Utah

Josh Green

Leaning my head against a door frame, I began to reflect on the events that led up to this moment. It had only been three days since this place went to hell in a hand basket. Just like any story, *that day* was like every other day.

I live in a place called Moab, Utah, which is a small town that's four hours from Salt Lake City. We have hot summers, cold winters, hardly any moisture, and it's basically a tourist trap. I was doing my normal thing, showing up to work fifteen minutes early in hopes that my boss would take notice and promote me to a foreman position. I put my construction bags on, then my framing hammer in the back-pocket hanger. I dropped some nails in my pockets, cranked the radio in my truck, and then slowly went to work building a new wall. I was the only one there.

That morning on the radio, I kept hearing about panic over on the east coast and other parts of the world. I would have paid more attention, but my friend Cley Buhler kept texting me pictures of this girl we nicknamed Hard-Body (HB for short) at the gym running on the treadmill. Someday, I'm gonna talk to her. But now, she's probably dead like everyone else on this stupid street I'm stuck on. If I only had one more day. Ugh, whatever. I'd probably waste that day by going in to work twenty minutes early at a dead end job that I was overqualified for. Damn economy.

Anyways, I was looking at Hard-Body's pictures, completely oblivious to the fact that everything around me was in total chaos. It was 10am by that time. I was just obliviously hammering my life away when I heard a loud crash behind me. I jumped and turned around to see my boss stumbling through a pile of 2x4s and trying to gain his footing. It was a very odd sight to see, especially since he could have just walked around them and not through them.

"Todd, are you okay?" I asked. I walked in his direction and I noticed that something wasn't right with him. He bled from the arm and had a laceration on his face. I hung my hammer up in my bag and rushed over to him. "Todd, what's up, man!? What's going on?" I shouted.

Todd looked at me through milky white eyes and lunged at me. As luck would have it, he didn't have good footing and he fell flat on his face. I freaked the fuck out and started to back away. Todd continued to advance towards me and I began to put some distance between us. I did my best to talk to him, and I even told him that if he was joking I was going to kick the shit out of him. Todd never responded once, and I knew something shitty was going on. I started to think about the radio and that's when I decided to pull my phone out and call 911. The line was busy. I called Cley to find out if he knew what was going on. He answered and his voice was muffled, then he disappeared from the line. My boss was hot on my tail and I fumbled with my keys to get the truck door open. I got inside the truck, put it in reverse and started to back up. My boss kept advancing, but then slowly turned and started heading another direction. I looked to where he was going and I saw a woman pushing her kid in a stroller. I honked the horn at her, but the stupid chick had headphones on and couldn't hear me.

My boss was getting closer and closer, so I just said, "Screw it," and threw the truck into drive. I gunned it forward and clipped him, but he somehow turned fast enough to grab hold of my bug shield. I eyed a tree just ahead of me and aimed the truck right at it. I think because I was so pumped up on adrenaline I didn't exactly realize how fast I was going. I hit that tree at thirty miles per hour. My airbag deployed and I was knocked silly. When I regained my bearings I could hear my phone ringing. I pulled it up to my ear and it was Cley. He was panicking because he had been watching the news while he was at the gym and he said that some guy said that the dead were coming back to life. I couldn't understand him because I was starting to fall into unconsciousness again; hitting that tree really messed me up. I passed out.

I was out cold for at least an hour. When I woke I was confused because I had this white pillow in front of me. Deflated and not soft at all. I realized that it was an airbag and I started to remember the details of me hitting my boss with my truck. First thing that I noticed was that I was still wearing my construction bags, which was funny to me because I never brought them into the cab. I always tossed them in the back in a plastic bin. I climbed out of the truck and walked up to the front of it. There, pinned against a cottonwood tree was my boss. He desperately clawed at the hood and tried everything he could to come get me. I stared at him in total disbelief and I remembered thinking: *This guy should be dead and he wasn't. But he was. Seriously, what the fuck is going on here?*

I got closer to him and he started biting in my direction. That's when I remembered that my friend said something about the dead coming back to life. I got to my truck and found my phone; luckily it had a pretty good charge left on it, so I called 911 first, but found a busy signal. I then called Cley and it went straight to voicemail. I called my parent's home phone number, but it just rang, and rang, and rang. I had other friends I could have called, but I assumed it would be the same everywhere. Using my phone I spent a good part of an hour reading about what was going on. I checked the social media sites and then I streamed the news. NPR was the only one that was really getting the story to me. Every other news site was telling me to stay inside and lock my doors. Social media though… damn. They were putting videos up of undead people eating living people. It was surreal. I looked to my pinned down boss and noticed that besides the scratching of nails on the hood of my truck, he was very quiet. No moans. No growls. Just… silence. When my phone died, I put it in my construction bag and went to my truck. I tried to turn the key over, but it wouldn't start. I opened up my tool box and pulled out my backpack.

Luckily for me, I'm an avid hunter and a part-time prepper. I made it a priority to keep a backpack in my vehicle with random supplies in case shit hits the fan. My dad always said it was better to be safe than sorry; I took that saying to heart. This backpack had food, a Camelback water source, flashlight, fire starting kit, poncho, a knife, sewing kit—almost everything you would need to hunker down for 72 hours. I threw it on and took a good sip out of the straw. I went over towards my boss's truck and started to go through it. Of course the keys weren't in it and I had no intention of searching my boss for them. I raided his ice chest and got a few waters out, as well as a few cans of soda. I also scored two bags of chips in the backseat. I stuffed them all into my backpack and adjusted myself under the weight of it.

I began to silently kick myself in the ass because I opted to not conceal-carry today. I usually didn't pack my .38 special with me during work hours, mainly because I like to wear it on my hip and my construction bags pushed it into my side. Whenever I got home, it was instinct to pull it out of my safe and tuck it in my pants whenever I went to town.

"Well Spencer, you got that permit so you could be prepared if shit went down…well, shit's going down and now you're unprepared." I scolded myself and then shrugged. Not much more I could do about it now.

I armed myself with my framing hammer and opted to keep my construction bags on me. It couldn't hurt, right? The more prepared you are, the better off you are. I started on my way and the street was eerily quiet. I knew I was at least five miles from my house and my plan was to get there, get my guns, and then get to a safe house somewhere. I had a gated community in mind that was just down the street from my place, but I'd have to better assess the situation first. At my house I had enough food to feed me for six months. I had a deep freezer full of venison and beef, plus canned food. And guns. Lots and lots of guns. I fully admit that I love to practice our Second Amendment rights with extreme prejudice. I kept enough ammo and weapons in the house to arm a small militia. Hey, I didn't have a girlfriend, so what else was I going to spend my money on?

I continued on and I eventually came across that woman with her baby. They were both being devoured by three zombies. My heart sank in my chest as I watched them yank away at her lifeless body. Her face had been eaten off first and now they were working on her stomach area. The baby was in the hands of another zombie and I wouldn't let myself see what they had done to it. I actually felt vomit enter my mouth, but I swallowed it back down foolishly. I should have just let it out, and then I had a burning throat. I sucked on the straw of my Camelback and crossed the street away from them.

Cautiously, I moved on and was soon met with the sound of gunfire. I found cover and saw a man who was covered in blood trying to reload a magazine while backing away from four attackers. He tucked the box of ammo under his arm, slid the magazine into the pistol and pulled the trigger. In his panicked state he forgot to slide the action back to chamber a round. He looked to the gun dumbfounded and that's when they took him to the ground; the box of bullets fell from his grasp and scattered everywhere. I could hear screaming and gurgling as they started to tear into his exposed skin. I hurried up to them and spun my hammer around to the claw side. I swung and hit one of the zombies in the head; it slumped over. I actually had to put my foot on its back and pry my hammer free. When I took on the next one, I used the business side of the hammer and started to smash away at its skull. I kept a rhythmic pace when I smashed the other two's heads in. They didn't even bother to look up from their fresh kill, too involved with their mouthful of skin and muscle.

I did a onceover on the guy and decided that he was a goner. Took the Glock 9mm out of his hand and saw that he had two magazines hanging out of his pockets. The ironic part of this is that both of those magazines were fully loaded. He was just too frantic to remember. I pulled them both free and removed his clip-on holster from his belt. I looked around for that box of ammo he was using to reload with and that's when his body started to twitch and spasm. I collected all the ammo that spilled and kept my eyes on the dude. He sat up and looked at me with milky eyes—those same eyes my boss had—and I figured out right then that the dead came back to life. I hit him with my hammer and continued on.

From that point forward it was a mad dash to stay alive, all while moving in the direction of my home. I spent the first night in the cab of a turned over pickup and nearly had a heart attack when a group of them stumbled by me when I woke up that following morning. They meandered out of sight and I slipped away unnoticed. Luckily, I came across a spewing fire hydrant and refilled my Camelback. I even got in a quick shower before continuing on.

That water felt refreshing because I was a stinky mess. I was covered in blood and I reeked of body odor and death. By the way, death smells a lot like shit, because every single one of those bastards I've come into contact with have soiled their pants. Even though I got washed up yesterday, I can smell my pits in a bad way. Body odor is an unfortunate side effect of being a bigger guy. I'm not morbidly obese by any means, but I am large and in charge. Genetically, I'm just a bigger fellow. I'm thinking it's because my entire family is made up of farmers and ranch hands. I'm guessing that somewhere down the ancestry line, my family's genes figured out that they needed to produce big kids in order to keep the farm going.

I continued towards my home as it got dark. I found the door to a shoe shop open and slowly stepped inside. I grimaced as the bell above the door made a ringing noise. I stood there for five minutes, waiting to see if something was coming to get me. When I realized that nothing was there, I decided to clear the place. I know this sounds kinda dumb, but I employed my paintballing skills to help me sweep the area. Back in the day I used to be a part of a local team that would tour the area. Our team leader was a former National Guard guy named Dustin Winkel. The dude didn't like to lose, and he pushed us very hard to learn how to maneuver around corners and check for blind spots. If I could see him right now, I'd give him a big fat kiss and tell him thank you. When I went aisle to aisle, I found one of the employees still hiding here. She freaked out when I shined my flashlight on her and she started to scream. I urged her to keep her voice down and she started to toss shoes at me. It was really, really weird. After a few minutes she finally calmed herself down and collapsed on the floor in a heap.

"You scared me so bad," she sobbed. I looked around myself to see if anyone else was in here. I holstered my weapon and clicked off the light.

"Are you in here alone?" I asked. The woman nodded and started to cry some more. I asked her if there was anything she needed and she said she needed a gun so she could get home to her children. I told her that I only had the one pistol, and she asked me to hand it over. Obviously, I told her no. But I also told her she could come with me to my house, and we could maybe stop over at her place on the way there to pick up her kids, but we had to wait until the morning. She was adamant about leaving this very minute, but I told her it was a bad decision. I talked her into waiting until the morning and offered her something to drink out of my backpack. She refused it politely and fell asleep sitting up across from me. I soon dozed off, but was awoken by that bell ringing again. I jumped up and pulled my pistol out. The woman was gone, and I rushed up front to see that she had unlocked the door and fled into the night. I shook my head and locked it all back up again. As I fell back asleep, I was hopeful that she made it to her children. But realistically, she's probably out there being snacked on right now. That's how life was now, sadly.

When I woke up the next morning, I was happy to see that the power was still on. That meant that my deep freeze was still keeping my food cold. I took a moment to enjoy the air conditioning, dreading the three mile trek I planned on taking. The June sun was going to be a bitch, and I wasn't ready to step out there.

I leaned against the doorframe, reflecting on how exactly I have gotten to this point. I probably had one of those "1000 yard stares" drool and all. I was suddenly brought back into the moment by gunshots ringing out from down the street. This wild haired guy had his back to me as he tried to reload his shotgun. He had on a hunter's vest, which I'm guessing he snagged at the general store a few blocks over. I wish I had made it there, but I imagined that it had already been overrun. I looked beyond his shoulder and saw about thirty of those undead pricks quietly advancing on him.

"Hey!" I shouted. I was so happy to see someone alive that I didn't even consider the possibility that I would startle him. He spun around and fired; I felt the air distort as the pellets missed me by inches. I pulled my pistol up and pointed it at him. "I'm a friend, asshole! My name's Spencer Adams! Get in here, I got this place cleaned out!"

The man turned back towards the mob, then back to me. He rushed in my direction and I unloaded a few rounds into the horde and dropped two of them. I said "fuck" out loud, mainly because I needed to work on my aim and start putting them through the heads and not the body mass area. Some habits are hard to break.

The wild haired man rushed up to me and shouted, "Ryan," as he ducked inside the shoe shop. I pulled the door closed and slid the bar over it. We watched as they stumbled up to the door and started beating against it. I chuckled because that door was made out of reinforced glass. Those fuckers could hit that thing with a cinderblock for an hour and it wouldn't phase it. In my cockiness I forgot one minor detail: I didn't even once think that they'd come through the big glass windows to either side.

I think we were up to about fifty zombies when the windows started to crack. I shouted out some obscenities as Ryan finished loading up his gun. He racked a shell in and aimed at the glass, frantically switching targets as the spider web cracks grew bigger and bigger. I shouted for him to follow me and he backed up. The glass exploded under the weight and the first two rows of undead fell down, tripping those behind them. We took advantage of that and ran towards the back. I let him pass me and I held my arms outstretched, knocking shoe boxes off their shelving in hopes to create tripping hazards for my silent predators. I never looked back to see if it worked. I was thinking on the fly. We rounded a corner and saw that there were two doors. We took the one closest to us and ran in. Of course it was a storage closet, and we were now trapped. Ryan and I pushed the door shut and I twisted the deadbolt to lock it. Within seconds, the dead were on the door and it began to creak and shake. There was no way it was going to hold.

I turned my attention to the new guy and did a quick once-over on him. The man was about 5'11 and had really long, dark hair that was matted with blood and other types of tissue. He was wearing a white, long-sleeved shirt that had massive amounts of red on it. Looking at his pointy noise, thin lips, and unshaven face, I guessed that he was in his early thirties like myself. The dude might be handsome to some girls, but right now he looked like shit. I assumed he was hungry and thirsty, so I swung my backpack around and unzipped it halfway. I pulled out one of the grocery bags that I had salvaged from the back of my bosses car and tossed it to him. The disheveled man dropped his shotgun and fell to his knees. I tapped him on the shoulder with a water bottle and he snatched it out of my hands, bobbing his head in an effort to say thank you.

I watched as he tore into the bag in the same manner that those zombies tore into that man I saw on the street the first day. The dude looked hungry. I had to break the silence, so I decided to ask him a stupid question.

"So I have a general idea of what's going on, but… what's your take on this?" Even though I had just witnessed some serious shit go down, I wasn't about to admit it to this Ryan fellow. I didn't want to sound crazy, which, ironically, sounded crazy.

"Look, all the dead people are starting to stand up and

move around again. They are attacking people, eating people, and just… it's a lot to digest. Thanks man, I'm starving so damn bad," Ryan said while digging through the ripped grocery bag. He pulled out the box of breakfast bars and hungrily tore into it, almost eating the wrapper as he scarfed down the strawberry treat. I scratched my head with the sights of my 9mm and finally accepted the truth: Zombies were real.

The sounds of fists pounding on the door behind me intensified our situation. We had to act fast, so I began to reload my magazine with what was left from that box of bullets I acquired earlier. "What's your plan then, Ryan? Because if you don't have one, I have one. I want to get to my house and to my guns. You should come with me. There's safety in numbers."

I only had three magazines on me—which meant that I only had forty-five rounds of "usable" ammo before I had to reload. If I could get Ryan to accompany me, that would improve my odds of getting home and getting to my gun stash. Plus, two people working together was way better than just one. Ryan was already chewing on his third fruit bar and untwisting the cap off of that bottle of water.

"My plan? My plan is to hole up in a hotel or something. They have food in the breakfast area that I could live off of for a while, and I could always chill up on the roof if things got bad. From there, I may be able to figure out where my girlfriend's at." He smiled.

I returned the smile and then shook my head. "No offense man, but that's a dumb idea." Ryan blinked and took a swig of water, legitimately shocked that I would say such a thing. I continued. "Look, a hotel has like, one hundred rooms, right? Average about two people per room, plus the staff, plus all other people who have the same idea as you. You're not going to last long." I stuffed the box of 9mm's back into my backpack and then sucked on the straw to get some water out of my camelback. My magazines were now fully reloaded, with an extra one in the chamber for good measure.

Ryan mulled over what I had said and then shrugged. "Okay, fair enough. I'll go with you to your house then. But afterwards, I want your help getting to mine." His words were muffled by the food he was chewing.

I nodded my head and clicked the safety off my Glock. "Deal. Let's do this. Let's get the hell out of here." I sounded so bad ass when I said that, I wished my friends were there to witness it.

Ryan stuffed the rest of the food into his pockets and finished drinking the water. I could hear the door creaking under the weight of the undead mob outside, and it was just a matter of time before they pushed through and started chowing down on my new friend and I. I secured my backpack over my shoulders and clipped the chest piece to keep it from bouncing around when I ran. I started to search the closet in hopes of finding a secret exit, but there wasn't any. I looked up and saw that there was no roof access from here. I punched the wall out of anger and my fist went through it. That's when I remembered that I still had my framing hammer and that I could try and bash my way out of here. I pulled it out and started slamming it into the back wall, which is where I was guessing would lead us to the outside. It didn't take much to break through the sheetrock, Ryan and I tore away at it as fast as I could break it. I got to the exterior surface and started to kick at it, taking swipes with my hammer whenever I could. We could see daylight through a small hole, which only got bigger with each kick. I pushed the plywood out and Ryan slid through. I heard the door crash behind me and they were on me faster than I thought they would be. I was halfway out the hole when they started to pull me back in. Their grimy hands tore at my hair and face. Ryan pulled with all his might on my chest straps, trying to yank me free. I could hear the teeth gnashing behind me as they started to bite my backpack. I would have just unstrapped myself to get away, but one had a pretty good hold on my hair and would not let go.

"Sorry man!" Ryan yelled out. I assumed he was sorry about running away and leaving me to be fed upon. To be honest, I couldn't blame him—I'd slow them down and he'd get free. But, my new friend surprised me when he slung his shotgun around and stuck it over my head. Ryan pulled the trigger and my ears rang like I had just had music blasted into them. I have a little bit of tinnitus from running a nail gun a good portion of my adult life, but this was way worse. I was sorta dazed by it, but he fired one more round and that brought me back into the moment. I got out of their grasp and was surprised to see that the dead ones had formed an "undead plug" to block the others from coming through. I did a quick assessment of where we were; a small alley that ran behind all the stores in this area. We were the only two back here, which caused me to let out a sigh of relief. I then started to laugh like I had lost my goddamn mind.

"I'm sorry man! I know that's loud!" Ryan yelled out. I stopped laughing and responded with a "What?" before I understood what he said. This Ryan guy seemed like a good person. I just knew he was going to leave me. Would I have left him? No. I'm positive I wouldn't have. We grabbed a wood pallet and stuck it over the hole. I got some nails out of my bag and drove four or five of them into the wall to hold it in place.

Ryan reloaded his shotgun and we assessed that he had about forty shells on him. As we walked down the empty alley, Ryan told me his story. Just as I had suspected, he had gotten the hunter's vest from the local general store. I was shocked to learn that it hadn't been hit yet, but a car accident out front had created a frenzy and people were set upon by the dead. The owner locked up the building, produced a handgun, chased his staff out of the store and then locked himself in, leaving everyone outside to die. Ryan had worked there for five years as a stocker, so while his boss was chasing everyone out, Ryan snuck behind the counter and snagged a 12 gauge Mossberg and a few boxes of shells. He snuck out of the pharmacy's back window and then locked it up before leaving. He had been on the run ever since, sleeping on the roof of a crashed 18 wheeler the first night, then sleeping in a tree last night. He climbed out of the tree in search of food when he stumbled across a group of them that had followed him for over four blocks. He told me he couldn't run anymore and started opening fire on them. I took that time to tell him that headshots were the only shots he should be taking from now on. He nodded and said that he had figured that out when he woke up the one morning and had to shoot down from the top of the truck to escape. He said that all he had was headshots and that the dead stayed dead then.

I took another drink of water and chewed on the end of the straw for a bit. We had reached the end of the alley and it was blocked off with an eight-foot high chain link fence with a locked chain around the gate. And if that wasn't intimidating enough, barbed wire was strung across the top to keep would-be thieves from getting back here. The street on the other side was dead quiet (pun, sorry) and there wasn't a soul around.

Ryan pulled on the chain and let out a curse. I looked around for a vehicle, but there wasn't one anywhere. If I had my truck, I would have just driven that big blue bastard right through this. But I don't have my truck anymore, because it's wrapped round a fucking tree right now and keeping my dead boss from getting free and eating people.

I miss my truck.

"Well shit," I said out loud. We both knew what we had to do, but neither one of us wanted to waste a round of ammo on this lock. Plus, it might draw some of them right to us. We both caught noise of a car heading our way and our heads jerked in that direction. A Cadillac with dealer tags came into view and was gone as fast as it was there. We both started to laugh, because obviously someone stole this car off the lot; it still had smiley-faced balloons tied to the antenna.

Well, at least there were *three* people still alive out there. That brought me some hope. "Dude, do you have any chisels in there?" Ryan asked, pointing to my construction bags. I had a head-slapping moment when I produced a small file that I used to sharpen saw blades. Ryan took watch and I started to file away at the lock. That was pretty fucking tough, so I started to file away at the chain. After ten minutes, I was through one link and the gate was ready to be opened. Damn, keeping my construction bags had been a damn blessing. We both agreed that this area was a good spot to fall back to, so we hung the chain up again so it looked like it hadn't been tampered with. If we made it to my house and got a good vehicle, we could come back here and nab supplies.

I'm glad this Ryan guy is thinking like me right now. I can't believe I've never seen this guy before. Turns out, his boss was an ultra-conservative asshole that didn't like long hair. He made Ryan work in the back and never let him out front. Ryan had a Bachelors in Arts, but as he explained, "Nobody appreciates art anymore," so he was never able to ply his trade as an artist. He has spent a lot of time out in the woods with his girlfriend, and he admitted to me that he spent a year in jail because of some hippie protest things.

I liked this guy.

We made our way to a parked car and we were both freaked out when we saw a woman still inside it. She had been bitten on the neck and must have climbed into this car to save herself. She died in there and now it was full of blood, shit, and piss. She had been fighting against the seatbelt and it had cut into her neck and stomach area; she must have buckled up before she left this world. Lifelessly, she pushed her face against the window and opened and closed her mouth. Snot and blood left streaks on the window and I felt my stomach churn for a second.

"I'm not driving that thing. Why couldn't she have died in the backseat?" Ryan complained out loud. I looked to him and he immediately looked ashamed of what he just said. He mumbled an apology and rested the shotgun on his shoulder. I looked back down to her and shook my head at what I saw. The worst part was that I agreed with him, and that made me feel like a big piece of shit. This woman probably died a painful, lonely death and I'm mad that she died in the driver's seat of HER car. I hated myself.

"Let's see if we can find another one," I said. We started to walk away and the horn began to honk. We both jumped and ran back to the vehicle. *Was someone else in there?* I thought. The horn stopped and the dead woman was now pushing her hands against the window.

"She's dead. She's not smart enough to honk a horn. We walked ahead of her and she tried to crawl towards us. Right?" I said to Ryan. Hell, I said that more to myself then I did to Ryan. I didn't want to think these things could get smart on us. If they did that, we'd all be dead for sure. Ryan shrugged and then his jaw dropped. He pointed down the street and I snapped my head to see what got his attention. Through the heat waves on the asphalt, I could see the outline of a mob heading our way. The horn had alerted them. Dammit.

"We need to kill her, or she's going to draw more of them," Ryan said. He aimed his shotgun towards her and I shook my head at him.

"Wait, I got an idea," I said as I holstered my weapon and pulled a nail out of my bag. I held it up to the window where she was gnawing at us and then swung my hammer. Just like I had planned it, I drove the framing nail right into her skull and she died instantly. She had a few "death twitches", but the nail was firmly in her forehead and the driver's side window. I was amazed it didn't shatter. I bet I couldn't do that again.

"Let's go before those get here." I motioned towards the mob with my hammer. We both ducked down and moved up the street, placing that car between us and them. I redrew my pistol and replaced the hammer in its holding spot. We got to a corner and placed our backs to it. I poked my head around and saw that there were a few stragglers out in the street. It looked like another car accident had taken place here. Seriously, I wonder how many of these things got their start from car wrecks. People run up to see if their okay, they pull them out to administer first aid, and then BAM! They are zombie chow.

"Did the ones behind us stop at the car?" I whispered. Ryan nodded his head and looked back to me "Yeah, they literally stopped right where the sound came from. How's it look over there?" He asked. I was still assessing the situation and saw that there were now five zombies stumbling around. My eyes caught sight of something glorious: a police cruiser was there and its door was wide open. I honestly thought I could hear the engine still running from here, but there was no way that I was that lucky. I leaned against the wall again and then smiled at Ryan as I formed a plan in my head. After a brief moment, I spoke.

"So, there's a cop car over there… but there's also five dead guys standing around it. Probably twenty yards out. I think it's still running, that's why they are standing there." I turned away from him and pointed at my backpack. "I got a soda in there, I'm going to shake it up and then throw it as far as I can. Hopefully the thing will make enough noise to distract them. Can you get it for me?" Ryan unzipped me and pulled the can out. He seemed onboard with my dumb idea, so maybe that meant that it would work.

I shook the can and stepped out from behind the wall. With a soft grunt, I chucked that can like my name was John Elway. It sailed beautifully past the cop car and landed with a "splishhhh" sound as it exploded on the road. The undead looked in its direction and started towards it, that's when I noticed that one of the walkers was a cop. I couldn't believe it, it fucking worked!

I counted to ten-Mississippi in my head and then I made my break for it. Ryan was hot on my tail and we made good time as we rushed the cop car. The engine still ran, which was a win for us. I pulled my pistol up and inspected the opened door to make sure that there was nothing sitting in the driver's seat. There was a little bit of blood on the microphone and police issued shotgun, but nothing dead in the front seat. I did a fist pump and Ryan ran around to the other side. He stopped in his tracks and started to back pedal, and then he fell down out of my sight. My heart dropped as I jumped up on the hood of the car to see what had happened. Ryan started to scream as an undead kid was clawing his way up his pant leg. It had started biting him through his pants, but I wasn't sure if it was breaking skin or not. I jumped off the car and holstered my gun. I reached down and grabbed the kid by the waist and then did a suplex-type move to throw him away. The kid slammed into the light pole behind us and I spun around to see if he was coming back towards me. The kid was trying to turn himself over, but both of his legs were broken and he was having difficulty doing so.

My best guess is that the cop ran over this kid and got out to help him. Then the kid died, came back to life and then bit the cop. Snowball effect from there and BAM! We have a street with dead people on it and they all were heading our way because Ryan was still freaking out. I couldn't quite understand him, but I could tell that he was relieved to only see bruising and no blood on his leg. Hooray for polyester! I drew my sidearm and decided that enough was enough. My first round went through the cop's head. The second and third rounds probably went through the kids family members. The next two sailed wide right, but I gained control of my shots again and dropped the last two zombies with ease. Ryan stood up and fired a shotgun round into the kid, thank heavens I didn't see it. I haven't had to shoot a kid yet, but I know that's going to happen sooner than later.

"Get in the car!" I shouted. Ryan nodded and climbed inside the passenger seat. I ran over to the zombie cop and pulled his weapon off of him. I then undid his tactical belt and yanked it free. I now had two pistols and some spare ammo. I could give it to Ryan, and he'd be set up as well. This was a good find.

I heard Ryan trying to get my attention so I spun around to see the mob that we had avoided earlier descending on our area. They were probably twenty yards from the car, so I had a few minutes. I yelled for Ryan to pop the trunk. He leaned over and did so. I looked inside and saw a first aid kit, a few cardboard boxes, shotgun shells, .45 cal shells, and a few more items that I didn't have time to look through. The dead were getting closer and I had to scoot. I grabbed a few boxes of both ammos and jumped in the driver's seat. I slammed the door and the dead started to pound on the hood of the car. They began to circle us, so I locked the door.

"Wow," I said out loud. Ryan let out a long, appreciative sigh and melted into the car seat out of exhaustion. I could hear them pounding all around us, so I leaned back in the seat and closed my eyes. I knew we'd be safe in here because police squad cars were built like brick shithouses. That means that it takes an awful lot to bring one down. I opened my eyes and nearly shit my pants when I saw a zombie head in my rear view mirror. Ryan let out a holler and turned to get away from it. Sure as shit, there was a zombie in the backseat of the police cruiser and we never even noticed it. The thin layer of Plexiglass was all that was keeping it held back and it actually saved our lives—had this been a normal car, we'd both be snack food right now. My nose finally registered the smell of shit and vomit, causing me to dry heave for just a second. The zombie was slowly moving its head against the glass and chomping its teeth at us, just like that dead woman we saw about twenty minutes ago. The only difference between the two is that this zombie had its hands cuffed behind its back and it was quite comical to see it moving around. Ryan and I both looked to each other and started to laugh hysterically. We both needed this. I wiped the tears from my eyes and took off my backpack.

"Let's get to my house. Then let's go find your girlfriend," I finally said. Ryan nodded and slowly put his seatbelt on.

For the first time in three days, we finally had the upper hand.

AND THEN THERE WAS THIS TIME

DENNIS PEKKALA

"Hey Bobby what you got for me?"

"A swift kick in the ass if you keep it up, I've told you time and again Harper my name is Robert," said the man as he entered the room. For Robert the passage of time had not been kind, especially after recent events. He had more wrinkles, more gray than not, and a lot less hair to go around.

"Did you bring me anything to drink? I'd kill for a rum and coke, hell I'd kill for a PBR."

"You know there's none to be had here. I did bring ya a thermos of Kool-aid though, made with REAL sugar!" said Robert with a smile.

"Ohhhhhh… you're spoiling me Robbie, give me that sweet thing."

Robert handed it over with a smile. Harper quickly poured himself a cup and took a drink. He spat it right back out.

"GRAPE! You KNOW I hate grape. I'm starting to think you don't like me," Harper griped and glared at Robert.

If there is one thing that time has taught Robert, it's a proper shit-eating grin. "Nawww I don't dislike you Harper, you just have an 'acquired taste.' So what did you want to talk to me about?"

"I don't know, don't care either, I just wanted to TALK to

someone, a guy could go crazy with all the solitude nowadays. Come on man all I want to do is jaw with you for a while" Harper held the cup out to Robert. "Sit and drink with me for a bit?"

"God no... I'll sit and talk with you, but I'm not touching that stuff, battery acid tastes better than grape Kool-aid." Robert pulled up a chair from the room's sparse furniture. "So where were we last time? The zombie stuck in a swimming pool?"

Harper laughed. "Yeah that was hilarious, stupid fuck stuck in 12 feet of water trying to catch the toy motor boat I was driving around the pool. Good times. Oh and then there was this time I found a TON of explosives in the basement of a house some army guys were using before they bit it. Saying I had a blast would be a complete understatement."

Robert rubbed his forehead. He could already tell today was gonna be a long day. "Alright lay it on me."

"Ok so this happened about a couple months or so after this all started, while I'm combing through a neighborhood for supplies. I noticed this military humvee at the end of the street. The place was boarded up tight and there were LOTS of DEAD people in the front lawn. After I called out and got no response I pried my way in and found the place literally shot to pieces. Seemed like someone died one way or another and then started in on his friends. Three of the guys inside were down and out but the fourth I had to finish with my crowbar, then I made sure the place was clear.

That place was a gold mine of useful stuff, but the best find was a case of grenades AND a couple blocks of C4! Oh YEAH! I had me some fun with that! I found myself a tall brick apartment building with a large adjacent parking lot. Slapped the C4 to a car, wailed on the horn and made my way to the roof of the apartment. When the silent masses came to investigate, BOOM! That explosion put all those action movies to shame. Then came the next wave of zombies. A couple grenades later, they were just a pile of shredded bodies.

Wash. Rinse. Repeat. Laugh maniacally. That was a great

day. Wish I still had one of those grenades. That joker Raymond from 3rd shift deserves to have one shoved down his throat. Let's see him make a wisecrack then." Harper glared at the door as if he expected the asshole to show up any second.

"Hey give the guy a break, he has a job to do, we all handle stress differently. Ray is a pureblood smartass, no denying that, but when he's stressed his cracks get sharper." Robert said in an attempt to placate Harper, who only grunted in return. "What else you got for me today?"

"Let me think… well there was this time I dressed a zombie up as a clown."

"You what?"

"Dressed a zombie up like a clown," Harper said grinning.

"…"

"Let me finish and you'll be laughing right along with me. So one day when I was in a mood I decided to do the most random thing I could think of; dress a zombie up like a clown, place them on a huge Slip-n'-Slide, and record the resulting hilarity for posterity. I found this one zed off by his lonesome, I trapped him under a blanket and I CAREFULLY gagged and tied him up. One rainbow wig, clown suit, shoes and make up later… and we have a winner! I combined several Slip-n-Slides into a fifty foot square in the middle of some parking lot, hosed that down. A quick snip of the bonds, a hard shove and Bozo was ready for his return to stardom."

"Proof or it never happened," Robert chided a grin.

"The tape should be with the rest of my stuff I had when I came here, ask Raymond he should know where it's at. Anyway whenever I moved along the edge of the slide, Bozo would attempt to get at me, but every time he managed to stand up, within a step he wiped right back out. This goes on for about an hour before Bozo is too beaten up from all his trips to the pavement that the best he can manage is a crawl… right into a face plant. This would have been an instant YouTube hit if the internet was still around." Harper practically glowed imagining the hit count his video would've received had the world been as it should.

"Haha I bet. I seem to remember you mentioning that you hooked up with another group of survivors at some point?"

"Way to go buzz kill, just what I didn't want to think about." Harper sighed. "Yeah, so early on a dozen of us stayed in this shitty two bedroom house. Only reason I willingly stayed in that cramped a space was because of the brick walls and the bars on the windows. There was the three from the Evans family; mom, dad and son. A couple of college kids. An elderly couple from across the street. Some random schmuck. And THEN there was Derryl and his two drinking buddies.

We had been cooped up in that house for a little over a week when the Evans kid ran out of asthma medicine. Sure enough the kid had a major episode and suffocated. This was before I knew that the dead got back up from more than a bite. The mother was holding the kid and sobbing uncontrollably, her screams of joy at her sons sudden return to life was short lived when he tore her throat out. In the resulting panic one of the college kids and the schmuck got bit as well."

Harper stops for a short while and stared at Robert. "Sometimes I really HATE how you poke and prod. Sometimes it feels like you do it just to pick my brain."

Robert just shrugged.

"Humph. So anyway it took a while before the Good Ol'Boys sprung into action. They clubbed mother and son 'til they stopped moving and strong-armed the other two that were bitten into one of the rooms. After seeing the kid turn without being bit Derryl and his buddies saw the elderly couple as a threat and wanted to get rid of them. With the commotion we made there were zombies surrounding the house and there was no sending them on their way to look for another place to stay. The only option as they saw it was to club them right along with the others that got bit.

Needless to say this didn't go over real well, and in all the commotion someone stuck a knife in Derryl's shoulder. And if that wasn't enough the asshole was right, the excitement was too much for the old bird, cause granny keeled over right then and there. Let's do the math; two dead-dead, two soon to be dead, one dead about to become undead, one distraught father, one distraught grandpa, one freaked out college kid, one bleeding buffoon, two angry stooges, and the whole neighborhood pounding on the doors, leaving me to somehow get the hell outta there before things got REALLY bad.

Just as it's about to really kick off between dad, gramps, college boy and Derryl's crew, before I could attempt to make a break for it granny raises up enough to bite my hand. Well, more accurately she attempted to gum my hand. Oh thank God for old age," Harper said as he shuddered. "I pulled my bruised hand back, I kicked her in the face, said fuck this then I ran down the hall and locked myself in the master bedroom. By the sounds that followed it seemed Derryl and his crew pummeled the others but apparently someone attempted to leave the house letting the other dead in. The sound of the dead… eating… is indescribable. I was holed up in that room for at least four days. Thankfully we had kept some food and water in there.

After the fourth day I couldn't stand it anymore. I yanked out the closet rod to use as a club and once the place was quiet I made a break for it. I hit anything that got directly in my path and ran past everything else. Thankfully the keys were in Derryls truck out front, the one good thing the douche bag did right. I drove until I was damn near out of gas, found an empty house that was isolated from any others and stayed there for a while. From then on I avoided the living right up until you guys found me."

Robert cocked his head to the side. "Considering what you went through, what makes you comfortable being around us?"

"Well Rob Zombie, truth be told I was starting to lose it a bit out there by myself. Plus you guys got your shit together, and this facility is about as zombie proof as you can get."

"Glad to hear you approve of the accommodations here." Robert smiled. "Any adventures that just about result with you ending as zombie food?"

"Other than my brush with death during the 'Derryl

185

Debacle?' I would have to say it was the time I was running over zombies and both tires on the right side blew at the same time on that humvee I found. What made that situation worse is that when the tires went it sent the humvee right into a parked car. In the crash my knee went right into the steering column. Attempting to out run a horde of those shambling bastards with a bum knee was anything but a breeze. More than a few times they made swipes at my back but thankfully none of them could grab hold."

"You are one lucky mother fucker you know that? Cheating death at every turn."

The comment managed to wipe the smile off of Harper's face. Harper glanced at Robert before lowering his head and staring at his feet. "Honestly I don't know how I survived as long as I did considering all the shit that I pulled. But I have the feeling someone was watching over me. It was like in those old cartoons, a little angel standing on my shoulder giving me advice, telling me what to do and that no matter what I was going to be ok."

"Hmm so you think an angel protected you from harm during your various 'adventures'?" Robert asked.

"Maybe, I dunno but you wanna know what else? It was like the Devil was on my other shoulder saying, 'Yeah listen to the White, you're gonna be fine, go big or go home bitch. Enjoy yourself, you're only gonna live once, so strap a lawnmower to your chest and SHRED that group of zombies into little bits.' And before you ask no, I did not strap a lawnmower to my chest and go to town on a zombie, that's just stupid."

"Good to see you're not crazy enough to actually do that," laughed Robert.

"A steam roller works much better anyway… what? Lionel was a pussy and there is no way in hell that a lawnmower would get the job done in the first place. It was that experience with the humvee that led me to find that steam rollers are the BOSS for running down zombies left and right. Fortify the cab, get that puppy going at a good clip and enjoy as 12 tons of steel barrels through masses of the undead with ease. Hahaha, I gotta take you for a ride one of these days. At least through that near death experience I found the mother of all rides for a zombie apocalypse." Harpers million dollar smile said it all. He'd *finally* rendered the Doc speechless. "Earth to Bert come in Bert, say something before I brain you."

"Fuck... You..." Robert said as he shook his head. "You are a special kind of crazy you know that? You don't know when to quit, but then again that's probably what got you here. Any idea how abnormal it is to deliberately put yourself in dangerous situations on the 'feeling' that nothing could go wrong?"

"Never thought about it, but I'll say this, I'll take God's love and the Devil's luck any day if it means I get to see tomorrow. That being said, as fun as killing zombies in new and exciting ways was, I'm glad you guys found and took me in. I finally feel safe enough to sleep through the night without the constant fear that the tiniest sound is one of those bastards creeping up on me. I *know* I'm safe here but I still can't shake the feeling that something bad is about to happen, and I'm talking thick shit like the day it all started." For a brief moment Harper scanned the room to reassure himself that there were no zombies.

"Hey don't worry about it. Between the walls, gates and security guards *nothing* is getting in here," replied Robert after seeing Harper's worried looks. "My shift is about up, got anything pressing to get off your chest before I go?"

"Other than to tell you to scrounge me up a god damn beer for your next visit... nope. Send Dumbass my regards"

"Right... I'll see what I can do. You gonna give me an idea of what to expect for next time?" Asked Robert as he headed towards the door.

"Well there was this time that I used these bear traps to..."

*****

On his way out of the room Robert closed and locked the

door behind him. He walked down the brightly lit hall passing by one of the guards. He nodded to him in greeting. At the end of the hall was the staff lounge. There were about a dozen people seated about the room, a couple on the couch, others seated around various tables. Robert walked up to the counter and picked up a mug of coffee. Once fixed with cream and sugar he leaned against the counter and took a sip. A man at one of the tables waved Robert over to sit with him.

"Hey Bobby how's it goin'?" asked the man.

"Fuck you, Sunshine," replied Robert as he took his seat. It was always the same old song and dance with Ray. Having known each other for years, Ray was the only one that got away with calling him Bobby.

"Yeah that's right I'm a fuckin' ray of sunshine. So, how'd it go with Harper?" asked Ray sarcastically.

"You know, 'And then there…'"

"'… was this time,' yeah but you gotta admit his stories are pretty entertaining."

"In a morbid sort of way. It would be a lot more entertaining if they weren't all about zombies and the end of the world as we know it." Robert sighed.

"Well what do you expect? The man's a fucking head case. He bashed that old guy's head in so bad that they had to identify him through his dental records and even then most of his teeth were either on the sidewalk or in his stomach. It still amazes me that he did it right in front of a cop, and when he was being dragged off the man's corpse he was yelling that he wouldn't have done it if, 'the pig had did his fucking job and shot the zombie in the head'. I shudder to think what those eleven individuals went through in that house, so don't even get me started." Ray finished his coffee as he finished his rant, with disgust. Hospital coffee is just as bad as the food. Getting up Ray asked Robert the question of the day, "You want another cup of this shit?"

"No thanks, I filled my daily quota for shit listening to Harper. So what do we do next? Any chance we can rid ourselves of him?" asked Robert.

188

"Not much we can do, in all likelihood he'll be found criminally insane and will be our problem till he dies. Only way we'll ever get rid of him is if we treat him to the point that he becomes 'sane', then he becomes the Department of Corrections problem. No more mental hospital for him."

"Well for the next two weeks… It's. Not. My. Problem. I am going to enjoy my vacation and there is nothing you can do about it."

Ray held up his hands in defense. "Hey you deserve a break Bobby, spending hours each day with Harper is enough to drive anyone insane. Going anyplace nice?"

"Taking the family up state, we're going to Gramps' camp on the lake. Think I will actually take one bit of advice from Harper, celebrating the 4th a couple weeks early by lighting off some illegal fireworks should be a blast." Robert got up and went over to the sink and rinsed out his mug. After putting it back on the shelf where his mug lived when it wasn't in his hand, he turned to leave.

"Hey Robert, watch out for the zombies… Don't get bit." Ray smiled.

"Fuck you too Sunshine. See ya on the 28th. Oh, by the way, Nut job sends his regards."

189

Women and Children First

A. Ben Carpenter

I used to have this neighbor who was a DJ. He was a good guy, and he worked nights, so we pretty much left each other alone. But on his nights off, he would work on music for the club. He would mix beats, spin tracks together, mess with tempo, and a bunch of other stuff that was above my head, technically speaking. The bottom line is, I had several sleepless nights before I got used to the constant thumping in the walls.

Thump, thump, thump, thump, "Yeah, boi." Thump, thump, thump, thump, "Shake that whatever."

At the time I found it incredibly annoying. Now, I just look at it as practice for the apocalypse. I can sleep through any loud, repetitive thumping noise. I'm calling it a win.

I know the drill. I've seen all the movies, read all the books, even some of the manga, like High School of the Dead (that one was good for several reasons, especially the anime jubblies.) This was a zombie apocalypse, possibly THE zombie apocalypse, and I knew exactly what to do about it. At least, I thought I did.

I used to live in the city, but I knew that staying in my apartment when it started was stupid, so I packed up my big back pack, got in my car, and drove as far as I could. It was chaos on the roads. I don't have to tell you what it was like, you were there. People were running through the streets, cars were on fire, police cruisers and fire trucks were everywhere.

Turns out driving as far as I could got me roughly eighteen miles from my apartment. At that point it just turned into streets filled with abandoned cars. I later found out that there were several major accidents on the freeway, multiple fatalities, and they were never fully cleared (most likely due to the multiple fatalities.) So I got my back pack, my hat, and my weapons out of the car and I started walking. I left my keys in the car.

Weapon Lineup:

1 Aluminum baseball bat

1 Glock 9mm, 2 spare mags, half a box of ammo

That's it. I had a few changes of underwear and socks in the backpack, and a bunch of travel food. Mostly granola and protein bars, and about a gallon of water.

I learned some interesting things that day. Firstly, that anyone who dies turns into a zombie, not just the people who get bit. That was a huge revelation, and possibly the most valuable piece of information I ever learned. At the same time, I learned that zombies have a hard time going down stairs, or even just down a steep hill.

A group of four zombies were staggering after a lady, trying to eat her I guess. She was running towards a cop, screaming for help. He was standing in one of those public fountain things, which was a few feet lower than the regular sidewalk. He saw her coming and pulled his gun, waited for her to get behind him, and then we all watched as the zombies fell down the stairs. They just stepped off into the air like it was flat ground, and tumbled onto their faces. It was only like three steps from the sidewalk, but they couldn't grasp the concept of elevation changes.

Once they stood up again the cop told them to freeze, but of course they kept coming. So he shot the front zombie in the chest. Sure, it made him stagger back a little, but the rest of them were still coming and, after a moment, ol' chest-wound was staggering forward again as well.

I yelled, "Shoot 'em in the head, dumbass!"

I don't know if he heard me, or just wised up, because the next shot went right though its brain. He dropped it like a rock. The other three went down right after it, easy as pie.

But on the last shot, I guess the bullet kept going after it left the zombie's head, and it hit some guy in the street who was pretty much directly behind the last zombie. He took it in the chest, and he went down hard. The cop didn't even see it, what with the lady who was still screaming at him.

Stupidly, I ran over to see if the guy was alright. He wasn't. I mean, other than the bullet hole in his chest, which appeared to have hit a lung, he was fine. But I also knew there was no chance of help arriving before he died, not at the rate he was bleeding out. Still, stupidly, I ran over and yelled for the cop, and we got back just in time for the guy's death rattle. It sounded desperate, and moist.

We were all still standing there staring at him when he started twitching. When he sat up, the lady started screaming again. I didn't even wait for the cop, who was slowly backing away. I just took out the bat and bashed his head in. It took three swings.

That is one of the things that alarmed me the most that day. In the movies and on TV, you hit a guy in the head with a bat and he goes down right away. But when he's already dead, one thump to the head is rarely enough. Fuck me, right?

So the cop asks me where I'm headed, and I tell him, "Out of town". He says there's a military base a few miles west of the city, I might want to aim in that direction. I say thanks, and start walking. That was two days ago.

So I made it to the outskirts of the suburbs that day. There's a lot of abandoned houses out there, which means plenty of places to sleep and a lot of food to scavenge. The power was still on, and the water was still running, but I didn't know how much longer that would last. Maybe a few weeks, maybe a few hours.

That night I crashed in a small apartment complex. I found a ladder, and pulled it up onto the balcony outside, locked, bolted, and barricaded the door, ate some food, took a shower, and went to sleep to the sound of pounding on the door.

Honestly, the pounding is comforting at this point. I mean, if the pounding stops, it means they got in, right?

On the way out to the 'burbs I stopped in at a post office and ~~stole~~ procured a map of the area. If you're looking for a good map, look in a post office or bus depot. Lots of good, up-to-date maps.

If I remember the street names correctly, then I was only about eight miles from the very edge of town (or the Edge of Madness, and I like to call it that), and then only another five-or-so miles from the military base. Walking, there was no way I could make that in one day, which meant I needed to get to the edge of town and then make a new plan.

Then the pounding stopped.

I looked at the door. Still locked and barricaded.

I looked at the balcony. Nobody out there.

I walked over to the door and peered out the peephole. The dead guy was still there, staring at the light in the hallway.

Then the power went out.

Not just in the hallway, or in the building, but in the whole city. I could hear the silence. I could feel it in the air. No power was flowing anywhere nearby.

Then the pounding started again.

Well, I decided, that was creepy as fuck. It was time to bug out.

I got all of my water from the fridge, snagging the orange juice as well. You gotta get your vitamin C where you can. I loaded up my bag and, snagged an ice pick from the kitchen. I figure, if the zombies get that close, an ice pick to the head will put them down pretty quickly.

I went to the nearest house and looked in the windows. It looked empty. I tried the door. It was unlocked. I went inside slowly and quietly, closing and locking the door behind me. I went through the place room by room, and it was thankfully empty.

I refilled my water from the sink, glad the water was still

running at least. I figured the water pressure should stay good until the water tower ran out. That meant I had either a couple of days, or a couple of minutes left before the water was gone. Get it while it lasts.

So I had to go past the school to get out of town, and I hated going around it, especially considering how slowly I'd been moving lately. I needed a car or, preferably, a tank. I looked at my maps and figured that it would either take another two or three days to go around the school, or I could figure out how to go through that hot-zone without getting eaten. Sounds like fun, right?

So for starters, I looted the house. They had some food, which I took, but nothing much else of use. Then I checked the garage, and just about crapped for joy. Two words for you: Motor Scooter.

Maybe it was for their kid, maybe they used it to get around the neighborhood, I don't know and I don't care. It was basically just a skateboard with a handle, and a three horsepower engine on the back. There was even a bike helmet and some pads I could wear.

It started right up and ran perfect. I checked the gas tank and it was only about three-quarters full. I wasn't sure how many miles it would go on a tank, but I knew it was better than walking.

I'm sure I looked like a total dumb-ass, but you know what I didn't look like? Zombie food. I didn't have a speedometer, but I bet that thing got going at least 25, maybe 30 mph. Downside, it was noisy as hell. All those zombies that were around the school turned and started following me, as well as some other zombies that were just in the area. Well, maybe it gave the people in the school a chance to get out. It was too late to undo the damage anyway. Beside, unless I rode right into a zombie, they weren't fast enough or coordinated enough to catch me.

That got me to the outskirts of town in like, 45 minutes. I was stoked, to say the least. I waited until I got to a nice, large, open, flat area, and stopped to look at the map. I was only

195

about four miles away from what appeared to be an Air Force base.

I ran out of gas three miles later and ended up walking the last mile. Not a problem, just an inconvenience. The problem came when I got to the turnoff for the Air Force base. There were a couple of humvees blocking the road, and six armed soldiers standing around. They stopped me when I walked up, but you know the drill. I'm sure you got the same story I got.

I could go to the refugee camp that was set up near the base if I wanted, but I would not be allowed on base. I would be debriefed upon arrival, then undergo a medical inspection (not an examination, an "inspection,") then I would be assigned to an area of the refugee camp, where I would then be assigned lodging (a tent.)

Was there food? For the time being, yes.

Was there water? Yes, they had several operating wells on the base.

Was the refugee camp behind a fence? They were currently installing a wall, and expected it to be completed within the next day or so.

Could I leave anytime I wanted? Yes, but they might not let me back in if I left.

Well, that was brutal honesty. But for the time being, it was still safer than being in the city.

That's how I got to camp yesterday afternoon. Since then, it hasn't been going very smoothly. During my "debriefing", it became very clear that they just wanted to know what was happening back in town. They were not very happy with what they heard. One of them was especially upset about the school. Maybe he had a kid there, I don't know. The medical inspection was pretty much just to check that I had all my working parts, and that I hadn't gotten bit by anything. Then there was the camp.

The 'wall' was just some sheets of high strength webbing filled with dirt and rocks. Is it effective? We'll see. It looks both very tough, but at the same time it also looks very fragile. Like I said, we'll see. The food isn't good, but at least it was available. The water was clean and plentiful, and we're right next to the base, which was sort of comforting I guess. Not anymore, but at the time it was, you know?

They got the wall done this morning, right before your group showed up. And you know what happened after that.

I'm sure there are some hard feelings right now, but I want you to know I don't blame you guys for bringing the undead with you. You were running, and they were chasing, and that's all there is to it. I would have done the same thing as you, so I can't really get mad, right?

Besides, I think we're all too pissed off at the military right now to hold a grudge against you guys. Those fucking meat sacks.

You didn't see it because you were at the front gate, but a bunch of people ran out the back gate and tried to get in the base. The soldiers at the gate didn't let them in, and they didn't tell them to get back behind the wall. They just shot them.

So now it's just us 'refugees' in this camp, with a couple hundred undead outside, and the only thing keeping them away from us is a temporary wall and a couple of chain link gates. And those gates aren't looking too sturdy, and I'm starting to wish I never quit smoking. Because, you know, lung cancer is suddenly very low on my list of worries.

All I'm saying is: count your ammo, dude.

Remember who that last bullet is for.

Eddie Smith, Part Four:
The First Virginia Republic

No, I don't know why the dead people suddenly stopped moving two days ago.

No, I can't explain why I'm sleeping better at night, beyond the obvious.

No, I don't understand why this is all happening, but I can tell you, that ever since we made the decision to head north to find this Adrian Ring character, I've felt smart. Not saying of course that the simple act of getting back behind the wheel of my rig has made me brighter. I'm saying that the decision to do this was the right one, and that we are helping the world be a better place, one mile at a time. I feel smart for having done this.

Each mile seems to make it better too. You know, did anyone else stop to put it all together that the dead folks went back to being dead on the third day, of the third month, at just about three o'clock?

There's some seriousness in that thought. I ain't that crazy. Not that kind of crazy at least. I'm a different flavor of crazy entirely. I need to tell people about that. Maybe I am crazy.

Wish I had a cigarette.

And a cold Shiner Bock.

Man. I'm happy and tired. Still damn cold. It's almost April and back home in Texas it'd be eighty degrees right now, and instead we're sitting here shivering, wearing coats we scrounged off the dead, and out of abandoned homes. We've had to dig through closets to find boots to keep our feet dry, and rummage through the glove boxes of abandoned cars to try and find enough winter gloves for us all. We weren't quite prepared for this weather, but the Lord provides if you work hard enough.

Hm? You're bored eh? You want something more exciting?

Road Warrior story?

Right.

Well, you boys were probably locked up inside the armored lock box when everything went batty on the Virginia/ Tennessee line near Bristol, so you heard all the action, but still don't know what happened. You wanna hear that? Yeah? Don't tell your mommas I told ya.

Now that the dead are back to being dead we're using the interstate again, but you know for the entire length of this here journey we've been on back roads. County roads, surface roads, you name it. Far from the highways and big cities whenever possible, and it's helped. We've had fewer accidents to skirt, far fewer dead to fight, and the road conditions have been good enough. Lots of potholes, and now snow which has slowed us down, but tomorrow before we leave I'm gonna try and operate that Pennsylvania plow truck we got a few days ago. If we can run that big boy's blades it'll be smooth sailing for a good long ways.

Right. Gunfight. Sorry.

We was on I think it was 633 heading this way just outside of Bristol in our convoy when we came around a little bend and came to a stop. I was third in line like always in the fuel rig, and your daddy Adam was in the front driving the Peterbuilt with the flatbed. Wedge we call it on account of it having that big steel wedge that looks like cheese on the front of it.

We stopped because the road had been blocked off by a pair of shipping containers. They had somehow been taken right off their truck and dropped in their own version of a V formation with both ends propped up against the sides of brick buildings. One of the buildings had a sign hanging half off the front of it that read 'Art's Vacuum Repair.' Don't ask me why that little nugget of memory is still clinging to the hole.

Standing on the rooftops of the brick buildings, and behind a row of sandbags on the tops of the steel shipping containers were a handful of militia-types. Most were wearing some combination of BDUs and camo, or police Kevlar, and they had assumed safe firing positions behind something sturdy by the time we came to a stop. These people were clever; they'd put their little roadblock in a spot where we couldn't back up to turn a semi around easily. The road was somewhat narrow too, which meant backing up would be a real pisser to boot.

One of them waves from the top of the container and pulls out this bullhorn, like police use during riots. You remember what he said? Could you hear him? No? Well he says, "Welcome to the First Virginia Republic!"

Mmhm. Right. First Virginia Republic. Not sure exactly what he or they thought they was achieving by declaring their spot in the road a safe haven and a new nation, but hey, more power to you. I personally thought it was a dick move to block off a road entirely with no visible way to get through, or back up easily. Not very American, but then again the founding fathers of The First Virginia Republic had their own ideas of what's right from wrong.

I got real nervous as your daddy got onto our bullhorn. He leaned out of the Peterbuilt's passenger's side and started talking back. "We're headed north from Texas, and didn't know this road was blocked or private property. We apologize. I'll get us turned around right quick and get on our way."

Your daddy got back inside the truck and the man with the bullhorn started talking again. "Is that fuel truck full of good fuel?"

That'd be the truck I was sitting in. Right about then I wished I hadn't had my SKS trashed in that little wreck we had when the zombie fell off the overpass and smashed into the windshield of Tammy's truck. Man I loved that gun. Tammy was good people too.

I put my window down, pulled out my Colt and switched it to my left hand after thumbing it to the 'shoot assholes' setting. I didn't want no wait if it got ugly. I made my target clear in my head; a woman leaning a little funny over the edge of one of the brown building's roofs. I could see most of her side, and could tell she had no Kevlar on. She had pretty red hair, but a face better suited for a mechanic's line of work.

"We're running low," Adam lied. "We only have enough to get our little group to where we're heading. If you need some diesel, we could spare maybe twenty gallons. Thirty. More if you've got trade that could help us." We could spare more than that, but you can't go all in on a hand without gauging your opponent. Doesn't make any sense.

Now what we've learned kids is that this is the moment where you find out who you're dealing with. Are you dealing with honest folks? Are you dealing with violent folks? Are you dealing with the desperate or the kind? The real… or the fake?

Right then the little walkies we've been using pipe up and Bud in the back truck with the horse trailer says a group of ATVs is heading up the road to our backside. No backing up for us now without running over folk. Which sometimes, you just gotta do.

Bullhorn man lifts the bullhorn and starts talking again. "For the good of the people of the First Virginia Republic, I am seizing all property in your vehicles. You are welcome to remain here as citizens, pending due process. Please put down any arms you have and surrender peacefully." Then the prick adds, "We don't want to see anyone hurt."

Now kids, pop quiz time. What's the one word you DO NOT suggest to a Texan that idjit said to us? I'll give you a hint; it ain't vehicles.

Oooh. That's right Nathan. He said the magic word that makes all Texas pull out their guns.

Surrender.

Your daddy didn't have to tell us what to do next. There would be no seizure. There would be no citizenship, and there sure as heck wouldn't be no surrender. I couldn't see it from where I was at, but I imagine Adam sat his bullhorn down on the floor of the Peterbuilt and picked up his AK. The next time your daddy leaned out that truck door it was with his rifle at his shoulder.

Of course just appearing with that weapon sent them into a tizzy, and the whole group of Republic shooters opened up on us.

Your daddy got off about ten shots before he took a round in the side and fell back into the truck. I watched as one of his last shots smashed the bullhorn right out of the hand of their leader man. Sad for leader man he still held it near his face. Right after the plastic shattered in his hands the top of his head exploded. Looked like a kid sneezed at the dinner table with a mouthful of spaghetti, cauliflower and red sauce.

I leaned out the window of my truck as your daddy fired and plugged seven pretty fast shots at the redhead on the roof of the vacuum repair place. My first five shots redecorated the brick right below her pretty good, and startled her. Bad for redhead though, instead of getting down she got up and looked my way, giving me a big old target. I took half a breath and put one right through her at the gut. She fell forward and hit her head on the edge of the building, and that was the last I saw of her. I slapped a new mag in and threw my truck in reverse.

The expression all hell broke loose describes what happened next. You gotta understand how loud it gets when two dozen people all start shooting guns at the same time. Then there comes the crying as people get shot. The screaming for help, for mom, for Jesus. Someone had the presence of mind to holler out, "Back up!" on the walkies and that's what came next, under heavy fire of course.

Bud in the truck at the back end with the horses tossed his into reverse and just about drove over two of the sumbitches - pardon my French, we ain't in France kids- two of them sumbitches in the four wheelers, and he made a path for the rest of us to start backing up. Now if you've ever seen several cars or trucks trying to back in a coordinated fashion you already know it's a plate of soup being eaten with a whisk. Now add being shot at like it's Viet-fucking-Nam -there's that French again boys, I apologize- and it's like trying to ride a unicycle during a hurricane after being told your girlfriend's pregnant.

It's a dang mess. Bud's wife Donna had her AR up and out the window and as the rearguard on the fourwheelers tried like a one armed wallpaper hanger to get the shit out the way she lit them up and sent them into the woods and the yards of the houses nearby. With Bud and Donna hightailing it and her shooting like it was the Alamo our whole column of vehicles started to inch backwards out of the firefight.

Bullets was pinging off the hoods and grills and doors all over the place and I watched as three holes appeared in my windshield right above where I'd ducked. I still got three holes there that look like little glass flowers. Little reminders of why prayers are important I say.

It was about two tenths of a mile before Bud was able to get his vehicle spun around in a side street, and we had to slow to let him pull back out heading south and away. One by one we turned around and those of us waiting patiently shot back at the Republic dickheads who were shooting at us. I pissed through all three of my magazines keeping their heads down as your daddy somehow managed to pull himself together and reverse the Wedge to catch up with us. He had to get away from those guns.

I took my turn backing around and headed south slow until Adam caught up to me. Over the walkies we started to make a plan and assess who had been hurt. Your daddy was shot up pretty good, and we needed to get pulled over somewhere safe to get Penny to him so she could get working on him. Thank God for nurses.

As your daddy told us -don't cry Nathan, he's okay, you know that. Your daddy ain't killable- as your daddy told us he was bleeding good, what was left of the four wheelers started riding up alongside us, and the jackasses started taking potshots at our tires. I remember looking out the window and seeing how *angry* one of those dudes looked. He had this face that said 'I hate you people' and that made me very uncomfortable. This ran on for about two more miles -BANG BANG- until they managed to shoot out enough tires to force me and Bud to stop. Granted that wasn't a lot of downed vehicles, but we couldn't risk crashing and losing the fuel or crashing and losing the horses. We made the call to stop, and boys… we let 'em have it.

I switched off to the 12 gauge I had on the passenger seat. I jumped down out of the rig and just racked 'em up until I was dry. I don't like killing people boys, but when you cross my kin or those who call me kin I will do what I must to protect what is mine. I shot two of the wheeler-men, and I know a few of the others took some down as well. I had to shoot the man with the angry face. One of the ATVs caught afire on account of taking a few rounds to the gas tank plus a spark, but for the most part, once we stopped, it was only a minute before the shooting ended.

Penny got to your daddy and started to patch him up, and we moved to Bud's truck and got his wheel off. Course you gotta understand at this time, we was worried the Virginia people were coming up on us for round two. We had to move, and move fast.

Felt like NASCAR.

Jack out, jack up, wheel off, wheel on, all tight, jack down, double tight, move on.

It's like a military march. Now changing a big rig tire is a much more involved process. It takes an hour, and all kinds of work and like many tasks, it goes better with beer, and a few friends who know what the hell they're doing. We caught a little bit of a lucky break on my truck in that the two tires I lost were on the same side, side by each. That meant we could limp further away after swapping but one tire instead of two or three, which would've cost us too much time.

I enlisted some help, and we got to changing it out. Lube up the rim, pry 'er off, pry the new one on after soaping it… It's all good. Took us twenty minutes, give or take with three of us posting guard to make sure we wasn't snuck up on while a few of us made sure the dead stayed dead, and dug them some shallow graves. A few heavy rifle shots came our way in the distance, but didn't hit us. I chalk that up to them being pissed off.

If you remember, they never came after us.

We got one tire switched out, drove south until we found a route that'd take us far and wide away from the First Virginia Republic, and we drove on for a few more hours until we reached a good spot to pull off, get the other tire fixed up right, and make sure your daddy was alright.

It was dumb luck and providence that we only had the one person hurt, and while bad, not bad enough to kill him. He's still not quite right, and if we can find a real doctor, I'm sure there's some work that could be done. Penny saved his life for sure, but a little more expertise would be a welcome gift.

Sure am tired.

How is it energy is wasted on the young, when you need so much more of it as the days pass? That's not a condemnation, boys. That's just the observation of an aging man who wishes he could run and jump and play like he did when he was your age.

So, I do hope that entertained. And yes, I'm still sitting here thinking about why all the dead are now dead. Funny isn't it? We spent so long thinking up the reason as to why they'd gotten up and started walking around that it's strange to think about them not being that way. Is this temporary? Is it over?

Really over? Or are we just at the center of the storm, and everything is swirling around us like a hurricane?

Maybe that Adrian character knows.

We got another day or two north and then we'll be near where we gotta be. Lord knows it'll be a challenge to find his exact location. Near a city, but in a small town. The directions Angie and Raef gave us aren't lining up on any map we've got. We'll have to scrounge for local maps somewhere. Supposed to be looking for some private school in the hills. With a big old dirt and wood wall around it.

And three people who may know why this is all happening.

Sounds like home to me. Still frigging cold though.

Go to bed kids.

ROSE

WENDI HAEGLE

The day before the world went to shit, Rose Gendron celebrated her 64th birthday. Well, celebrated may not exactly be the right word; Rose very rarely 'celebrated' anything beyond the sheer joy of being miserable on a daily basis. Oh, yes, Rose knew just what an uptight bitch she was, and quite frankly, fully embraced being just that. Of course, it hadn't always been that way. No, she'd be more than happy to tell you that marrying that useless turd of a husband had been the impetus of her downward spiral. In fact, it just that uselessness that Rose was pondering as she and her cart wobbled their way forcefully through chaos of the grocery store aisles.

"Useless bastard," she muttered. "I told that God damn son of a whore to just leave the God damn windows alone. Didn't I?" After all, she thought, only a dipshit like Walter Randall Gendron could manage to drop a sheet of plywood smack on the top of his foot.

Rose angrily snatched a handful of items off the nearest shelf, not even looking at what they were... concerned with nothing but wallowing in her own rank pool of loathing and self-pity. Today, that pool was fairly boiling at the fact her husband was sitting at home, perfectly comfortable in his ratty-ass La-Z-Boy with his poor widdle foot elevated. Rose couldn't help but think her foot planted in his ass just might have served to fix his little 'owie' in no short order.

"But, I can't *WALK*, Rosie," he'd whined.

Pussy. Useless, 62 year old, good for nothing turd. She'd

told him as much, and then told him that he'd better hope the world *was* ending or she'd surely kill him herself before the week was out. Oh, yes, Wally was convinced the world was coming to an end after listening to all those bullshit news reports about weird people and weird goings on.

Of course, Wally believed the world was coming to an end every other God damn day. Just so happens that THIS day he decided to haul his ignorant ass out to the garage, pull out his useless little tools and his useless little plywood and board up the house. Board up the house like some paranoid, delusional freak; like the neighbors needed something else to talk about. Oh, yes, and she'd told him THAT, too. Just before he started bitching that they needed 'supplies' to 'tide them over.'

"Tide us over?" she'd sputtered. "And how long will we need tiding, oh wise one? Eh? How long before..."

"I don't know," he'd snapped; interrupting her. He'd fucking interrupted her. Rose opened her mouth to respond, but Wally cut her off again.

"Just please go to the damn store and get us some things, Rosie; and not Simpson's on the corner. Go down the road to the big market." He'd shifted in the chair then, to look directly into Rose's eyes.

"Then, when you get back, you're going to help me board up the last window."

Rose had gaped at him for a moment; partly because Wally never looked her in the eye and partly because, if it were any other day, his old balls would be too shriveled and puny for him to dare to tell her what to do. Rose liked it that way; this way? Not so much.

"Really, Wally? Really," she spat, venomously. "Or when I get back you could just... oh, I don't know... go shit in your hat maybe? How 'bout that, Wally?"

But, still, she'd grabbed her purse and her keys and driven down the God damn road to the next God damn town to get Wally his God damn supplies.

*****

Leaving the snack aisle, still muttering, Rose levered her cart around and into the canned goods where her progress was promptly halted by a wall of people and carts. No one was moving, primarily because the store was full of 30-something pissant soccer moms and yuppie dads who, clearly, wouldn't be able to fight their way out of a God damn paper bag.

"Stupid shit heads," Rose grumbled, wedging her cart firmly against the back of the man blocking her progress. If she had to suffer being stuck amidst these ignorant shits, then someone else was damn well going to suffer with her. As the man turned to glare at her, Rose sneered at him and leaned even heavier on her cart. When he finally turned away, with a snort of disgust, Rose reached out and randomly swept an arm's worth of cans from the nearest shelf straight into her cart. As the last can clattered atop the pile, she suddenly sensed someone looming behind her.

"Ma'am," the voice said quietly, "can you please back away a little so the folks in front of you can get out of our way?"

She could feel the breath of his words on her neck, which only heightened Rose's annoyance at the big set of un-Wally-like brass balls this fucker had to even speak to her. Without even looking in his direction, an unnecessary expense of energy because she knew he'd just be another yuppie cocksucker, Rose politely told him to go fuck himself, buddy.

"Ma'am, I am NOT your fucking buddy." Rose froze even as he continued speaking. "And if you don't put some of those cans back you just scooped up, and get the hell out of the way for everyone else, I will see to it both your hips get busted right here in this aisle."

Who the fuck… Rose thought; tightening her grip on the cart and feeling that familiar surge of adrenaline that usually preceded her succumbing to a full blown conniption. Fully planning to lodge Mr. Yuppie's testicles in his throat, Rose half turned to face the idiot who was determined to make her day even more unpleasant than usual… as if a useless lump of a husband and the apparent end of the world weren't enough.

What she saw over her shoulder, however, fairly pinned her would-be testicle launchers to the floor. He was enormous. A tattooed freak that looked, for all the world, like he could squash her like a gnat. To make matters worse, he was smiling at her as if he would enjoy doing just that. Uncharacteristically, Rose hesitated, hastily weighing her odds of winning this particular battle, before deciding that this hulking brute would probably not be as easy to smack down as Wally "Uselessturd" Gendron of La-Z-Boy Land.

Forced to swallow an altogether unfamiliar lump, which had suddenly taken up residence in her throat, Rose returned several of the now dented cans to the shelf and removed herself from the aisle. As the aisle cleared, Rose caught many a snicker and smirk from the surrounding patrons. With that, whatever small, uncharacteristic wave of shame and submission that had overtaken Rose in confrontation with the huge, tattooed man quickly dissipated. In its place, Rose's ire returned two-fold.

"Oh, just wait. Wait until I get home, Walter Gendron," she fumed. "You and I are going to have a fucking talk about you and your foot and me being in this shit hole right now instead of you."

*****

The tattooed man had, to her amazement, allowed Rose to return to the canned goods aisle ahead of him. Not that Rose cared that he was suddenly all ass-kissy. No, she simply, again, randomly swept cans into her cart; daring him to say something else. To Rose's disappointment, he didn't. He had been utterly disinterested in her since she complied, and she quickly lost track of him in the mayhem.

Leaving the aisle, Rose realized how heavy her cart had become, and a renewed burst of fury swelled within her. *Uselessturd had better be ready to gimp his lazy ass out to hump all this shit in,* she thought. *Because I sure as shit am not lifting it*

212

twice.

As Rose eventually made her way into the final aisle, a sudden commotion at the front of the store erupted. She turned to watch as shoppers rushed from the checkout lines to gaze into the parking lot. *Crazy fuckers,* she thought with a derisive snort. As Rose leaned into the weighted cart to resume her trek, a sharp crack resounded through the store, followed by screams.

"What the..." she muttered, thinking it had sounded remarkably like a gun shot.

True to form, however, Rose couldn't be bothered to actually care what was happening. Instead, she simply moved forward to gather the rest of Wally's 'tidings' before making her way to the cashier. Forty-five minutes later, as she finally reached the register, Rose was fairly certain her fury could not escalate any further. Until...

"$313.69," said the pimply girl, tiredly.

"Are you shitting me?" Rose growled; fumbling for her wallet. "It ain't gold, for fuck's sake, it's food! God Damn highway..."

"*For fuck's sake*, Lady, just quit bitching and pay for your shit would you please?" blurted the gangly, yuppie puke behind her. "Some of us have people waiting for us!"

"Is that so?" Rose quipped with a sneer. She then, very slowly and very meticulously, counted out fifteen twenty dollar bills, two fives, two ones, four quarters, five dimes, and three nickels while yuppie boy went positively apoplectic with frustration.

"Well, they can just bite my ass," Rose said gleefully, sliding the last four pennies to the cashier.

*****

As she made her way home in her aging Civic, Rose pondered the blanket shrouded figure she'd passed in the parking lot. Clearly, the sound they'd all heard had been a gunshot, as she doubted the blanket was covering a steaming pile of shit. So, who had been shot and why? And, who'd done the shooting? She seemed to recall that the hulk back at the canned goods had a shotgun with him. Was it him? Rose felt vaguely lucky that she'd not confronted him further. At least, she thought that was what she felt... luck was another emotion she was unfamiliar with. Suddenly, as she rounded a bend, Rose was forced to slam the brakes to avoid colliding with the passenger side of a mangled vehicle blocking the road.

"Christ on a crutch!" Rose bellowed, clutching the steering wheel and thinking, for a nano-second, that her heart might stop beating right then and there. Throwing the car into park she began to open the door, intending to take a closer look, when she realized that the other vehicle was already empty. Wondering where the police or a God Damn tow truck were, Rose glanced around and realized it was eerily quiet on the street. Although she had passed an occasional car along the way she noticed that, like Wally, the people who resided in the nearby homes had also evidently decided the world was coming to an end. Windows were boarded all around, and yards were void of people. Like the entire populace was bunkered down, waiting for something.

"Everyone's just gone fucking bat shit." Rose muttered, slowly reversing and then pulling forward to skirt the wreck. As she rounded what had been the front end of the other car, Rose glanced to her left. There, under the hanging driver's door, was an enormous pool of blood. Blood and... sausage?

What the hell is sausage doing in the road? she thought. Squinting, Rose realized suddenly that it wasn't sausage, but intestines.

Are you shitting me? Rose thought. *What kind of people work in this God Damn town? Take the dead bodies and leave the fucking body parts behind? Way to traumatize the poor widdle soccer mommies!* Rose actually laughed at that last part. *I'd pay to see that shit*, she thought. *Tossing their organic cookies and fainting like the coddled little bitches they are!*

Still chuckling, Rose continued toward home; suddenly

remembering just how bad Wally was going to get it when she arrived. Laughing aloud, now, she pushed the Civic to 35mph so he could get it sooner rather than later.

*****

Twenty minutes later, turning into her driveway, Rose was struck by three things simultaneously.

Her old-ass neighbor Frank -two houses down- who had been bed-ridden with cancer for the last year and a half was lurching around in circles in his front yard. Wally had managed, while she was gone, to put the final sheet of plywood up over the front window. Wally was standing in the open doorway with his shotgun slung over his shoulder.

Heaving herself from the driver's seat, Rose glared at Wally. "Looks like your God damn foot wasn't so hurt after all, was it, shit head?" she spat angrily at him. "You'd better get your ass down here..."

"Hey, Rose?" he called, interrupting her *again*. "You might want to be a little quieter or Frank over there might hear you."

"Fuck Frank," Rose replied, heading toward the walkway to the door where Wally stood. "Get down here and unload your shit, I'm not fucking around with you and your apocalyptic bullshit anymore."

That Wally made no move to exit the house as he was told stopped Rose in her tracks. "What the fuck has crawled up your ass, Walter Gendron? Who do you think you are? Are you really..."

Suddenly, Rose sensed someone or something behind her. Stepping to her right and turning, she found herself face to face with Frank who was, inexplicably, reaching to grasp at her. Slapping his hands away, Rose backpedaled, nearly stumbling over the toolbox that Uselessturd had, of course, left on the lawn.

"What the HELL?" she squealed. "Frank... what the fuck are you doing outside?" As he continued to shuffle towards

215

her, Rose realized that something more than cancer was wrong with Frank today. His eyes looked… dead. Suddenly, he lunged at Rose, grabbing at her clothes.

"Wally, do something! Get this fucker off me!" she howled, swinging wildly to keep Frank from catching a hold of her.

Wally didn't move. Rose grabbed Frank's wrists and kicked in vain at his nuts. What should have dropped him to his knees had, seemingly, no effect.

"WALLY GENDRON WHAT THE FUCK ARE YOU DOING? HELP ME!" Rose screeched.

Wally took a step. Then another.

Suddenly, Rose's grip on him slipped and Frank bit fiercely into Rose's cheek. She flailed blindly at him; connecting with an adrenaline fueled thump to the side of his head that momentarily pushed him back. Rose spun, flinging bits of flesh and blood from her face, and ran several steps towards the house and Wally.

"ARE YOU FUCKING CRAZY? SHOOT HIM OR I SWEAR TO CHRIST I WILL KILL YOU, YOU USELESS…"

But, then, Frank was on her; all gnashing teeth and clutching hands. As Rose struggled, screaming, Frank sank his teeth into the gristle of her neck with a sickening pop.

"Wally," Rose sputtered through the sudden, coppery rush of blood in her throat, "Wally… you fuck…"

Wally, with a smile, brought the shotgun down and closed the door.

Storm Crow 602

Rob Roche

"Culbert Tower, Sierra Charlie six zero one"

Lieutenant 'JG' Wentworth glanced over at Capt. 'Doc' Hollis, Doc didn't look back. "Needles are dark," he said. "Runway lights are FUBAR too."

"And nobody's awake in the tower either," JG said, finishing the sentence.

The C-2 Greyhound they rode in bucked and jerked through the turbulent night sky. They had left Andrews Air Force Base a short time earlier with a mixed load of VIP's and civilian passengers.

Everything had gone to shit in the last 24 hours. Some kind of virus had begun sweeping through the country and so far, nothing was stopping it. As unbelievable as it was, the dead were not staying that way. Little was known other than transfer of bodily fluids spread it and those infected quickly died. Then reanimated and attacked the still living, thus spreading it even more rapidly. Lt. Wentworth and Doc Hollis were far too busy to keep up with all the gory details, only catching bits and snippets in between missions. One flight had a cargo of Spec Ops guys that left the aircraft at 20k feet over some GPS point in North Carolina. Another had a load of congressional staffers that got booted off at some podunk airport in Virginia. The flights became a blur after that. The log book stayed closed and the aircrew scrambled as best they could to get the bird turned around -aka preflighted- for the next flight. Chief Ryker and PO Yellowfeather were top notch and handled problems like they always did. Quick and efficient.

This was the last mission. "RTB and you're on your own after that," according to the last comms from the squadron CO CDR Mike "Davey" Allison. Andrews AFB had fallen silent shortly after they had taken off, and it appeared that Culbert field was also quiet.

Easing back on the throttles, JG keyed the ICS, "Wakey-wakey Chief, Final coming up."

Doc, in the right seat broke out the landing checklist and began rattling off things the flight crew had to do in preparation for landing a Navy aircraft at a shore installation. In back, Chief Ryker broke out his own checklist and along with PO Yellowfeather got the cabin and its passengers squared away for landing.

"Major Sir, you need to put that laptop away. Can't have anything loose in the cabin while on approach or landing," Yellowfeather said to the officer.

The Army Major just nodded and put his gear away as requested. The dozen or so heavy hitters in his team just sat like statues, staring at the closed ramp 10 feet in front of them.

In the front office, Doc and JG were peering through the patchy fog that haunted this part of Chesapeake Bay. The partially functioning airfield lights made it a challenge, but no more than landing on the pitching flight deck of an aircraft carrier.

Landing checklists complete, the aviators aviated and Chief Ryker kept a sharp eye on his charges in back.

The Greyhound bucked and wobbled through final approach and touched down without incident. Few lights were on at NAS Culbert Field. They taxied up to the 'Crow's Nest,' the VRC-39's hanger. A dark colored SUV was just pulling into the parking lot nearby. Headlights illuminated the causeway and road leading up to the squadron's hanger. Families were arriving.

In back, Chief Ryker lowered the ramp as soon as they turned off the active. Pulling up in front of the hanger, he lowered it the rest of the way. Everybody unbuckled and piled out en masse. Everyone except the major and his group.

Lt. Wentworth and Doc Hollis shut the engines down and Lt. Wentworth unstrapped from his seat. "You coming?" He asked his friend.

"Staying here JG," Doc replied. Looking JG in the eyes he said, "I got one last mission before I'm done. You get Sally and the kids and bug out. I'll take the Chief and his with me."

"Roger that Doc," he said as they grasped hands, "been a pleasure flying with you Man."

"Same here, now git boy!"

JG passed left the cockpit and passed through the cargo compartment. Stepping off the ramp, he looked around at what had been a familiar sight during the four years stationed at VRC-39 and NAS Culbert Field. It felt cold and alien now. Mist shrouded parts of the field. The tower, normally ablaze with light and activity, was dark. The windows looked like dead eyes staring down at the still living. A smell like a mixture of baby shit and vomit wafted on the still air. Activity in and around the hanger was frantic, but still professional. Ground crews had the remaining squadron aircraft backed up to the hanger doors and refueling trucks were plugged into them.

As he walked across the ramp, a voice behind him called out, "Sir, coming through!" JG jumped out of the way as the bird labeled SC 601 was backed up to an open hanger door. The tail and wing walkers making sure they didn't hit anything as it moved ponderously.

Sally Wentworth, JG's wife of ten years and their two kids John and Mikaela, ages nine and seven stood silhouetted by the lights inside the hanger. JG ran up and grabbed them in a big hug. "C'mon, we're leaving. Get your stuff in 602!" he said, pointing at another C-2.

Loud, piercing gunfire erupted inside the hanger and people began flooding out through the open hanger doors. Half dragging his two kids, JG and Sally stormed up the ramp into SC 602. "Strap them in!" he shouted as he continued on to the cockpit. Sally threw their bags into the cage and turned to begin strapping the kids in. People were flooding across the ramp and several had already jumped into seats in the cargo bay. More were running toward SC 602 and others parked on either side. Up front, JG blew through the preflight routine and began flipping switches and tugging levers. The APU roared to life with a shrill scream. Shadowy figures lurched out of the fog and heavy mist in the distance. Seemingly attracted to the noise. Gunfire could be heard on a 360 radial. Something splacked off the armored windscreen leaving a small chip. Glancing at a gauge, JG started wind milling engine #1. A few seconds later he hit the 'start' button and the low moan of a T-56 Turboprop coming to life joined the chorus of its mates also waking up.

Master Chief Petty Officer Waylon White shouted from the cargo bay, "Sir, get us the fuck outta here NOW!" Waylon had 35 years of Naval service and was as unflappable as they came.

The staccato roar of an M-4 carbine erupted from inside the rear of the cargo bay. Sally Wentworth, a licensed private pilot, plunked herself into the co-pilots seat beside her husband and began strapping in. Engine #1 was up and running by now. Hydraulic pressure came up in the plane and the ramp in back -its actuation lever almost bending under the frantic pushing by the Master Chief- finally got the ramp up and closing.

Airman Piesceki, SC 602's assigned plane captain pulled the chocks and flung them off to the side, and then jumped into the aircraft as the ramp began closing. He barely got his legs inside before the clamshell door slammed shut.

JG advanced the throttle on #1 and began taxiing as he engaged the starter on #2. Looking left and right, he saw other Storm Crows moving away from the hanger. Flashes of gunfire and staggering figures could be seen inside the Crows Nest behind them. Some of the people appeared to be feeding on still-thrashing shapes lying on the ground.

#2 engine spun up to full power and like a million pissed-off hornets, the eight bladed T-56 turboprops bit into the clammy night air and pushed the C-2 Greyhound out onto the taxiway.

The ICS crackled with Waylon's voice from the rear, "Cabin

secured sir, lets un-ass this LZ."

Pushing the throttles forward, JG turned onto the active.

Humanoid shapes staggered and shambled along the edges of the runway. Some began wandering out onto the mist soaked asphalt in their path. They wouldn't be able to take off if their runway was obstructed.

"Shit," he muttered as he slammed the throttles all the way forward.

Storm Crow 602 lurched forward under the combined thrust of both engines. Vortices spun off the propeller blades as they went supersonic. Airspeed picked up and shapes appeared in the gloom. Some directly ahead. JG danced on the rudder pedals in a desperate attempt to miss the 'people' wandering across the runway. A prop strike could end their night quicker than he could blink.

At somewhere near flight speed, another mass of forms lurched out of the gloom. Hauling back on the stick, JG and Sally coaxed the heavily laden Greyhound into the air. Barely clearing the mob below, he threw the gear lever up and pushed the nose back down into level flight. Milking the flaps up as airspeed increased, they stayed on the deck as SC 602 roared out across the open waters of Chesapeake Bay.

A little left rudder brought them around on a 90 degree heading at around 1500 feet above ground level. Below and to the left, JG saw a different C-2 drift off the runway and cartwheel into a ball of flaming debris. The plume of black smoke crept into the sky like tendrils of nightmare. Another C-2 barely cleared the wreck and vanished into the gloom. Right on its heels, the last Greyhound also lifted off and disappeared into the night sky.

"All Storm Crows, good luck and god's speed shipmates," JG transmitted over the squadron's frequency.

Nobody replied.

"Honey?" Sally said as she looked over at JG with huge scared eyes, "What's going on and where are we going?"

"I have no idea Babes." He looked back at her, "Pick a direction."

In back, Master Chief White surveyed the mass of human wreckage packed into the cargo bay. The red lights in the cargo bay cast everything in a blood red glow. Capacity for the plane was around thirty souls. He guessed fifty plus were stuffed in there. The two Wentworth kids had given up their seats to others and crawled into the baggage cage. The Master Chief stood beside the baggage cage with his back to the closed cockpit door.

Dozens of scared people stared at him and each other. Nobody could hear the muffled scream and crunch of teeth tearing into living flesh over the shriek and scream of the engines.

Ten of the fifty died and turned before the rest realized what was happening. With nowhere to go, the carnage spread like wildfire. Those that didn't die from a flesh rending bite, died under the crush of panicked humanity trapped in a confined space several thousand feet in the air.

Master Chief White ripped open the cockpit door and shoved the two Wentworth kids through. The pilot looked back at him with a shocked expression. "We're fucked back here El-Tee." He threw the lock on the cockpit door after slamming it shut.

Sounds of a struggle and a lot of salty language that only a salty old Chief could put forth came over the open mic.

"Open the doors!" was the last thing anyone heard from Master Chief White.

Reaching over his head, Lt. 'JG' Wentworth pulled a yellow handle. Hydraulic fluid at 3000 PSI rushed through lines and forced the locks open, pushing the rear cargo ramp open.

Having already thrown the pallet release handle on the port side, Master Chief White plunged his arm into the writhing mass of feasting undead piled on top of the remaining pallet release handle. Teeth ripped at his arm, stripping flesh from it in bloody chunks. The pain was ungodly. He flipped it open and the floor, along with the passenger seats attached, shifted aft. Pulling his arm free he punched a freshly turned zombie in the face, shattering its jaw. It dropped free to the tilted floor only to be replaced by another of the hungry dead. The milk white eyes of a small child glared in hatred at him as he bashed the unruly corpse against the baggage cage to dislodge it.

As the ramp descended further, the wind howled and shrieked throughout the cargo hold. The shift in weight threw the aircraft into a climb. The cargo pallet sliding aft jammed. The ramp wasn't open enough yet.

In the cockpit behind the locked door JG and Sally fought the controls in a desperate effort to regain level flight. A stall would be unrecoverable at this altitude.

The mass of undead still inside the cargo hold began falling out the now fully open ramp. The previously jammed up cargo pallet soon followed, taking the rest overboard. They plummeted into the sky, leaving the chaos behind. With the sudden departure of the passengers and cargo pallet, the C-2's center of gravity returned to normal.

The Master Chief collapsed to the floor, tangled in his ICS cord and a loose cargo net. His heart stopped beating and his eyes turned milky white. The floor all around him was slick with blood and gore, body parts and now an undead Master Chief. He thrashed around, finally untangling himself by pure chance.

He sensed living flesh.

Hunger filled him. Something dim remembered that food was inside the shut door nearby.

Waylon lurched towards the front of the plane and crashed into the locked cockpit door.

JG and Sally looked at each other as something heavy crashed into the cockpit door. John and Mikeala screamed.

JG had an idea. He pulled back on the control yoke, throwing the C-2 into a steep climb.

The dead and furious MC White was thrown back away from the door. Reaching the end of the ICS cord still attached to his helmet, he jerked and crashed around inside the cargo hold. His angry arms flailing all about as his body crashed back and forth in the cargo bay he somehow hit the 'ramp up' lever.

JG continued to reef on the yoke, throwing the aircraft

around the sky. John and Mikeala, not strapped in, were also thrown around in the cockpit. Sally and JG, taken by near panic by now, were oblivious to the plight of their two children.

The crazy movement of the plane sent the undead navy man all about. In back, a tool box broke loose as the undead Master Chief crashed into it. The heavy steel box began to fly around, crashing into things that should not be crashed into. A wire bundle here, a hydraulic line there.

Warning lights began to flash in the cockpit. Sweat poured into the eyes of the pilots. Engrossed on what they were doing, oblivious to everything else. Nine year old John fell limp as his head impacted the radio rack. Seven year old Mikeala screamed as she fell under the co-pilots seat, her arm snapping as it got tangled up.

Stomping on the left rudder pedal, the C-2 groaned and slewed to port. The extreme nose up attitude threatened to stall the aircraft. JG dropped the left wing and kicked the rudder, bringing it out of the climb, but putting a tremendous amount of stress on the airframe.

That loose tool box kept soaring in the back with its ugly friend Waylong. It found another critical part to smash into.

A fuel line, used to transfer JP-8 from various tanks located in the wings and fuselage was punctured.

Mikeala was bleeding out. Under the seat her arm had a compound fracture and an artery had been severed. She fell into shock and passed out. She would die soon unless the bleeding was stopped.

John had a nasty head wound, but one that was survivable with medical attention.

Full of panic, JG and Sally were still fighting a runaway Greyhound.

The ICS cord attached to MC White's helmet finally snapped as he continued to ricochet around in the cargo bay.

Training eventually overcame panic and JG, along with his wife's help, was able to bring the bucking Greyhound under control.

Only 10 minutes had passed, but it seemed an eternity.

It was then that they saw the instrument panel and all the warning lights flashing.

Master caution.

Fire warning.

Hydraulic pressure, and a host of others.

In back, The zombie that had been MC White regained his feet. Hunger throbbed. Fresh meat lay beyond that flimsy cockpit door.

He charged it.

His arm -lacking flesh- snagged the ramp door handle again in between the bones of his tattered forearm. Jerking the upper part of his limb free, the ramp began opening again. It opened slower this time as there wasn't sufficient hydraulic pressure left in the plane, only gravity.

Leaving his shattered forearm behind, he charged the cockpit door again.

"#2 engine is smoking," Sally reported as she looked past JG and out of the cockpit window.

"Roger that," he replied. Glancing at the gauges he noticed more bad news. "RPMS is dropping as is fuel pressure. Oil pressure is at zero." JG reduced the #2 throttle to idle and hit the feathering switch.

Only with no oil pressure, the feathering mechanism failed to operate.

"Shit," he muttered.

The aircraft began to slew to the left as the dead engine now acted like a big speed brake. The wind milling propeller also began to speed up.

Something slammed into the cockpit door, the latch almost giving way.

Under Sally's seat Mikeala opened her eyes. John groaned, but didn't open his. Blood ran down his face and covered his shirt.

Another tremendous crash came from the battered door.

In back, fuel mixed with air swirling about in the cargo bay. A wire bundle leading to the aft anti-collision lights shorted out. Damage from the errant tool box was the culprit.

225

Fuel pressure to the #1 engine began to decrease.

More warning lights illuminated as the #1 engine began to starve of fuel.

The #2 engine was reaching critical RPMs, and both props were shrieking a death song.

Searing pain enveloped Sally's right leg.

JG turned to look at his wife, her features gone white in agony. He looked down.

Mikeala's milk white eyes returned his gaze. She shook her head, ripping a chunk of meat and skin from Sally's calf. Blood spurted.

The cockpit door burst open.

Master Chief White (NAC/EAWS/ESWS/Undead) crashed headlong into the instrument panel between the two pilots. His body pushed both throttles to max.

JG looked again at his wife. The undead man between them thrashed and flailed. She returned his gaze.

"I love you Babes," he mouthed.

"I love you too sailor, numbah one long time," she replied through gritted teeth.

JG pushed the control yoke forward, putting the stricken Greyhound into a shallow dive.

Fuel and air reached critical mass. An opportune spark ignited the cocktail of fuel and oxygen in the cargo bay.

MC White gathered his one armed self and pushed away from the instrument panel as the plane dove. He cast his ravenous gaze on Sally, then at JG.

JG began punching wildly at the snapping teeth bearing down on him.

In back, Vulcan roared.

The explosion blew the tail off and ignited what fuel remained in the tanks under the floor. An instant later, #2 engine shed five of its eight blades. Three of those passed through the fuselage severing more fluid lines, adding to the conflagration.

The #1 engine, screaming past max allowable RPM's like a runaway train pushed the dying aircraft further and faster into its dive.

3500 feet below on the ground, a shrieking fireball appeared out of the mist and gloom in the sky, if anyone had been alive to see it.

Storm Crow 602 plunged into the great dismal swamp at near vertical.

The shrieking cacophony inside the plane silenced with a metallic wet "Whoomph" as it buried itself in the swamp.

On the flat, featureless gray plain of earth, five more souls died, and joined the milling masses already there.

No Fucks on Timmy

J.C. Fiske

He's got demons they say. He's crazy they say. He's drunk and stoned again they say. Well, that last part's usually correct, but not right now. You know how I know? The voices in my head are louder than usual. They get this way sometimes. Bastards are practically having a throw-down up there. I suppose it's a blessing. They're much more entertaining to listen to than my king shit of a boss. Can't really make out what he's saying, but I think he's yelling. Hold on, you who's listening in. I better focus for a second just to make sure... yup... definitely yelling. Most likely at me from what I can tell. I am the only one here in this pricey office that just screams I don't get laid.... Damn is he loud when he yells, but not loud enough.

'Roid rage. It's a real thing. I've had experiences with roidheads before. Not by choice of course. Thing is with roidheads, their moods don't just go from hot to cold. They go from volcanic to frozen. How do I know my boss does 'roids? I'm the janitor you see. You want to really know someone? Look through their trash. And no, fuck you! I don't go routing through people's trash for shits and giggles. I learn these things like I usually do. The hard way. For example, Trish? From accounting? Yeah, the prissy one. Hypocrite dips after hours. I dumped her trash bin a little too fucked up one night. Next thing I know, Tinkerbell's spit cup spills all over my good jeans and my Metallica Master of Puppet's shirt. There's a 'swallow' joke here somewhere, I know it, but I'm too sober currently to think of one.

Sorry, where was I? Oh, yeah, my boss... Let me see if he's still yelling... Yup. The guy's neck is bulging, getting red. He's starting to sweat. His bald head is getting red too. Fuck, I mean sure, I've referred to him in passing as a 'prick' before, but damn, he's really starting to look like a throbbing shlong. If he blows a load out the top of his head I'll shit a brick... but that's not what pisses me off about him. It's his goddamn pink shirt. He looks like a fuckin' Ken doll on 'roids! God, I know his wife dresses him... poor mother fucker... prolly is on a short leash. I'd be miserable too if I had to slave away for some princess just to get laid, but damn, I know there was a saying for men who wear pink shirts somewhere in this brain of mine... oh, wait, he snapped his fingers at me. What am I? A dog? Well, I didn't shower this morning. Probably smell like one...

I must have really done something to piss him off now, but what? I suppose if I just paid attention for a second I'd figure it out, but, nah, sorry, don't give a fuck really. Heh. I'm suddenly reminded of an internet meme that got passed around a while back. Not much speaks to me, but this one sure did. It portrayed a group of children huddled together. Above them was a line that read, "Everyone just wants to be liked, and accepted." Then off to the right it showed a boy holding a bundle of balloons floating away from everyone with a proud, sturdy middle finger raised at the children below. Above this lone floating boy it read, "Except for Tim. Tim doesn't give a shit." I never really believed in signs, or miracles, or a higher power, but let me tell you something. When I saw this, I felt like the universe spoke to me. Something out there sent me a message. And what was that message? I think it said, "You know what, Timmy? You're ok! Keep on keeping on soldier!"

My name's Tim you see, Tim O'Kane. Write it on my gravestone; Timmy never gave a fuck.

Suddenly, my boss is on his feet. Oh, now he's smacked the desk with not one, but both hands as if loud noises will get my attention. One of his many autographed celebrity pictures falls off the wall. That's the thing with these muscle-bound freaks. It's for intimidation only. If one truly had it in them to fight they'd be, I don't know, in martial arts, MMA, a dive bar on a Friday or Saturday night. The desire, the hunger has to be there. This guy? Not a chance. What kind of man aspires to wear a monkey suit, sit in a cage of a cubicle, and slave his days away doing mental gymnastics for money? Fuck, sounds like a zoo! I feel for the guy in a way. Everyone knows what it's like to feel weak, powerless --especially me-- but some overcompensate. Oh, well, I'll give him some eye contact and let him vent away for a bit...

Ok, that's enough. I'm bored now and I've had enough of this job anyway. Time to take my leave, but first... do my eyes betray me? Or is that a bottle of whiskey on one of his shelves? Looks expensive as all hell too! That son of whore is coming home with me! Seems your luck is turning up, Timmy! Suddenly I'm upset. This prick didn't even send out a Christmas bonus this year. I got the job because I was promised a Christmas bonus. I will get my Christmas bonus you greedy mother fucker. And just like that, seems I'm on my feet. I'm walking past him, and, ugh, damn prick is still yelling. Fuck, he just sprayed a whole shit ton of spit across the back of my neck with his yelling. I'm suddenly reminded of Trish's spit cup. Ok, spit on me once, shame on you, spit on me twice... shame on me. Maybe I've been a bit dishonest. Yes, on the whole, I'd like my tombstone to say, "Timmy didn't give a fuck." BUT, well, I'm only human. Every now and then Timmy does give a fuck. And when he does? Well, I have no idea what will happen! Things go white, sometimes red, and then things tend to break and people, the right sort of people mind you, get hurt. And now? Now just may be one of those times. Suddenly, everything comes into focus, like coming up out of a dream, my boss's words are coming in loud and clear, and I don't like his tone...

"NOTHING BUT A LOWLIFE PIECE OF SHIT! YOU THINK YOU'RE SO GODDAMNED TOUGH!? YOU'RE A FUCKIN' LOSER! A FUCKIN' NOBODY! LOOK AT ME! TURN AROUND AND LOOK AT ME YOU FUCK! I AM YOUR BOSS! WHEN I SAY TO TURN AROUND YOU FUCKIN' TURN

AROUND! WHEN I SAY..."

My boss didn't get out much else after that. Uh, oh... Timmy gave a fuck... one thing that makes Timmy give a fuck? When someone tells me what to do. This may get deep for a second, but every now and then my head comes up with something of substance, but I'm a firm believer that free will is not an illusion, and the only illusion we have is that some of us honestly believe another human being can have authority over you. A boss is just that, a boss. Someone just as lost as you and me pretending they have all the answers. You've heard 'em. I have a degree! I make this much a year! I've read this many books! I've sucked THIS much dick! Right... now, I'm not saying I know everything. I know I never will. And that's just my point. Be wary of pricks who say they have all the answers. Chances are they're just as, if not more lost than us! Me? I got one life to live. I'm going to do whatever the fuck I want, when I want. It's worked out so far! Oh, right, back to the present moment... I tend to get ahead of myself... my fist, it seemed to move all on its own. Damn, sorry, boss. I cracked him right in the throat. Leaned my bodyweight in a little too far. Fuck. Now I feel bad... fuck... better say something, help him up.

"Jesus, man... get up! Christ, stop crying... everyone's watching... come on, dude, man up! Be a man! Just, ah, fuck it." This one's a lost cause. I tried. Life's too short for this bullshit...

Ok, where was I? I know I got up for a reason... oh, right! My bonus! I quickly grab the expensive bottle of whiskey, or is it scotch? I'll find out soon enough. The label is in some foreign language I don't understand. Foreign liquor... should fuck me up good! Maybe just a taste? There's an actual cork. Fancy! I pop it off, take a smell. I take a quick swig. Smack my lips. No burn at all. Oh, shit, Timmy's got the good stuff. Wait, that's right, everyone's looking in on me now. Think someone's calling the cops.

Oh, well.

In situations like this there's only one thing to do. In my mind, I pull an invisible rip cord. Balloons appear, and begin to carry me out of the office as I whistle the Star Wars Empire theme song all while raising a middle finger proudly, making sure I hover it over everyone so they all get a turn. I'm sure to linger it lastly over Trish, why? Because fuck, Trish.

The balloons have drifted me safely to the doorway. No one's saying a word. That's a good thing. Here it is. The moment. I sort of live for this. Shocking societal sheep with a dose of reality. I enjoy giving people like this a wake up call. A wake up call that says there's far more to life than keeping up appearances. Sure, you know what you want. You got to do what you do to live the way you want. I get that. But make sure it's what you want and not what someone else wants for you. If you live in any other reality besides your own? You're gonna have a bad time... so, here we go. I have my audience. They're waiting for me to say something, anything... I think long and hard... heh, long and hard... and then come up with the perfect phrase. With my middle finger still raised high and proud, I clear my throat, and remember now why I was so pissed to begin with. My goddamn boss's pink shirt!

"Listen and listen well, and weigh the gravity of the situation here. Pay attention to the man who leads you. The clothes make the man as they say, and pink is the color of just two things in life. Uninfected vagina, and an asshole. Girls wear pink because they enjoy taking it in the pink. Guys who wear pink, also like to take it in the pink! Never forget that folks!" I then take another swig from the bottle like the drunken asshole that I am, close the door, walk down the office hallway, down the stairs, and I'm out the door.

The sun is shining. It's a fine late June day. I take a deep breath of this fine New Hampshire weather. Live free or die bitches. I live for it. Hm. Well. Let's take a reality check. I'm jobless, but got plenty in the bank for what I need. I'm a man of VERY humble pleasures. Give me a thirty rack, Netflix, my friends, a curvy blonde with boobs so big they can suffocate me, and Timmy is one happy hombre. Well, I guess I'll take a week off then find some kind of new employment and some more people to fuck with and spread the good news all while

233

keeping the faith and living the dream. I hope Jesus would be proud of me. What would Jesus do they ask? Well, Jesus would probably drink some red wine, light up a J, put on some sandals, and strut around being awesome, inspiring people to enjoy the gift of life, and putting high society dicklocks in their place. BOOM! I have the moral high ground here. I really do live to inspire people. Fuck. Where did I park again? Oh, right... that blue Camry I hot-wired. Belongs to some local writer fuck. I hate writers. They're all assholes. Especially this prick. Drives around advertising his series like he's hot shit. He was passed out in a snow bank this winter with a bottle of Jack in his hand. Amateur... keys were right there! Mine now, you pretentious fuck. I should peel off the decal on the back of his car for his website eventually. I hate that I'm giving that fuck free advertising. But where the fuck did I park it? Oh, right! I parked in the back today! Time to roll a fresh one, blast some Rush and have the best ride home ever! Wait 'til Reckin' Ball Ryan hears this story! Wait, hold the phone... what do we have here folks? Jackpot! Holy shit, Timmy! Your day just gets better!

I don't have a lot of weaknesses but I do have one, and that's a curvy blonde with boobs big enough to suffocate me. Hell, there's one right now, and, well, this is new, seems she's humping my car... kinky. I'm just going to stop for a second. Take this in. Make sure what I'm seeing is actually real. May as well take another sip while I'm observing this. AH! It's so fuckin' smooth. Ok, on my second observation I realize she's not humping it, but keeps like, bumping into it. Her boobs jiggle and bounce every time her hips hit the side of it. Suddenly, everything that just happened seems so unimportant. I may even forget about it. I'll find out tomorrow I guess. Uh, oh. Timmy's giving a fuck again. Twice in one day! Hot bosomy blonde, dressed to kill, business professional, and seemingly born without motor skills is walking into the side of my car, bumping into it, looking confused, then does it again. It's like watching someone with a blindfold trying to play pin the tail on the donkey. Ok, take a deep breath, Timmy. You either have hit the jackpot today, or something's seriously wrong. Most likely the latter, but hey, consult the liquor a few more times and then go start up a conversation! She's obviously really digging your wheels... You have an in already! Ok, I'm going in...

As I get closer to the blonde bombshell, my gut churns. I immediately think it's my usual hangover cure. A Baconator from Wendy's. It's happened. Finally got food poisoning. It was bound to happen, but quickly realize that's not it. Something's off about this chick. I got pretty shitty vision as it is. I'm nearsighted. My prescription sunglasses are in the car. Most women from my point of view look pretty good from afar until I get close. Then they're far from good. I saw curves and blonde hair from afar. Her face is even pretty. What I can't get past though? Well, on the other side of her, my blind spot, there's a crowbar jammed firmly in her side. Blood's running down her legs, well, everywhere actually. I'm not even thirty feet from her and I smell her stank. Don't know if it's a yeast infection or what. I went down on a girl with a yeast infection once. I manned up. Even went back for seconds. That's how much of a pleaser I am in the sack, but this girl? I just can't get past that crowbar in her side... call me old fashioned, maybe picky, but that crowbar would just be a distraction! Ok, think hard, Timmy. How do you start this conversation? "Nice crowbar... um, wanna fuck?" No, no! That would never work! Ah, fuck it. Just say the first thing that comes to your mind.

"Nice boobs..." I say. Fuck. No, Timmy. Wrong, WRONG! Suddenly, she spins my way and that's when I see her eyes. Eyes are the gateway to the soul so I've been told. Hell, this may make me sound a little romantic and shit, but some ladies, damn, they could get me off with just their eyes. This bitch though? Ugh... her eyes are pupiless and milky... fish eyes... Jesus Fuckin' Christ, if I didn't know any better... If I dare say... this white eyed broad with the crowbar implant? She's either taking the worst walk of shame of her life from the frat house down the road, or she has a serious condition! Wait, holy fuck! What if she's a zombie? Goddamn it... I knew this would happen. I haven't read or watched the news since 9/11. Too damn depressing. Don't tell me I missed out on some goddamn zombie apocalypse! Maybe that's why people were all glued to the TV today. I dunno. It wasn't Netflix so I didn't give a fuck. Come to think of it. My boss was all in a hissy fit... think he said something about my lack of janitorial skills got a bunch of people sick, and how there were excrement's all over the toilets in the ladies room.

Thing is, I know I cleaned that shit. Women's bathrooms for the record? Oh, FAR worse than the men's room. Don't let women fool you. There's a reason they put on makeup, make themselves look like perfect, little composed dolls. They are DISGUSTING and that coming from a guy who scratches his ass and balls and smells his fingers after. Oh, shit, if this girl is a zombie... FUCK! She's making her way toward me now. But, damn, despite everything else, her rack... Jesus, they are perfect... oh, fuck! No fuckin' way! Bitch tried to bite me! Just lunged at me like a goddamn cat! Fuck does she smell bad... Damn, it... what do I do here? What do I... fuck! Ok, that was far too close. But damn, I still can't take my eyes off her rack. Focus, Timmy, focus... no, not on her rack. Get to your car. You can't hit girls. Even Zombie girls! Fuck! Back to the mission. Stop giving a fuck. Get in your car, roll a joint, and get out, Timmy! Move! Move!

I quickly side step her, hop in my car, slam the door closed. Start her up, and pull forward. Bitch is staring at me as I drive away. Better not think about it. Better do something I haven't done in years. I turn on the radio and go through the stations trying to find the news. All I get is static. Fuck. Is this really the Zombie Apocalypse? Well, best get home to Heaven's Shelter. My sanctuary. See if my fellow knuckleheads know anything. See, thing is, I did shit right. Bypassed college, busted ass for four years doing odd jobs since I was sixteen, lived off humble pleasures, and instead of owing $100,000 I pocketed it. Now? Purchased myself some land way up north in NH where only moose, bears, hermits, and other people like me tread, and everyone who isn't from there? We call them flatlanders. Hell, all my neighbors are cool as shit. We got a brotherhood. We've already PLANNED for something like this. We built a rigging system to block the only entryway in. One pull, down come about a hundred or so of the thickest logs you've ever seen, and we're as safe as a virgin in Sunday School. Let me tell you something. I know you city pricks think you're all smart in your fancy hybrids, but I've read the graphic novels. Zombie outbreak happens? You're the first to go. You know why? You fucks are already zombies! Like the good little robots you are, you wake up, do what you're told, get a job, bust ass for someone other than yourself, buy shit you don't need to impress people that don't care, and fuck! There's even laws for WALKING for fucks sake in cities! I've been called a lot of things in my life, but one thing Tim O'Kane isn't is a goddamn sheep! I got one life, and one life only and I discovered real early there isn't a whole lot of things that make me happy except cold beers, a finely rolled blunt, and good friends. It ain't about what you have, but who you have. Remember that.

The ride is quicker than I realize. Must have downed the rest of my joint and time traveled. Happens when you're stoned at times. Feels like I blinked and here I am. Rush's 2112 album will do that to you, takes you on a digital trip. Try it!

I drive up our immensely long driveway and pass under the ranch-like sign where in big bold letters it reads, "Welcome to Heaven's Shelter." I get out. The air is so much nicer up here! Spruce trees all around me. They can only grow up in high altitude you see. They look like tall, thin Christmas trees. Finally, I've washed off the stink of flatlanderville.

I'm home! I stumble a bit as I make my way to my trailer. Yup. A double wide. See, me and all my best friends, we all pitched in, bought some land up here, built ourselves eight trailers in a neat circle with a fire pit in the middle. We all have fully stocked fridges with beer. We each grow about three plants of different herb for us, and us only. No need to sell. We get in enough trouble as it is, and New Hampshire, the Live Free or Die state, STILL hasn't legalized this shit. The people in charge of New Hampshire are all on moral high horses. Any one who seeks power shouldn't have power or be in power. As it's said, we would be better off being run by the first twenty names in the goddamn phone book. Now you know why America is fucked up. But anyway, I digress. Seems that shit's finally come to an end! Woo! Let life begin! We have junk food galore up here. Freezers stocked with deer, moose, partridge, and trout. We have smokers for the meat, dehydrators to make jerky of all kinds. We have the fastest internet possible. Gaming laptops, every gaming system imaginable, and best of all? All linked together so we can play in our trailers against each other. You know, just in case we're too stoned to take a thirty foot walk to each other's trailers. Like the sign says. This is heaven! Hunting, fishing, video games, alcohol, weed, and yes, despite my rather haggard life, yes people. We get laid! Girls are ever so lonely way up here. Thing is though, way up here in a place like this. It's not about who's fucking who. It's about who's turn it is... but nobody cares. Literally. Everyone here? They're like me. Don't give two fucks, because giving just one might mean you care.

Fuck. I got to rock a piss terribly. Ah! Speaking of pissing... there's one of my best buddies, Reckin' Ball. Yup, that's all you need to know about him. He got the nickname because no matter what, you give that guy liquor, and he'll crash into everything important and break it. Currently, he's wearing a Stone Cold Steve Austin shirt that says, "Been there, destroyed that," on the front. How appropriate. He's leaning against his trailer with one hand, and pissing in the other. Even more appropriate. Oh! He's already swaying, anddddd boom! He's on his face. Jesus H Christ, Reck! Get yourself together! We still got loads of...

Fuck.

I just tripped over my own feet on the way over to him and took a digger. I already hear him laughing. Bastard. Hope he pissed on himself. I get up and dust myself off as he tries to stand only to fall again. I stand over him.

"Ok, before anything, zip it up," I say.

"Ugh, we got to do something about this gravel. Dick's all cut up again," Reck said as he sits up, and zips up, tries to

238

stand, but topples over. "Jesus, Timmy! How long you been standin' there watching me piss?"

"Long enough..." I say.

"Like what you saw did ya?" Reck asked. Before I can respond, I see he notices the bottle in my hand. Reck, you see is what you call a liquor connoisseur. If there's a label he doesn't recognize, he needs to drink it. He's passionate you see. His eyes light up like a damn kid at Christmas. Some people are just lucky like that. They discover their passion and hobbies early in life!

"What, what the fuck is that and where did you get it?" Reck asked.

"Stole it from my boss... think it's French..." I say. Reck rubs his hands together.

"Seems the Reckin' Ball's going to be out in full swing tonight, Timmy! You, you do plan on sharing that, right?" Reck asked, and then I noticed that despite him falling while pissing, his glass beer mug is untarnished, and he hasn't spilled a drop. This, this people is what a champion looks like. Fuck Wheaties and their choice of athletes. Put Reckin' Ball on the box!

"AH! But look at this, Timmy! Still intact! Like a champ! And, and I think there's still a little left down there," Reck says, as he finishes up the last swig.

"All right, buddy, up we go!" I say, and reach out with a free hand, which Reck grabs, and a moment later he's hoisted up.

"To the bar?" Reck asks.

"To the bar!" I say. We both cheer. It's what we do. Literally, this place we've built here. It's like fuckin' Diagon Alley in Harry Potter, except instead of us being wizards, we're just raging alcoholics. Next question!

We walk past several friend's trailers. They are empty. Everyone's still at work. Reck is the only one still unemployed. Well, that makes two of us now. He's taken a break you see, planning his next job carefully, and how to quit it in a blaze of glory. It's what we do... if we don't, we won't have any drinking stories to tell each other. The last job he quit was a seafood restaurant. His boss was a 6' 3" ex-college football star who got into a bad party one night, got kicked out, lost everything, and now throws his weight around the kitchen as a manager. Except he had one problem. He threw his weight at Reck one day which is something you just don't do. See, Reck is Irish Italian and stands in at about five foot six. Listen, you know the whole saying of, it's not the size of the dog in the fight, but the size of the fight in the dog? Yeah, I've seen Reck beat the ever living shit out of guy's nearly twice my size and I'm a big dude. He's grounded. Like a lightning rod. You just can't knock him over when he's in fight mode, and boy, does he fight dirty, like a fuckin' Wolverine. Even as kids, we couldn't beat each other up, so, we just decided to be best friends instead. He's the only one who can keep up with my drinking in this park and it's always good if say, we go down into the flatland to raise some hell, that he knows, and I know, no matter what, cops? Jocks? 'Roid freaks? Wiggers? Those fucks are going down.

Now, I said Reck was the only one unemployed right now, but he's not the only one in the park right now. My good friend Molly, a sort of off and on, friends with benefits thing, she's our official bartender, and we tip her better than a whore in a strip club. Sorry, performer I mean. They really hate being called whores. Whores never take their clothes off for money. Molly could strip if she wanted to, but this woman is CLASSY and honestly, I have just as much fun hanging out with her as I do with Reck. We built her a bar, now when I say built, we fuckin' built it. Honestly? This girl rakes in more in a year catering to us drunk fucks than she would at any corporate job. She's got a shit load of student loans you see, over 100k worth, and just two years hanging with us? She's got maybe a few more months to freedom. Sure hope she doesn't leave... it would break my heart. What little of it is left that is...

"So, how'd you get the French shit?" Reck asked. I'm about to tell him when I see Sammy struggling pulling a keg out of her pickup truck.

"Hey, assholes, come help me with this thing," Molly said.

"Well, top of the morning to you too!" Reck said.

"Fuck you, Reck. It's one in the afternoon, now help me," Molly said. Together we lug the full steel keg inside, and within moments the Keg containing Harpoon IPA, a New England Specialty, is hooked up and running fine. We pay the lady upfront around $100 each. Gonna be a long day considering it's not even five O'clock yet. I raise the bitter, hoppy brew up, and knock it back. Amazing. Head's starting to clear a little now. Beer has that magical power. Once it hits your lips... just no going back!

"So, saw a hot blonde today," I say.

"Why isn't she here?" Reck asked.

"Think she was a zombie..." I said, then tell them both about the scene that took place at my car before I left, not before telling them my recent retirement from the working world. I don't know what it is exactly, but at this point, Molly does something no one really does out here. She turns on the radio, and we listen in to what's going on in the outside world. Even Reck seems fascinated. I pick up a few words on the broadcast, 'sickness' 'plague' 'outbreak' and all of these other fancy words but I know the truth. A zombie outbreak started, no idea how, or why, but fact of the matter is, I don't care. The Dow Jones? Zombies? Drunk Hermits? Doesn't matter... the life we've built here for ourselves? Nothing can touch us. This was the point. That's the thing with Redneck ingenuity, or, I suppose it's more accurate to call us Notherners 'hicks,' but we all figured out real quick we don't belong in society. We drink too much. Drive too fast. Talk too loud. Swear too much, and dress as if we are colorblind. Stress is the major killer, and no greater stress than trying to fit into a world that isn't your own. If you have the ability, like us, to create your own reality, be very careful who you allow inside... so, if you're somehow listening to me, if you don't hear anything I say, just remember this. If society ever breaks and America goes to shit, find yourself a Redneck.

FUCK! And then it hits me, hits me so fuckin' hard... I start breathing heavily, I start sweating... I'm shook. Ridiculously shook. Like, I doubt I've ever been more scared in my life. I'm just paranoid is all. I had a long day, adrenaline must be

241

wearing out. Reck and Molly look at me with surprise. I doubt they've ever seen me this way. I need to get out of here. The walls seem to be closing in. I feel claustrophobic. Fresh air. Need fresh air. I nearly spill my beer, a cardinal sin around here, in my attempt to get out of the trailer. I hear Molly and Reck's voice but they sound distant, underwater... I immediately hack up the French stuff, followed by my beer. Fuck does it burn. I then feel Molly patting and rubbing my back, bless her, what a woman, and Reck asking me questions. I don't hear him right away. I tell myself to calm down, calm down, it's going to be ok, it's going to be...

"Timmy? You fuck! What the fuck's the matter with ya?" Molly's voice comes through clear now. Reminds me of a lot of good times, sleepless nights she was there for me. I cling to her voice, and as always when I get low, which isn't a lot, I'm up out of the darkness of my mind, and I'm back to the light, breathing hard, but most certainly back. God bless this woman...

"Dude, ok, ok, he's back. I can see it in his eyes. What the fuck was that all about man? Thought you were going to have a nervous breakdown or some shit!" Molly asked. And then it hits me. So much pent up shit. This is what happens you see. You go through life, push down all your darkness, and eventually, a fear so powerful comes up, something you can't process, and the floodgates open, and you collapse... fear's hit me for the first time since I was child...

"What is it? What the fuck's wrong? I don't like seeing that look in your eyes, Timmy!" Reck asks. Before I can answer, we're interrupted by the sound of loud motors, muscle car motors. I look up through hazy vision to see everyone, my family, come screeching in all at once. I see my brother Ramsey with his glasses, a ridiculous look on his face, smiling, laughing, cheering. He worked at an office building. Said something about zombies, society being over. He's happy. He runs into his trailer, takes all his suits, and ties, throws them into the firepit, and helps himself to a beer at the bar.

I next see my brother Brian. A tall beast of a kid, usually

quiet, not a big drinker, pull in from his job at Best Buy. A huge, child-like grin on his face. He goes to his trailer, grabs a shotgun, and starts open firing at the sky. Tears are streaming down his face. He's happy. Then Mike, my real life brother pulls in, stumbles out of the car, the joint in his mouth nearly out, but he sucks it back, burns his fingers a bit, tosses it to one side, and rips up his court summons with a big grin, runs to his trailer, grabs his favorite bong --a three foot behemoth-- goes into the bar, and does what's known as a 'Strikeout.' You inhale a huge rip of smoke from the bong, hold it in your lungs, chug a beer, do a shot, then blow the smoke out. I see his eyes water and turn as red as the Devil's prick. I've seen Mike happy plenty of times, but never this happy.

Next up comes my brother Josh. It's like destiny happening before my eyes. My fear started to dwindle little by little as I suddenly see all my friends, one by one arrive, Josh being the last. He has the ability to light up every room he enters, or in this case, possibly the entire bit of Heaven's Shelter. He's been through restaurant after restaurant all to support his music habit. Now? Society's over. He celebrates by grabbing his guitar, a cigar, and big mug of ale as he begins playing and singing 'American Pie.' When suddenly, they all notice me on the ground. They rush over. Fuck. I hate being the center of attention, but they've got me now. They've never before seen me this way. Only Sam has, and she looks worried, especially at a time when everyone else is happy, ecstatic even. The rapid fire of questions fly at me. Timmy's balloons have burst. I've finally fallen down after many, many years of repression, all due to my number one fear, now made reality. I shudder at the thought of it again. Sam holds me. It's comforting. Just comforting enough. I ask for breathing room. Everyone steps back, waiting, eyes bulged. I hate to say the thing everyone else hasn't thought of yet. I hate to be the bearer of bad news...

"What is it, man? You look like shit! I ain't never seen you look so, so..." Ramsey starts.

"Sober?" I say. I grunt. "Fear will do that..."

"Listen, man. This zombie thing? We'll handle it! No one can

243

get up here! We're prepared for anything! We're..." Josh starts.

"No. That's not it..." I start. I then begin to cry. God, is it glorious, freeing. I've felt so numb these past ten years. What a release this is. I don't care how everyone is weirded out by this suppose weakness to cry. I let the tears come, and have my fill, and when it's over, it's over. I dust myself off, stand up, walk out of the group a bit, and look up at the sky for a moment, before I hover my hand over the cord, the magic cord that will release the logs, and trap everyone else outside, and keep our world safe, for as long as our lives have coming. I think once again of that other cord, the Timmy doesn't give a fuck cord in my mind. When I pull this cord, it's always the end of something, and the beginning of another. Fuck do I hate these moments. I turn around and look at everyone, those who have stood by me and realize the one thing seemingly people go through their whole lives not knowing...

It's not about what you have in your life, but who you have in your life. And I am so thankful, and fortunate to have the greatest friends anyone could ask for. Whew! I actually gave a fuck! Maybe they'll have to change what's on my gravestone now. Well, that's enough for one day. They're all looking at me now to say something. Anything. So, I tell them the truth.

"I hate to be the bearer of bad news, but do you guys realize something? With society being over? That means... no more internet... ever again... which means no online gaming, no more internet memes to laugh at, and no more Netflix... ever, again..." I say. The fear hits my chest again. It nearly knocks me over, but I stabilize it. There's only one thing to do when fear hits you. I look out at everyone as I hold the two cords. One in my hand, and one in my mind, and with that, Timmy does what he does best. He pulls the cords, out come the balloons, and I float away to the Promised Land...

I KNOW. I COUNTED.

KRISTA BLASEVICK PULLIN

"Anything new?" Carol whispered urgently over my shoulder.

"A few more zombies but nothing to write home about." I didn't bother to whisper in reply. If the half dozen dogs barking non-stop in their kennels wasn't loud enough to mask normal conversational tones then the car alarms out front certainly were.

"Scott, we've got to get out of here." Again with the whispering. It grated my nerves. Made me want to open the door and shove her out. Out into the dead's waiting arms.

"They can't get in here Carol. Not with the bars on the windows. Not through the brick walls. Not unless we make a mistake." It was then that I tore my gaze away from the fourteen undead outside. Yes. Fourteen. I'd been counting since the first trio shuffled forward and started banging on the door.

She was young, barely out of her teens, and still a bit pudgy with baby fat. Her rounded cheeks and short hair reinforced what we veterinarians had known for years; pets and their owners eventually begin to look alike.

In Carol's case, the fat black cat that annoyingly scratched at its carrier in agitation and indignity managed to match not only her appearance, but also the tendency to rake nails down the chalkboard of my nerves.

"You're welcome to leave though, Carol." Her expression of horror made it plain that I was well and truly stuck with her. And Mr. Jiggles.

Another man outside, missing part of his right arm from the elbow down, stumbled forward to join his peers as they slowly surrounded the clinic. I watched him stand still for a moment, swaying slightly before raising his one remaining fist against the front door. Recognition took hold as I stared at his face. Clem Burrows. A pair of pit bulls. They were overdue for their shots.

I turned away and closed the paw-printed curtains, blocking the view from my office window and surrounding us both in darkness. Night had fallen, the electricity was as dead as the people outside and only the tire store across the street had provided any light. The scent of burning rubber still hung thick in the air as flames danced beneath a heavy column of black smoke rising above.

"What are we going to do?" Carol asked as she fell into step behind me. I ignored her and checked each window and door for the eighth time in an hour. Eight times. Yes I counted.

"Stay put until someone comes to rescue us, I suppose. Nothing else we can do."

My circular trek led me through examination rooms with their short, metal tables, small offices and larger spaces where x-ray and ultra-sound equipment were kept. All empty now. All dark from curtains pulled shut. Around back, where animals recovered from various treatments or were simply boarded by our loyal customers, lay cages stacked three high. Most were empty save for six dogs, two cats and a rather plump bunny. I tried to soothe them but animals, being as intuitive as they are, simply weren't buying it. A cup of Snausages given to each worked where words failed and for a few moments there was blessed silence. Until Carol spoke again.

"What if there's no one left to help us?"

"Then I'll simply put everyone to sleep once the food is gone. You don't mind Purina, do you Carol? It's a bit crunchy but I suppose some water added will soften it up nicely. No?"

Mr. Jiggles hissed dramatically in his crate as his owner recoiled at my words.

I ignored them both and finished my inspection in the clinic's waiting room. There was Mrs. Winkler, seated calmly where I'd left her, reading an old magazine aloud to the ancient bulldog resting comfortably in her lap. Ginger was the dog's name. It snored softly without a care in the world.

"Everything secure, Dr. Scott?"

I nodded to the older gentlewoman in reply.

"Ironic isn't it? The robbery last year driving you to have bars installed in all the windows?" She smiled and shook her head slowly from side to side. "Likely the only reason we're still alive."

"He wants to euthanize us when the food runs out!" Carol shouted. Mrs. Winkler's reply caught her off guard and sent blood rushing to fill full cheeks with a bright, unflattering blush.

"Far better that than to starve, though I suspect it will be the loss of water that sees our end before a lack of food." Calm as you please, the old gal went back to reading her magazine aloud. Ginger's feet kicked slowly in the midst of a little puppy dream.

One hundred and sixteen minutes passed before anything changed. Yes one hundred and sixteen. I counted. That change was subtle at first. Barely noticeable really. A slight change in the air pressure. Just a hint that something new was afoot. Or more correctly, ablaze.

The tire store across the street had collapsed with a quiet groan as the fire within destroyed inner supports. Nothing explosive, mind you. Just an old man rolling his head to the side before breathing out his final breath. Flickering orange lights made shadows dance across the waiting room's far wall when shuffling bodies drifted away to investigate. Three remained behind.

Yes, three. I counted.

Carol's voice rose to unintelligible hysterics as a burning tire rolled from the wreckage and struck the line of undead. Their forward movements halted. Slack neck muscles allowed chins to lower and heads to droop as they stared dimly at the flaming doughnut. No reaction stirred within the first, a young woman with five earrings dangling from her lobe, as her jeans caught fire.

And yes. There were five. I counted.

The scent of roasting meat wafted our way and, God help me, my mouth watered. Despite my earlier bravado, I really had no desire to eat dog food. A glance at my watch told me it had been seven hours and twenty three minutes since the tuna fish sandwich I'd carefully made for lunch disappeared down my throat.

Stomach grumbling, I watched as the girl slowly turned and shuffled back towards the clinic.

"Oh dear," Mrs. Winkler commented while Carol devolved into a blubbering mess nearby. Vaguely understood words dribbled from her lips as she raised one chubby hand and pointed towards the walking torch. I believe she said 'neighbor,' but I might have been mistaken.

Regardless, the fire began to spread. Bodies packed tightly as the zombies, for what else could they be, began to cluster outside the shatterproof glass doors that separated dead from living. The stench of burning hair soon ended the fit of hunger my stomach had suffered.

"Not to worry. This may, in fact, be good news." Both women glanced in my direction before I continued. "The animal hospital's outer walls are brick so I doubt we're in serious danger. I cannot imagine it will take long before muscle burns away and they are reduced to little more than ash. At that point we can make our escape."

"Oh how very clever Dr. Scott. My car is parked in the handicap spot just outside the door." There were seven keys on the keychain that Mrs. Winkler dug from her purse and jingled before us. Yes seven. I counted.

I hurried after that, dashing into the secured room where various medicines used to treat our animal patients were kept. Pain medicines. Antibiotics. Bandages. Armfuls were shoveled into a cardboard box and set by the front door. A glance outside showed me several of the zombies had dropped to the ground, smoldering and unmoving even as others stepped into their place. And the burning remnants of their clothing. Like the Olympics, the flame never died.

"What about the dogs?" Mrs. Winkler asked once I'd slipped on my coat and an old pair of jogging shoes bought the year before. New Years resolutions. My immortal enemies.

I spared a glance over my shoulder and chuckled. "I never really liked animals to begin with." A nod of my head guided their gazes towards the final zombie as he collapsed into a smoking heap. "Now or never."

The three of us stepped cautiously outside, pausing long enough to determine no undead lay hidden from our sight, and made great speed to Mrs. Winkler's car. It was a rather large Cadillac of late model. I opened the door as soon as I heard the locks lift from its owner's remote. Unfortunately, a series of events brought disaster to an otherwise simple endeavor.

First, it was at that moment that Mrs. Winkler's heart gave out. Clutching her chest, she collapsed to the ground eighteen steps from the car. Yes eighteen. I counted. Ginger bounced as the bulldog was dropped and landed with a yelp directly in Carol's path.

Ass over teakettle is the term, I believe. Head over heels the young girl went, the infernal Mr. Jiggles spilling out of his cat carrier in a black roll of fat, fangs and fur. Sensing the presence of his kind's mortal enemy, the cat then proceeded to expend more calories by attacking Ginger than he'd likely used in a year.

I stepped out of the car to aid Carol when movement flashed in the corner of my eye. Four zombies had approached and were rounding the car's backside with remarkable haste. Heedless of the danger, Carol simultaneously held her ankle, cried with pain, and tried to recapture Mr. Jiggles with one chubby hand.

Writing the young woman off as a lost cause and, truth be told, hoping the cacophony of noise coming from her direction would distract the unwelcome newcomers, I dashed across the distance to grab Mrs. Winker's keys. To say the old gal had a

CHRIS PHILBROOK

death grip on them would have been both morbidly amusing and entirely accurate.

Eyes opened as I struggled to pull the key ring from her bony grasp. Words gurgled from her slack lips. Apparently she wasn't dead. Carol's voice rose in pitch somehow, threatening to shatter glass and my eardrums in one fell swoop. Having had enough, I simply stomped down on Mrs. Winkler's hand until brittle bones snapped like twigs. The keychain came free and I half expected a spear of light to descend from Heaven and illuminate the glistening metal. Needless to say, I was back in the Caddy a heartbeat later.

Zombies are rather messy eaters. I learned that while watching Carol's bulk feed an army. Literally. Seventeen undead had drifted into the clinic's front lot and were enjoying their all you can eat buffet.

Yes, seventeen. I counted.

As the feast got underway, I did not. Get underway that is. Key in the ignition and obscenities flowing freely from my lips, I cranked and cranked the damned engine over and over to little avail. The battery wasn't dead. Dinging chimes and blinking lights told me as much. Fists started to bang on the exterior just as I remembered to lock the doors.

And so I sat, watching Carol disappear bite by bite as Mrs. Winkler slowly rose and looked about with dead eyes. Of the embattled animals there was no sign though the sound of dogs barking inside the clinic carried easily to my ears.

On unsteady legs came my former valued customer, shuffling towards my position as I helplessly watched. A mangled hand, fingers splayed out at entirely wrong angles, slapped against the window inches from my face. Five times. You know I counted.

It seemed for a moment that she paused, staring down at the door with a slack-jawed expression. Other hands and fists were pounding in all directions, setting the car to rocking back and forth beneath the assault.

I decided then to take a fatal dose of painkillers and reached into the back seat for my cardboard box. Naturally it was not

250

there and in that instant I recalled leaving it on the roof. Cursing my bad luck, I began to search the glove box when I heard the door locks open. Sitting upright quickly, I barely managed to lock them from within before Mrs. Winkler's shattered hand glided past the keyless entry once more.

Fingerprint scanners apparently continue to work when you're dead.

We played a game then. Her fingertips would brush the sensor outside the door. I'd relock them from within. Over and over it went. One hundred and thirty six times before I finally gave up and let them open the door.

Yes, one hundred and thirty six times. I counted.

- About The Authors -

Chris Philbrook is the creator and author of *Adrian's Undead Diary* as well as the fantasy series *Elmoryn* and *Tesser: A Dragon Among Us*.

Chris calls the wonderful state of New Hampshire his home. He is an avid reader, writer, role player, miniatures game player, video game player, and part time athlete, as well as a member of the Horror Writers Association. If you weren't impressed enough, he also works full time while writing for Elmoryn as well as the world of Adrian's Undead Diary and his newest project, *Tesser; A Dragon Among Us*.

Check out Chris Philbrook's official website thechrisphilbrook.com to keep tabs on his many exciting projects. Sign up for his email newsletter to stay informed about the latest developments and special announcements, or follow Chris on Facebook at www.facebook.com/ChrisPhilbrookAuthor.

ALAN MACRAFFEN is a writer, illustrator and book designer. He is the author of the science fiction novel *Carnival of Time*, as well as the novella *The Doom of Eldrid Cole* and the Unhappy Endings story *The Only Thing That Matters*. He lives in Maine with his wife, artist Molly Brewer, and their cat Husker. As a child, he loved monsters, dinosaurs and mythical creatures. He still does.

Learn more about Alan MacRaffen's books, design services, and other upcoming projects at macraffen.com, or follow Alan on Facebook at www.facebook.com/alanmacraffen.

JOE TREMBLAY is the author of the Unhappy Endings story *Fear*, as well as the paranormal thriller *Subject 15*: Follow Jack McCoy into the nefarious clutches of the CIA, and experience the mind experiment through his eyes. Discover more at www.subject15.com

Joe aspires to tell stories via the written word and film. He recently returned back to the sticks of New Hampshire upon completion of film school at the Art Institute of Las Vegas. He now attends Ashford University where he intends to obtain his Bachelor's degree in Marketing.

Joe is a US Navy Veteran who spent six years as an Electronics Technician onboard USS Reuben James FFG 57 and USS Dubuque LPD 8. He presently writes full time and works a third shift job that he hopes to retire from soon to become a full time storyteller. He enjoys the outdoors, role-playing games, a good cup of coffee, watching movies, football and spending time with his family and friends.

J.C. FISKE is an American author born in Manchester, New Hampshire. He is an avid reader, martial artist, and metal fan. He received his Bachelor of Arts Degree from Southern New Hampshire University in 2008. The first book in his Young Adult Fantasy series, *Renegade Rising*, was published through Tenacity Books in 2011. Currently, he resides in New Hampshire and is hard at work on the sequel series to Renegade.

Learn more about Gisbo Falcon and the world of the Renegade Series at the official website: www.JCFiske.com

You can also email J.C. Fiske at JCFiske@Gmail.com, or find him on Twitter: @GisboFalcon

Can't get enough of AUD?

Visit the School Store at **adriansundeaddiary.com** for stickers, hats, and a wide variety of awesome shirts!

Stickers!

Hats!

T-Shirts!

Can't Wait for More?

Look for Chris Philbrook's **FREE** short fiction eBook, *At Least He's Not on Fire.*

Find it on Amazon, Goodreads, or Smashwords today!

Amazon: http://www.amazon.com/dp/B00JSGEKIK

Goodreads: https://www.goodreads.com/book/show/
21948978-at-least-he-s-not-on-fire

Smashwords: https://www.smashwords.com/books/
view/430970

Made in the USA
Monee, IL
12 December 2019

18487056R00150